THE PROTECTOR

A JACK WIDOW THRILLER

SCOTT BLADE

D1566739

BOOKS BY SCOTT BLADE

The Jack Widow Series

Gone Forever

Winter Territory

A Reason to Kill

Without Measure

Once Quiet

Name Not Given

The Midnight Caller

Fire Watch

The Last Rainmaker

The Devil's Stop

Black Daylight

The Standoff

Foreign and Domestic

Patriot Lies

The Double Man

Nothing Left

The Protector

Kill Promise

1

Out of breath, I sprinted for almost a half-mile, straight out, chasing after a car that barely swerved to miss me. Driving fast, more than sixty-five miles an hour. The car nearly slammed into me. The force would've flung me into the night air, legs flailing about. It would've been a hard landing. At best, I would've ended up in the hospital with two broken legs from crashing into God-knows-what. At worst, the paramedics would've pronounced me dead at the scene. My head could've bounced off a desert rock and busted wide open, spilling out the contents like a split coconut.

Before the car nearly killed me, I walked on the highway shoulder, thumb out, in the middle of a beautiful autumn night. An endless blanket of stars canvased the sky. Hulking rock formations and mountains lingered in the distance. A breeze blew off the Arizona desert, chilly but not unpleasant. I welcomed the slight chill in the air. It was a nice change of pace from the blistering heat that swept across North America this last summer.

I tried to get a ride for hours without luck. Honestly, I didn't expect a car to stop for me. Not out here. Even if I hadn't been on this dark, quiet highway, the odds of getting a ride were against me. No one picks up hitchhikers anymore, not at night, not out here, and especially not ones who look like me. On a good day, I wasn't the ideal candidate to offer a lift. I was unkempt on this night, as I was lately. It might be a phase I was going through where I just didn't care how I looked. A two-week beard covered my face and the hair on my head was full and a little bushy. I looked like a caveman who was just thawed out of ice after a hundred-thousand-year nap. The wind blew my hair around like it was at war with it. Strands danced and billowed across my forehead, blotting over my eyes, slightly impairing my vision. But the strands didn't stay still long enough to impair it enough for me to brush it out of my face.

I looked like the sketch artist rendering of the nightmare drifter who'd been killing drivers up and down some dark superhighway and dumping their bodies across state lines. If the FBI was involved in a manhunt for someone like that, they'd arrest me on sight, throw me in a cell, and close the case. No questions asked. And that's only if they didn't shoot me first.

Even if I hadn't looked menacing, hitchhiking was still a dying enterprise. I was surprised I got as many rides as I had this far into the twenty-first century.

I heard of the *good ole days* of hitching for rides from two old timers who hung out together on an interstate cloverleaf back at the foothills of the Rocky Mountains.

They educated me on the ways of the hitchhiker, like older guys did to younger guys. They had that attitude that anyone younger than them knew absolutely nothing about anything and they knew absolutely everything about everything. I don't consider myself young. Not anymore. I think that happens as we age. There comes a point where you think your youth is gone, until you meet someone decades older, and they think you're a newborn baby. These two saw me like that. Apparently, they considered a former Navy SEAL and undercover NCIS agent hovering around forty to be *young* and inexperienced. They acted like it was a miracle that I could tie my shoes.

Some people thought that way. Others didn't. Apparently, they did.

To these two guys, I was a greenhorn, a rookie, a new blood— someone who needed schooling. I've met a lot of interesting people ever since I started wandering around with no clear destination, but these two deserved to be on the most memorable people list.

They were two old guys, one white and one black. Between the two of them, they didn't have a full mouth of teeth. Their faces were dirty, almost soot-covered like two ancient, old west California gold prospectors on their last dime and last shred of reality. They were dressed like California gold prospectors too, only they weren't reclusive. They were friendly, as friendly as any other two old guys would be to a stranger.

They saw me and immediately invited me over to them. Pleasantries were exchanged and conversations took place as the sun descended in the sky, at which point, I said goodbye and hit the road again on my own. They offered to walk with me. I didn't want to be rude, but I felt I had a better chance of scoring a ride with some daylight left—and without the tooth-less, crazy prospectors on my tail.

Rides, for me, were scarce enough, but nighttime was ten times scarcer. Getting a ride for me at night was like praying for rain in a years-long drought.

Most people didn't pick up hitchhikers. At least that's true in my case. Then again, maybe they just didn't pick *me* up.

I'm what kids call a *big dude*—six foot four inches in height and two hundred and twenty-five pounds of muscle and bone. I was blessed with half-unknown, but good genetics. My mother was a small-town sheriff. She was tough, the toughest person I ever knew. But she was a tiny thing, meaning I must've gotten my ape-man genetics from my father. He was a drifter, like me, but I never knew him. And I rarely give him a second's thought.

I've got massive arms, the size of caveman clubs, the kind used to crush the skulls of Wooly Mammoth and prehistoric big cats. My biceps are as big as cannonballs fired on the battle-field at Yorktown. And my hands are big, like bear paws, but with long fingers. Both of my arms are covered with sleeve tattoos. Some of which serve meanings for me. Some don't.

People avoided me based on my appearance, which was okay by me ninety-nine percent of the time. I liked not being both-ered. If people kept to themselves, I kept to myself. There's always an exception to any rule. That exception for me was when I needed a ride.

But that's how it went sometimes. Often people avoided me when I needed them, and were evasive when I didn't.

Usually, I'm surprised whenever anyone stops for me. Even if an exhausted driver, after a long day and night of traversing endless highways, hooking interstates, tolls, and copious bridges, stops for me, I'm surprised. I shouldn't be, because on the surface it all makes sense. It's simple commerce. It's economics. Hitchhikers need rides and some drivers want company. Others need someone to take the wheel for the last leg of their trip. It's fair trade. Road company for a ride. Or free labor for a free ride. You drive for me, and I give you transportation to get where you're going, all in a climate-controlled vehicle. Not a bad exchange. It's a capitalistic approach to a common, everyday problem. It's the old age of you scratch my back and I'll scratch yours. It's not rocket science.

I knew as the sun went down the odds of someone engaging in this trade with me diminished to nearly zero. In the middle of nowhere, in the middle of the night, on a quiet Arizona highway, I was the last thing someone wanted to see. That goes for any quiet nighttime highway in America. Hardly anyone stops for me under these conditions. Obviously, this isn't always the case. Sometimes people stop for me. It's a matter of numbers. On any day, hundreds or thousands of cars will pass me by without a second glance. But in those numbers, there's bound to be one person who'll stop.

Statistics.

So, when I saw car headlights barreling straight at me on a quiet Arizona highway in the middle of the night, in the middle of nowhere, I thought maybe it was going to stop and offer me a ride. I thought it was the exception to the rule. It was the one in a thousand. But I should've known better. My judgement was slightly impaired because I wanted a ride so badly. I wanted to sit in the front passenger seat of a car and get off my feet.

My legs ached and my feet throbbed from standing and walking for a couple of days straight. I haven't stayed for more than a night in a single location in several days. I just felt like moving with no interest in staying anywhere. My shoulders stung from sleeping on the ground under a tree. Many miles back, and the night before, I was tired, and the only motel I found was at full occupancy. Desperate, I laid up under a tree off the highway, down a hill out of sight, and slept there. Why not? When I was a SEAL, my team and I slept in worse conditions, outdoors, in rocky terrain, and with enemy combatants hunting us all night. We slept in the cold, in the pouring rain, all while keeping one eye open in case the enemy stumbled upon our camp. Crashing under a tree in Arizona wasn't the end of the world.

But I overestimated how tired I was and overslept the next morning and woke up with my shoulder hurting from laying on it. A large tree root had pressed against it all night. My body cramped up. It was bad for the first part of the morning. It wasn't the end of the world, but it was still sore.

Moments before I leapt out of the way from being plowed at sixty-five miles an hour by the car, I saw inside the vehicle. It was just a glance, but it was like slow motion, the way time slows when you're being shot at. I couldn't see the driver. I thought I saw two occupants. They looked to be scrambling for the wheel. There was no one in the backseat.

It looked like there were two people in the vehicle's front, fighting over control of the car, maybe? Perhaps the driver was fighting with a passenger, like a carjacking or something. Perhaps it was a friendly conversation turned bad. Conceivably, they fought because the passenger was an unwilling participant on their journey. Maybe it was a kidnapping gone wrong? Or perhaps the driver was victim to a bad hitchhiker, someone with malicious intent. Whatever the reason, I didn't like almost being hit by a car. Maybe I should've let it go. But I wasn't the kind of guy who let things like that go. Not after it almost hit me. Not after I had walked for hours. Not after I slept on the hard ground the night before.

I saw the car's headlights coming at me. I stayed on the shoulder, watching it, thinking it was coming at me, thinking it was going to slow and stop as it neared me. But it didn't. I leapt out of the way, diving off the shoulder and rolling away in the dirt. The car barreled past me and weaved from lane to lane. It dipped down over a hill, into a valley, and then back up another hill. It ramped up into the air at the apex. The tires came up off the ground and the car landed on the pavement. Sparks flew, and the suspension hissed, but the car kept going. It weaved from shoulder to shoulder, across the highway, until the taillights faded away into the blackness and the car was lost to sight.

I didn't think the car would make it far. Not in the reckless state of driving that it was in. My fear was it would crash into a tree. And that's exactly what it did.

2

THE CAR's make and model was a violet Ford Fusion.

The vehicle's year I didn't know. It looked less than ten years old, but older than five. Whether it was an LS or XL, I didn't know, or even if it came in LS or XL. What I knew was that it crashed into a tree about fifty yards off the side of a forgotten section of Route 66. The engine coughed and spurted and choked like it was about to die. The headlights were still on. They were bright halogen bulbs. They lit up the dark road ahead, beyond the tree. No headlights approached from the opposite direction. Nothing approached from behind me. We were alone for miles. Minus the starlight and the occasional streetlight, the road was dark. The night was black. But I was used to the dark.

In the last four hours, I had walked in the dark. The last sign of civilization I had seen was a couple of hours ago. I had seen lights off the highway from a small town. I was in a rural part of Arizona, somewhere west of Flagstaff but east of California. The Grand Canyon was probably within a hundred miles of me. If it was daylight, I'd probably go visit it. I liked to do things like that on a whim. Too many people didn't stop to enjoy things.

Today, too many people walk around with their eyes half on their phone screens and half on the road ahead. I had seen it in cities. I had seen the same in the small towns and the same in the medium-sized towns. The same on trains. The same at day. And the same at night.

I had seen people driving the same way. Maybe a little less occupied with their phones, but that had only been because the ones who were more occupied with their phones had lost their driving privileges. Probably. Or worse. They had lost their lives or limbs.

Either way, most people lived their lives the same way that they drove their cars or walked the city streets or small towns or medium towns—half distracted.

Most people were too busy to live. In too much of a rush to look and see what was around them. Often they're too busy looking to see. Maybe I was getting lame, but I liked to stop and smell the roses. Whereas other people simply walked right over the roses, not even noticing them.

Maybe not everyone would agree with me. Not necessarily. But that's the kind of thoughts that you get on the road, when you're alone.

I was never one for meditation. However, walking from place to place without complications is like surfing. The sun beats down. The wind gusts. The trees wave. The desert sand blows. The mountain terrain hovered on the horizon. It all had a way of cleaning the mind, of making everything clear, of resetting the brain.

Speaking of sand, the wind blew sand and sediment off the desert and batted my face. I swept it off my cheeks and approached the rear of the crashed car. The engine idled and exhaust pooled behind it and rose into the brake lights, creating a dark red smoke.

The night sky was clear and starry. No moon that I could see. Probably dark somewhere hiding among the stars.

I walked to the car's rear bumper, staying in the rearview mirror so that I could be seen by the driver. I didn't want to frighten her. I figured the driver was a woman just because of the type of car. No kind of statistics told me that. It was just a guess. The car was more in the feminine category than the masculine. Although that meant nothing.

I stopped at the rear and stood near the trunk. I bent down and peeked in through the rear window to survey the situation. The interior was dark, and the backseat was empty. No passengers. The only person inside was the driver. I couldn't make out any details from this angle. I knocked on the trunk lid, hoping to get her attention.

But there was no response.

I knocked again.

No response.

I knocked a third time.

Nothing.

"Hello?" I called out.

The driver didn't respond. So, I walked around the vehicle from the driver's side and up to the window. I bent down and peered in. The dash lights illuminated the interior in a soft ambient blue light. It reflected an indigo color across the driver's torso.

"Hello?" I asked again. There was no response.

I saw a few new key pieces of information that either I was wrong about before or I hadn't known. First, the driver wasn't a *she*. *He* was a man. And he looked knocked out but alive. He breathed at a normal pace. His chest expanded on inhales and shrank on exhales.

Second, a gun laid in the footwell, near his feet, under the gas pedal. It looked like a Glock 22, a .40 caliber pistol. It looked like it fell out of his hand. I peered down into the car and saw the passenger door was closed. There was no one in the passenger seat. I had been wrong about that. It was just the driver. He must've been bouncing around and the sight of it appeared to be two people struggling. But it was only him.

The engine spurted and coughed louder than before. It didn't seem at risk of catching fire, but I didn't want to take the chance. I reached in, turned the key, and killed the ignition. The engine noise died away to nothing.

I grabbed the guy's suit jacket and shook him. Easy, not like I wanted to rattle his brain inside his skull, but hard enough to wake a man out of a deep sleep. I said, "Hey. You with me?"

The guy grunted and twisted like he might've been in a deep sleep, but he didn't wake up. To be safe, I popped the lock on his door, opened it, and backed up as the door swung open. I reached down and grabbed him by the arm and hauled him out of the car. My hands are pretty big, the size of shovels. I used one to palm his head like a pillow, to keep him from banging it on the door pillar, or the ground, as I pulled him out of the vehicle.

The guy was probably five feet and nine inches tall. Nothing special about his height. His weight was a different story that belonged in an entirely different section of a library. He must've weighed two hundred and fifty pounds, twenty-five pounds more than me. For a guy his height, he was heavier than what was normal. Of course, I tried not to judge others on their lifestyle choices. Live and let live is my credo. Variety is the spice of life. However, in that moment, in that situation where I needed to move the guy to keep him safe, I wished he might've taken more stairs and ate less fast food.

I was tired. I struggled to get him out of the car. I set him down in some witchgrass and dragged him from behind his shoulders, until I got him to a decent distance away from the car; in case it caught fire.

I dragged him far enough and laid him down on the shoulder of the road with his head in what paramedics call: *the recovery position*.

He breathed normally.

I poked at his chest and said, "Hey."

No response.

I poked again and said, "Hey."

Nothing.

I felt his pulse. It was weak—weaker than it should've been. It was strong enough to be alive, but weak enough to need a hospital.

I looked around. Nothing in the distance but darkness. No oncoming headlights. No sign of nearby houses. There was nowhere for me to go to get help and no one passing by to flag down.

I shook the guy, soft at first, then a little harder and harder still.

No response.

I shook him a little harder still.

Nothing.

I looked down at the guy. His face turned a shade of blue. It was bloated. This guy needed an ambulance. I reached down and searched his coat. Maybe he had a phone I could use to call 911. The guy looked like he might've been an underpaid college professor. He wore stonewashed blue jeans and a tweed coat. It was whitish, or possibly gray. I couldn't tell in the dark. He wasn't wearing a tie.

I searched his jacket pockets for a phone. I found one in his inside right pocket, slipped it out. It was an iPhone in a case with a sports logo on it—a Dallas team. I touched the screen, and a lock screen popped up with a message that read *Slide to Unlock*.

I swiped across the screen. Another screen popped up, asking for a passcode or fingerprint. It was an older iPhone. I knew the newer ones used face recognition and not fingerprints. So, I grabbed the guy's hand and put his index finger on the phone's only button.

The phone shook like a scolding parent saying: *No. Try again.* Then I saw the word *Emergency* written at the bottom of the screen. I pressed it and a call screen came up. I dialed 911.

A voice said, "911. Fire, Ambulance, or Police?"

Before I could answer, a cold hand grabbed my wrist. I looked down, and the guy was awake. He muttered, "No... No...Help."

He was having trouble speaking, like he was drifting in and out of consciousness. His eyes rolled in and out of his head, like they were being called back to sleep, and he was fighting it.

I looked at him and said, "You need an ambulance."

He shook his head and said, "Have to stop them."

I stayed quiet.

He said, "Have to save her."

The guy reached slowly into his other inside jacket pocket, but his head plopped back down onto the hard ground, and his eyes rolled back into his head. This time they didn't come back out.

The emergency operator said, "Hello? 911. Fire, Ambulance, or Police?"

I put the phone to my ear and lips and said, "Better send paramedics. There's been a car accident. I pulled the driver out of his vehicle, but he's not looking good."

The emergency operator asked, "Where are you, sir?"

I paused, looked around, but there were no recognizable landmarks. Not to me. I wasn't intimately familiar with Arizona. I'm sure a local could've looked at one of the looming rock mountains and knew the name. But I wasn't a local. So, I said, "I'm on Route 66, somewhere west of Flagstaff, but south of Las Vegas. The Grand Canyon is north, I think."

The emergency operator went quiet for a moment, then she asked, "Are you still on I-40?"

"I don't think so. This isn't an interstate. It's more like a highway."

The emergency operator said, "Okay. Got it. I think I know where you are based on that information and your GPS signal. Leave your phone on, we'll find you."

I stayed quiet.

The emergency operator typed some keystrokes and said, "Sir, the computer is showing that this phone is registered with Homeland Security. Are you a federal agent? Can you tell me your agency and badge number, please?"

I paused, looked down at the guy. He was still unconscious. I said, "It's not my phone. I found it on the driver. He ran his car into a tree. I'm just a pedestrian."

"I see. And sir, what's your name?" the emergency operator asked.

I paused a beat. It was instinctual. My brain asked if I really wanted to give away my name like that. Before my civilized brain could answer the question, my primal brain answered for me. I said, "John Capone."

In the past, I used dead presidents, baseball players, basketball players, and Olympic gold medalists names as aliases. But I ran through them all. Out of boredom, I started using famous gangster names. Only, I couldn't use many of them as they were. No one would believe me if I said my name was Al Capone or John Dillinger, so I started mixing and matching them. Today, I was John Capone.

I heard keystrokes. The emergency operator typed something into a computer. The line crackled like it was a radio. The emergency operator asked, "Is the driver conscious?"

"No. He's out cold."

"Is he breathing?"

"Yes."

"Do you see any physical injuries on him? Is he bleeding anywhere?"

I glanced back at the car and down at the driver. Blood trickled out of his nose. There were cuts on his face, but nothing life-threatening.

"The airbag deployed. It bloodied his nose a bit. But it doesn't look broken. He's got some cuts and scrapes on his face. Nothing that bad. It's all superficial."

"Is there anyone else in the vehicle with him?"

"No."

"Are you injured?"

"No. Like I said, I wasn't in the car. I'm just a pedestrian."

The emergency operator paused a long beat, like she was keying the information into the computer.

I stayed quiet, and let her do her thing. She said nothing for a moment. Then a new voice came on the line. A male voice. He said, "Sir, this is Lt. Daniel Moreno. I'm the night watch CO here in Ash Fork. We're about twenty-five miles east of your position. That phone's GPS shows us you're near Cedar Springs. Our nearest ambulance is fifteen minutes out. I've dispatched them. They'll be with you shortly. Our nearest sheriff's deputy is coming from here as well. He's leaving now. He'll probably get there after the ambulance."

I asked, "Why're they coming from Ash Fork?"

"What's that?"

"If I'm closer to Cedar Springs, why not send help from there?"

"Cedar Springs is on the Hualapai Indian Reservation. They can't help you. It's not their jurisdiction. They don't have an ambulance. It'll come from here."

I stayed quiet and wondered why this guy's phone was registered with Homeland Security. I asked, "Lieutenant, why is this guy's phone listed with Homeland Security?"

Moreno said, "The phone that you are using is registered under a United States Marshal."

"Marshal?"

"Yes. I'm sure he'll be grateful for your help."

I ignored Moreno and looked down at the driver. I cradled the phone between my shoulder and cheek, like it was a portable house phone from an ancient time. I used both hands to search the guy's other jacket pockets. I found his wallet, took it out, and opened it.

A younger picture of the guy stared back at me from a picture ID that was behind a milky clear plastic window. Across from it was a gold badge. It was a circle of gold with a five-point star in the middle and the US Marshal seal on the center of the star. The ID was a US Marshall Service identification card. The card identified the driver as *Patton Fry: Retired.*

3

THE CEDAR SPRINGS paramedics arrived closer to twenty minutes later and not fifteen.

Their time was better than I expected, but not much. A small town with limited resources a good distance away from my location wouldn't be the fastest imaginable savior in a rescue situation. However, a couple of paramedics on-call all night with nothing to do might be inclined to respond fast. They probably waited with a combination of coma-inducing boredom and eagerness for action. That's small-town life. I know. I grew up that way. They got the call and not just from anyone but from the night watch commander from the nearest sheriff's office and the subject of the call was more than just an automobile accident. It involved a retired US Marshal and a tree and an unknown, middle of the night passerby.

The paramedics arrived, sirens blaring, lights strobing. They jumped out of a blue square van with medical emblems plastered all over the sides and the back. They leapt straight into action. They were like power tools that had been neglected but were eager for action.

They went right to Patton Fry and lifted his head slightly and checked his pulse and talked to him. He didn't respond. He was out cold. One paramedic held Fry's wrist and looked at his watch, like he was counting Fry's heartbeat while the other guy readied a stretcher for extraction.

I stood on the highway shoulder and looked around. No sheriff cruisers came at us. Not yet. I returned to the paramedics and asked, "Where's the sheriff deputies? I was told they'd come out here?"

The paramedic taking Fry's vitals ignored me. The other didn't look back, but he said, "They told us you should wait here for them."

I stayed quiet.

He said, "They told us you should stay and wait."

I said, "Where are you taking him?"

The paramedic said, "Cedar Springs."

"Is there an ER in Cedar Springs? The cop on the phone said Ash Fork."

"Cedar Springs has an ER. It's small, but closer. Just a couple of floors of a federal building. As long as this guy doesn't have major internal bleeding or extensive head injuries, then we'll keep him there. They'll take care of him."

"And if he has those things?"

"We'll send a helicopter for him out of Flagstaff for anything worse."

I nodded and asked, "Can I ride with you guys into town?"

The paramedics began lifting the guy onto a stretcher. The one said, "We don't care what you do."

The other finally spoke. He said, "The cop wanted him to stay behind."

Then, the same guy hushed his voice to a lower octave, but not low enough to where I couldn't hear him. He said, "He could be dangerous. He could've attacked this guy."

The first paramedic looked at me and shrugged. He said, "Help us put him in the back."

I went to the ambulance and held the back doors open wide, preventing them from swinging closed. I didn't need to move too far back, because of my arm span I could hold both doors open through the whole procedure. There was plenty of room under my arms for the paramedics to maneuver.

The paramedics wheeled the guy and the stretcher onto the floorboards of the ambulance and pushed him all the way forward along a track. The first paramedic hopped in after Fry and tapped his foot on a mechanism at the base of the back wheels and I heard a rusted sounding *snick*. The wheels locked in place to keep the stretcher from rolling all over the place.

The paramedic said, "Hop in if you want to ride with us."

I climbed in the back and sat across from the first paramedic on a bench that stretched the wall. The second paramedic shut the doors behind us. Then, he scrambled around the outside of the ambulance and opened the driver's side door and hopped in. The engine was already on. The paramedic took the gear out of park and hit the gas. We were off the shoulder and back on the blacktop, headed for Cedar Springs.

4

RETIRED UNITED STATES MARSHAL PATTON Fry woke up and repeated his earlier concerns. He looked at me with weak eyes. He faded in and out of consciousness. He reached over to me and grabbed two fingers on my hand and squeezed them like a newborn and said, "You've got to get to her first."

I asked, "Who? Get to who? Who is she?"

He repeated, "Got to get to her first."

The first paramedic said, "He needs to stay calm." And he put an oxygen mask over Fry's mouth, but Fry reached up with a shaky arm and grabbed the guy's hand. He shook his head slow and mechanically, like it took all the muscles in his neck.

The paramedic said, "Sir, it appears you've had a cardiac event. I need you to stay still and calm."

A cardiac event?

I looked at the paramedic and realized that must've been why Fry swerved all over the road. He probably was speeding to help whoever this girl is that he keeps mentioning, and then, he saw me on the road and was hit with a mild heart attack, all like a perfect storm. It caused him to drive recklessly and crash into that tree.

He was both a lucky and an unlucky guy. Unlucky because of the heart attack. Lucky because the tree was there to save his life. It stopped the car and stopped him from ramming into a ditch and flipping. Or, worse yet, slamming into another car on the road and killing someone. Either way, he could've been dead and, in my book, any guy who survives a career in law enforcement, a heart attack, and a car accident to boot, was a pretty lucky guy. No matter which way you cut it.

Fry said, "Wait. Wait."

He breathed heavily, like he was gasping his first breaths from being deep underwater. Fry squeezed my hand again, tighter, and pulled, like he wanted me closer. He stared into my eyes and said, "You. I need your help."

I scooted down the bench past some medical equipment, some of which was foreign to me and some I had seen before. I neared the edge of his stretcher, as close as I could. Fry relaxed his squeeze on my hand.

The ambulance sirens were off because there was no traffic or even a car on the highway, but the lights swirled through the air, ricocheting red beams through the front windshield and into the rear of the vehicle.

The red lights flashed across Fry's face as he spoke, taking quick, deep breaths between pauses, slurring his words. He said, "Help her."

I asked, "Who? Help who?"

He said, "Kara. Kara. She's in danger. They know where she is. They're coming. Now."

I said, "Who is?"

"I don't know. Them. Men, who want her dead."

"Who is she?"

He said, "Kara is a witness. She's in protection."

I glanced at the paramedic. He looked up at me. He was processing what Fry was saying, but he stayed quiet. I asked, "Where is she?"

"Six years," Fry said, and he took another breath. The paramedic strapped an oxygen breather over his face. It was a plastic face cover with hoses leading to a tank.

The paramedic said, "Take it easy."

Fry took deep breaths from the breather, and then, he said, "She's been off the books for six years. I promised her she'd be safe, and her son."

"I can call her for you."

"I tried. She won't answer me. She might have a new phone now."

I asked, "Where are they?"

Fry's eyes faded in and out.

The paramedic said, "He needs to breathe."

I said, "Where is Kara?"

Fry looked at me once more, took away the mask, and said, "Diner. Waitress. Please."

That was the last thing he said. Within seconds, he was out again.

The paramedic hovered over him and put two fingers on his neck. Then, he forced the breather over Fry's face and watched as Fry took slow, deep breaths.

The paramedic said, "What's he talking about?"

"Nothing. He's out of his facilities. Obviously," I lied.

I was no expert on the US Marshals, but I knew they lived within a brotherhood, just like the SEALs and NCIS. And a brotherhood carried with it a code of honor. If Fry had a witness, he was keeping *off the books* for six years, then it must be for a good reason.

5

SIX YEARS WAS A LONG TIME. The only information I had to go on was the witness was a woman named Kara, and she had a son—age unknown. Fry mentioned *waitress* and *diner*. I presume he means she's a waitress in a diner. Since Fry was headed to Cedar Springs, that's probably where she is.

I couldn't be sure because I knew nothing about Fry's case. Not for a fact. I knew nothing about the good guys and nothing about the bad guys. All I knew for sure was it forced Fry to drive all night down Route 66, alone and not in the best of health. I think he knew about his heart condition. You don't get to that level of heart attack without at least being suspicious.

Fry was obsessed with Kara's protection. This leads me to believe she is that one case that haunts him, even after he retired. Every cop's got one or two of them. Perhaps he had become personally involved with Kara and her son. Perhaps he felt a sense of responsibility for their well-being. Perhaps it was more than professional to him. It was very personal.

I could only guess because right then I only had two certainties about Patton Fry. One was that he wasn't going to help anybody, not tonight, and not for a few days. The second thing was Fry had no idea who to trust.

One of the primary functions of the US Marshal Service was to protect witnesses to major crimes. Witnesses whose lives were often in grave danger.

The US Marshal Service is tasked with overseeing the witness relocation program, or WITSEC.

From the circumstances of Fry's current predicament, and his last words to me, I could assume that he was headed to Cedar Springs to warn a witness from a six-year-old case that she and her son were in jeopardy. That somehow Kara and her son had been made by the bad guys. Patton Fry had taken himself out of retirement, told no one of where he was going, and hit the road toward Kara's last known residence.

I presumed he told no one, because it would've been ten times easier for a retired US Marshal to just pick up a phone and call the local field office and warn them of his fears. The closest local FBI field office is probably in Phoenix, which wasn't that far up the highway. Certainly, it was a lot closer than he was. He looked like he had been driving for hours. So why not let them handle it? I think I knew the answer to that question. He trusted no one.

Being an outsider, I trusted no one. And I was just a random guy. It made me a better advocate for Kara than someone he'd get through official channels.

The ambulance pulled into the town of Cedar Springs, if you could even call it a *town*. It looked more like a nook than a full-blown municipality. It was tiny. There was one three story building, which was the federal building that the paramedic had spoken of. There was a gas station, a McDonald's which was closing its doors and turning off its sign as we passed, and about a dozen other buildings, a Walmart Super Store that barely qualified as super, and finally, off at the end of the main street, there was an all-night diner.

The ambulance pulled into the federal building parking lot. There was no overhang like other emergency rooms had. No clear markings except a pitiful blue and white sign with fading bulbs in it. They flashed and blinked.

The ambulance stopped, and the driver slid the gear into park and opened his door and stepped out. I slid back down the bench to the rear doors and undid the latch and pushed the doors open. I stepped out and helped the paramedic with the gurney and lifted it up and out of the van and laid it on squeaky wheels on the pavement.

The paramedic, who had spoken with me earlier, said, "If you head east, you'll reach the interstate. Step off the road and follow alongside it. That should keep you out of sight. If that's what you want. To avoid the cops, I mean."

I asked, "What if I want to talk to these sheriff's deputies?"

The paramedic said, "You can wait here. You must stay in the parking lot. But if I were you, I'd get going. Whatever they want with you probably will inconvenience you at the least and at the worst... Well, let's just say out here the cops are bored. So, when they see a stranger come to their jurisdiction and get involved with a US Marshal who ends up in the emergency room, they'll be inclined to detain you. You should get going while the going is worth getting."

The paramedic turned his attention back to Fry and his partner. They headed toward the emergency room's uninteresting entrance and rolled Fry through a pair of automatic doors, which sucked open, and stayed open a long time after they left.

I watched them leave and stood in the night air. Wind gusted from out of sparse trees in the distance. I pulled up the collar on my jacket and shoved my hands into my pockets. It was December, officially wintertime. Although it didn't quite feel like it. The fall weather had maintained itself around the sixties in the daytime. And that applied to most everywhere I spent the months of October and November. I'm not sure if it's climate change or what have you, but temperatures seemed to be warmer this year. Tonight, the temperature was cool, maybe fifty degrees. Apart from the car accident and the impending danger, this was a nice night.

I looked toward the main strip and traced the closed daytime businesses. They led into other businesses that were open at night. The first building I saw was a bank, then a church—Protestant. Next to it was a pharmacy and a dry goods store, which looked like it was cut straight out of an old west movie set. After that, I saw the more nighttime establishments. There was a coffee shop, opened late, then a bar, and a fast-food joint that I'd never heard of, which was across from the closing McDonald's.

The main street was straight at first. Then it wound slightly to the left. On that side of the street, there was a motel with a red neon sign. Across the motel's parking lot, there was an all-night diner. It must be the one Fry mentioned because it was the only thing that classified as a diner in the whole town that I could see. And I could see the whole place. The car count in the parking lot was enough to count on one hand. Out front, a short staircase led up to the entrance. Another neon sign glowed in a window. It had two lines that read: *Ceanna's Diner* and *We're Open*. The diner had half wall-length windows that stretched from one corner to the other and then wrapped completely around the building.

I crossed the street and headed toward the diner's lights without even thinking twice about the coffee shop. Which was unusual because I liked coffee. But diners had coffee. Coffee shops had more expensive blends. Most of which I'd never heard of. Even though they were pricey, I liked to try them. You never know when you might find a coffee bean you like.

In my current state of affairs, I wasn't in Cedar Springs for the coffee. I was there because Fry told me his witness needed protection. It was time to find out how true that was. So, I did what I did a thousand times a day. I put one foot in front of the other and marched up the strip to the diner.

6

THE THING about hunting unknown bad guys in a small-town diner, where everyone knows each other, is that the most suspicious person is *you*. And when you're a stranger who walks into a small town, off the beaten path, everyone suspects you.

Inside of Ceanna's Diner, the place looked like a ghost town. It was pretty empty. There were two tables with people and a room full of empty tables. There were two patrons sitting at a long, white counter, on the customer side. A cook, dishwasher, a waitress, and a waiter stood behind the counter. The cook, dishwasher, and the two patrons were huddled together, like they were at a craps table. They spoke to each other in hushed tones like they were relaying dirty jokes.

The waitress was a young woman, somewhere between twenty-five and thirty years old. She stood five foot nothing and looked like she weighed a hundred pounds soaking wet. The young waiter and she wore the same uniform—the same white top, the same black apron over their bottoms. But that's where the similarities ended. The waitress's uniform had a black skirt, cut short. It was above the knees and just low enough to leave something up to the imagination, but not much. She had long dark pantyhose under it, which I guessed helped keep her legs warm. Her top was basically the same as his, only hers looked better on her. Her sleeves were short, which revealed some tattoos on her arms. She had long black hair with a partial shave underneath on one temple. It was a style I'd seen before. I kind of liked it. It was rebellious, yet not overboard.

Her eyes were big and blue, like oceans trapped in a sea of white. I felt instantly drawn to her, like two characters on a stage. She glanced at me with a stare that could stop an oncoming train.

The waiter was a young Native American guy—probably right out of high school. He wore thick glasses. Underneath the glasses, there was a look on his face like this was his first night working. There were patrons sitting in his section with angry looks on their faces like they had been waiting for their change or their checks forever. Perhaps they hadn't even gotten their food yet. Whatever the thing was, they looked angry. My guess was they had already eaten because most people would just get up and walk out with that kind of angry boiling on their faces. Of course, in this town, where else were they going to go? I guess to the coffee shop, which probably had a limited menu. Maybe it served food, but a lot of coffee shops only serve cold food. No grill. No selection of home-cooked meals.

The patrons in the young guy's section had already eaten. Now, they waited, with decreasing patience, for their bill. Which was good for me. It meant that they would get up, pay their check, and walk out, eliminating them as suspects. That left me with only the two guys at the counter. However, they didn't fit the bill either. The staff were talking to them like they were all friends. I doubted the staff knew the bad guys that I was looking for. That would make no sense. The guys I'm looking out for would be out-of-towners. No one would know who they were when they walked in, except maybe Kara, which I guessed had to be the only female staff member, the waitress with the eyes.

I approached the counter and looked around. The waitress stepped over to me with a smile on her face. She was an attractive woman—no doubt about that. Besides her eyes, her smile would set a loyal dog out on a path of betrayal. One of her visible tattoos took up the length of the bottom part of her forearm. It was writing. Some kind of cursive font that I couldn't read, not without staring. And I had already stared at her enough. Any more and I risked ogling. I didn't want that. I was trying to be anonymous, undercover.

I glanced at her nametag. It claimed her name was *Beth*. But it wasn't. This was Kara. It had to be, unless Fry misled me. She was the only woman working that shift. Unless there was another one in the back, which I guessed was possible.

Kara said, "Hi there."

She spoke with a hint of an accent but not a western one. It was more blurred between southern and generic, like someone from out of the DC area. She is in WITSEC. Maybe she's originally from Virginia or some place south?

I smiled and said, "Howdy, ma'am." Which made me feel lame the second I said it. It was like the right words were shredded in my brain before *howdy* fell out of my mouth.

She said, "Are you here for dinner?"

"Yes, ma'am. Where shall I sit?"

"Have a seat anywhere you'd like."

"Where's your section?"

She said, "I'll take you wherever you want."

I cracked a smile at the proposition, inadvertently. It was a reflex. I'm a gentleman, but not a dead man. Of course, I doubted she was attracted to me. I'm probably fifteen years older than her and scruffy looking. She looked up at me and smiled, but that was her job. I heard my mother somewhere in the back of my mind reminding me to *be a gentleman*.

I nodded, turned, and stepped away to a back-corner booth. I sat down, back to the wall, so I could see the entrance and the parking lot through all the windows.

Kara grabbed a menu and walked over to me. She placed it in front of me. The menu was a simple eight-by-ten construct; paper laminated in plastic. It was double sided.

I scanned it. It was all the basic Americana types of foods, including a breakfast section that stated it was available twenty-four hours a day.

Kara stood close to the edge of the table. Her apron was so close I could've reached around her and untied the knot in the back with little effort. She asked, "Can I get you a drink to start? We got beer in bottles."

I asked, "Got fresh coffee?"

"I wouldn't say it's fresh. It's been sitting out for an hour. The owner scolds us if we make a new pot after only an hour. But it's good. Best in town. Better than the coffee shop's I think. I drink it. Then again, I like my coffee strong and black. I don't do creamer."

I smiled. Kara just became the most beautiful woman in the world to me. A black coffee drinker and not bad on the eyes was all the information I needed to know she was a good woman.

"I'll take a cup," I said, then I heard my mother's voice again in the back of my head. *Where're your manners?* So, I added, "Please."

Kara nodded and returned behind the counter. She went to the young waiter and made a hushed comment. He glanced at me, smiled. They giggled together like old friends. I realized he might've been gay, which must've been hard for a teenager on a reservation. If he lived on the reservation. I wasn't sure, but being in such proximity to it meant it was a likelihood.

He ignored me and returned to his dilemma of trying to figure out whose check was whose before his two tables started grabbing pitchforks and torches. They were getting restless.

Kara returned to my table after a moment with a piping hot cup of coffee. She set it down in front of me, stepped back, folded her hands together, and said, "I've never seen you here before."

"I've never been here before."

"What brings you here? We get the same people here."

"I'm just passing through."

She said, "Few people come through here unless they're lost. Are you lost?"

"Not lost. I'm in the right place. Don't people stop here at night? After a long day of driving? I imagine you get a lot of customers who grab something to eat before going over to the motel?"

"Not really. We're off the beaten path. Sometimes people end up here. But they're usually lost. We get many people stop in here and ask for directions to Flagstaff and drive away."

Fry sent me here to protect an off-the-books witness named Kara. Before I could do that, I needed to confirm this was who he was talking about, without giving myself away. So, I changed the subject and asked, "Have you lived here a long time?"

She said, "Since I was a little girl. Well, I wasn't born here. I grew up in Flagstaff. Now I'm here."

She might be telling the truth. And she might not. It was hard to tell. If she was Kara and had been lying to everyone for five-plus years, then she'd be damn good at it by this point. So, I took a different approach. Fry said she had a son. I asked, "Got any little ones?"

"One. I got a son."

"Ah. How old?"

"He's nearly seven. Wanna see a picture?"

I said, "Yes. Please."

This was her. It was Kara. It had to be. It added up.

She reached into her apron and pulled out a phone. She put in a passcode and swiped to a photo and reversed her phone, showed me the image. It was a picture of her and a little boy. He was about five or six in the photo. He had thick blond hair and big blue eyes, like hers. They both wore Mickey Mouse ears.

"We took this one last year at Disney Land," she said.

They looked happy, which also made me think of my mother. She was dead now, but I missed her. I wished I had more time with her, but I didn't.

Kara must've noticed I was lost in thought because she asked, "Are you okay?"

"Oh yeah. Sorry. You look happy together. He's a good-looking kid."

She removed the phone, stared at the photo one last time, and smiled at it. Her smile was all big white teeth. She glowed. Then she returned the phone to her apron.

She said, "I'm Beth, what's your name?"

I reached a hand out to her, open palmed for her to shake, and said, "Jack Widow."

She slipped her hand in mine and squeezed, hard too, which didn't faze me. My hand was like a bear's paw compared to her dainty one. Even though her hands were dainty compared to mine, they were worn, like she'd been waitressing a lot of years.

"It's nice to meet you, Jack."

"Just call me Widow. No one calls me Jack."

"Oh, okay, Widow. That's strange."

I shrugged and said, "It's a military thing."

We stopped shaking hands. She slid her hand out of my palm, slowly and tenderly. She asked, "Were you in the military?"

"I was, but that's ancient history now."

She smiled again and asked, "So, you want food?"

I glanced at the menu and back up at her. I scooped up the coffee mug and said, "Just the coffee for now. But I'll hold on to the menu. I might be here a while. If that's okay?"

"Sure, you can hang out all night if you like. We're open twenty-four hours."

"Will you be here all night?" I asked.

"Yes. I'm working the grave shift. Be here till morning," she said and turned to walk away. She stopped and said, "If you need anything, just holler."

"I will. Thank you."

Kara turned and walked back to the counter. Back to work.

7

KARA RETURNED to doing work behind the counter. I sat, drank coffee, and studied the room. The counter was a long, off-white thing. It was clean and tidy and organized, but faded from age. The white color would eventually fade away, losing all traces that it had once been white at all.

There were five chairs at the counter. One had a black garbage bag covering it as if to signal the chair was out-of-order. Probably broken, or perhaps it was too torn up to leave out for people to see.

The two guys sitting at the counter were not together. Although they sat a chair apart, they spoke to each other occasionally. Both middle-aged guys, drinking coffee. No food or plates or silverware in front of them.

One guy faced the kitchen. His back was to me. The other sat diagonally across from the first, around the counter's corner. Both men wore trucker hats. Both wore thick beards, speckled with gray over black. They were truck drivers, obviously. There were two trucks parked across the street, stretched across the back of the motel parking lot. They were acquaintances, but not friends. They knew each other from the road. Maybe they even had similar routes. Maybe they both stopped here every so often at the same time. They were two men in the same industry, sharing the same route, sharing the same all-night diner.

Whatever the case was, these two guys weren't my suspects. They weren't who Fry wanted me to look out for. That was obvious. I had to keep my eyes peeled for anyone who came through the door. It wasn't long before I signaled Kara back over to refill my coffee. This could be a long night. I figured I better get the fuel in now.

Kara refilled my cup. She smiled at me the whole time. Then she returned to the counter. She appeared to be doing some kind of side work, which was probably required by her employer.

The other patrons in the diner were finally paying their checks. The young waiter had gotten it all straightened out and was at the register closing out his customers.

After all the checks were paid, both of his two tables piled out the front entrance like the building was on fire. The door's buzzer dinged every time someone opened it. The customers strolled out to the parking lot and piled into their cars and vanished into the night.

The young waiter looked relieved. He sighed the moment his customers all left, like a mountain of stress had just drained from his life. He went over to Kara. They spoke out of earshot. Eventually, their conversation ended, and he walked back through the kitchen. He returned after a couple of minutes, wearing a windbreaker, and holding a pack of cigarettes. It was a fresh pack. The young waiter tore the plastic off as he passed the counter. He patted the end of the pack on the palm of his hand. I don't smoke cigarettes. I've only smoked them a handful of times in my life and that was out of social circumstances. But I knew the reason smokers did this was to pack the tobacco down into the tube more tightly.

The young waiter passed through the nearly empty dining room and went out of the front door. The door alert chimed and slowly sucked shut. He turned back and nodded at Kara once more, before disappearing around the side of the building.

The only people left in the diner were Kara, the cook, dishwasher, the two truck drivers, and, possibly, a manager in back. Although I had heard no noise coming from the back, the whole time I sat there. Usually, diners had a supervisor posted on all shifts, even the grave shift. The cook might've doubled as a cook and a supervisor. Or perhaps Kara doubled as waitress and supervisor. It was possible. The only thing I knew for sure was it wasn't the young waiter.

Kara finished whatever she had been doing and moved down the counter. She joined the conversation between the cook, dishwasher, and the two truck drivers.

After I emptied another cup of coffee, Kara left them and came over to my booth. She leaned on the tabletop with one hand, but not putting her weight on it. She held an old brown service tray down by her side. She said, "So, where ya headed?"

I said, "Nowhere in particular."

Kara said, "Are you lost?"

She'd already asked me that question. She might've forgotten my answer, but I didn't mind. Kara was stunning. She could've forgotten my name and I wouldn't have minded. I said, "No. Just not headed anywhere in particular. I got no plans. I'm just going."

Kara tilted her head, shot me a sideways glance. Then she looked down at my empty coffee mug. She said, "Wow! You really like coffee."

I said, "It's my drug of choice."

"I'll get you another round," she said, then turned and walked away. She stopped at the two trucker drivers at the counter and checked on them. They responded with cheery demeanors. They did that every time she spoke to them. Every time she approached them, they perked up. I was understanding why they stopped in here.

Kara walked to the coffeepot sitting on a burner and picked it up and returned to my booth. She said, "There's plenty of coffee, so don't be shy. Drink as much as you like."

She refilled my cup and rested the pot on the table's end. She propped one knee on the empty seat across from me, like she had probably done a million times with a million other strangers. A waitress's way of both being extra friendly and working harder for tips. Flirting was a moneymaking tactic used all over the world in every tipped profession.

I didn't mind. She could use this tactic on me until the sun came up. I wasn't going to cry about it. Plus, I was supposed to keep a close eye on her. It wasn't my job. I wasn't being paid for it. But who else was going to keep her safe?

I couldn't keep guard her forever. I could stay all night. I guess. Tomorrow, I could reassess the situation. Maybe Fry would be well enough to talk. Another thought I had was that cop I spoke to, Moreno. He might figure out where I was and send a deputy here. Perhaps they would take over. There was too much I didn't know about this case. Fry was going to have to elicit help, eventually. For now, I was all Kara had. I thought about asking her point blank, but I decided against it. Better she knew nothing until she needed to. Right now, there was no reason to alarm her.

Kara asked, "So what do you do for work?"

"Nothing."

"Between things?"

I nodded.

She asked, "What do you do with your time, then?"

"You're pretty much looking at it."

Kara folded her arms under her breasts and asked, "What do you mean?"

"I drink coffee. That's about all."

"What? You just drink coffee all day?"

"Not all day. I sleep sometimes."

"That seems unlikely if all you do all the time is drink coffee."

"Not really. When it's time for bed, I sleep pretty good."

"You learn that in the army?"

"I was in the Navy, but yeah. When you go on deployment, you learn to sleep when you can. Coffee has zero effect on that for me."

I paused a beat, then I said, "I have to pee a lot though."

Kara giggled and asked, "So, what do you do? Really? For money?"

"Really, nothing."

"No job?"

"Nope," I said and took a pull of my coffee, which I was thinking about half the time. The other half, I was distracted by her being so close. She made me sweat a little.

"Why not? You can't get one? Or you don't want one?"

"I don't need one. Not interested in working away the years I got left."

She shot me that sideways stare again and said, "You ain't that old. What're you? Like forty?"

"Something like that."

"Well, I'm twenty-five. That's probably too young for you."

She said it with a certain tone at the end of it, like it was a question. It was like she said it, thinking it was what everyone would think. But then, she left a question mark on the end, like maybe she wondered if I thought that.

I said, "You're old enough to drink, right?"

"Of course. I'm twenty-five. I told you," she said and smiled again—big, white teeth. She glowed without the smile. But with it she radiated.

I smiled back at her and took another pull of my coffee.

She asked, "How do you pay for things?"

"I have savings, some monies invested, things like that."

"Sounds expensive. What will you do when you run out?"

"I don't need much. Just enough for clothes, coffee, food, and bus tickets."

"What about shelter? Where do you sleep?"

"I sleep in motels."

"Doesn't that get expensive?"

I said, "I don't go to the Ritz Carlton."

"Will you run out?"

"Someday. I don't really think about it. Guess I should though, but I don't. I live in the present. I don't think about the future so much."

Kara shifted her weight from one foot to the next. Her hips reacted accordingly. For having a small stature, she had nice curves. A set of metal ring bracelets jingled on her wrist. She smiled again, and again, it was all teeth and glow. She asked, "Will you please take me with you? I'd love to get out of this dump."

"Why don't you?"

Her smile rescinded a little. Her shoulders slumped a little. And her eyes gazed off into a thought. She appeared sad for a moment. She said, "No. I couldn't do that."

"Why not?"

Kara paused a beat and said, "I got reasons. It's complicated."

I stayed quiet.

A silence fell between us, and a bit of awkwardness set in. Kara reared back and glanced at the parking lot, like she sensed movement. And there was the faint sound of big tires on gravel. I craned my head and looked around Kara's curves to see the lot through the windows.

There was a new arrival. A big, black Ford Explorer, a newer model, pulled in slow and chary, like an undercover surveillance vehicle. It stuck out and seemed more of an outsider than I was. I checked Kara's eyes. She didn't recognize the vehicle.

Just to be sure, I asked, "Regulars?"

She stayed facing the parking lot and said, "Never seen them before."

"Better get ready for them," she said, and turned back to me, smiled, picked up the coffeepot, and returned to the counter. She waited there, fiddling with the various machines like she was preparing for a new batch of customers.

Kara waited behind the counter for the new customers to get out of their vehicle and enter the restaurant. But that never happened.

8

THE YOUNG WAITER returned from behind the building where he had smoked a couple of cigarettes. I watched him through the windows. He walked up to the front of the diner and stopped on the steps leading to the entrance. Before he started up them, a man rolled down the passenger window of the Ford Explorer and called him over.

The young waiter turned back to the guy and walk over to the Explorer.

The vehicle's interior lights were switched off. I couldn't see how many people were inside. I presumed there were at least two—the driver and passenger. Light emitted from two lights in the parking lot. They were high on poles. Exhaust billowed from the Explorer's tailpipes. The engine idled. The head-lamps were off, but low red brake lights reflected off the Explorer's rear panels, over the back tires.

The young waiter walked toward the passenger window, but stopped suddenly five feet away, like something scared him from stepping any closer.

Kara watched with impatient eyes. She went through the trouble of returning to her default waitress position to welcome these guys in. But they weren't coming inside. Not so far.

The truck drivers at the counter continued speaking in murmurs to each other. I drank the rest of my coffee. The primal part of my brain was alerted. I figured if these were the guys I was waiting for, it was best to down the coffee now. I hated wasting coffee. I never left a drop behind. Never.

Kara had a look on her face like she was saying to herself: *What in the hell is taking so long?*

My hope was these guys were stopping to ask directions. Or maybe they were asking the kid if the diner had food worth stopping in for.

The young waiter turned and glanced back at the diner and back to the passenger in the Explorer. He nodded like he was answering the guy's questions. Finally, the passenger in the Explorer rolled his window up and the young waiter turned, shrugged, and came back inside. The conversation was over.

The young waiter climbed the steps and stopped at the entrance door. He gazed at me, like he was surprised to see me. Then he pulled the door open. The door alert chimed again. The young waiter entered, threaded through the dining room, stopped at the counter, and spoke to Kara. I could hear them well enough.

She asked, "What's that all about? They coming in or what?"

The young waiter said, "Not sure. They asked if we were busy. How many people were in here, and stuff like that."

"That's weird."

"They asked about you."

"What? Why?" Kara asked. She leaned out and glanced past him at the Explorer. It just sat double parked. The engine idled and exhaust pooled out the back. The occupants ran the heater, but they were just sitting out there, waiting, like they were waiting for another vehicle to arrive to join them.

The young waiter said, "They asked if you were working. Never said why. Guess they want you to wait on them."

Kara paused a beat. A look came over her face, like she was deep in thought. She pondered the next words that she'd use. She asked, "Did they ask about Beth?"

The young waiter stared at her dumbfounded. He said, "Yeah. What else would they call you?"

Kara smiled and said, "Nothing. Never mind. Did you tell them I'm here? I'll be here all night. Like usual."

"I know. I told 'em."

"Guess they're waiting for someone."

The young waiter nodded. He looked around the diner, threw his arms up in the air, and remarked about how empty the place was.

Kara said, "I suppose you wanna go home?"

The young waiter nodded and asked, "Is that okay?"

"Sure. Get your side work done and you can leave."

"I did it already."

"Fine. Get out of here. See you tomorrow."

The young waiter smiled. He was so happy to leave early that he half skipped back behind the counter. He stopped at the register, keyed in some code, and printed out a pile of receipts from it. The machine was ancient in terms of cash registers. The entire process took several minutes. Finally, the young waiter finished. He took the heap of printed receipts over to an empty spot on the countertop. He sat down and counted up his check totals. He used an app on his phone to calculate what he owed to the diner.

After he was done adding things up, he pulled out wads of rolled up cash-money. He set it all down on the countertop.

One of the truckers lifted his head and stared at it. The guy licked his lips like the thought of jumping the kid outside in the parking lot and stealing his tips was crossing his mind. The temptation subsided, and the trucker went back to his coffee and conversation with the cook, dishwasher, and the other trucker.

The young waiter continued his calculations, and after another few minutes, he was satisfied. He piled the dollars into two piles—one large pile and one small one. I assumed the small one was his tips because he looked disappointed.

After he gathered up the money, he handed the large pile to Kara, who took it and his paperwork. She spent half the time it took him to count it all up, and she was done. The young waiter said goodnight to everyone, except for me, and left. The front door chimed again.

I followed the young waiter's departure as he walked out the front door, back out to the parking lot, and past the black Explorer. The Explorer's engine continued running idle. The interior lights stayed off.

I tried not to stare. In case they could see into the diner, I didn't want to make it obvious that I was watching them. But who knew how long they'd sit out there waiting? I got another refill from Kara. It looked like I was going to need it.

9

Two HOURS PASSED, and the Explorer didn't move and neither did I. I stayed in the booth, watching there the whole time. Kara spoke with me several times. By then, I was the only person left in the joint. Occasionally, she looked back to the parking lot to see if the Explorer was still there. And every time, she commented on it. It worried her. I recommended she should call the cops if she was so worried, but she didn't. Without giving away why I was there in the first place, I told her it was reasonable to call them.

"What if they're casing the joint, waiting to rob it?" I said to her. It was a plausible scenario. It tempted her to call the sheriff, but she didn't.

She stood near the edge of my booth. The coffee pot rested on the tabletop. I took matters into my own hands. The Explorer was making her nervous. And it did the same to me. I finished another cup of coffee, and I asked, "Gotta payphone?"

"No payphone. But you can use mine. The owner won't let customers use the diner's phone. Just no international calls."

"It's local."

She took a phone out of her apron, unlocked it, and handed it to me. She took up the coffeepot and walked off to give me some privacy, but she didn't go too far. No one is completely trusting of a stranger using their phone.

I looked at the screen. The phone's wallpaper was a photo of Kara and her son. He was a good-looking kid. Great smile. Great coif of hair. Her hair was jet black, but his was beach blond. He didn't have her hair color, but he sure had her smile. He open-mouth smiled and there were big, white teeth, like hers. But his were all crooked, and hers were all straight. He was still at that age where kids had crooked teeth, before years of dentists and braces and tooth fairies and quarters under pillows.

I swiped on the phone and pulled up the *Google* icon. I tapped it and Googled the nearest hospital and memorized the number so I could dial it. But when I tapped the number, the phone asked me if I wanted to call it. I forgot phones do that now. I pressed yes, and the phone rang twice. A hospital staffer answered.

"Hello, Cedar Springs emergency room?"

I said, "Yes. My father was admitted earlier. I wanted to check and see how he's doing."

"What's your dad's name?"

"Fry. First name Patton, like General Patton."

She went quiet. I heard keystrokes on a keyboard. She came back on the line and said, "Here he is. Good news. He's stable."

"Is he awake? Can I speak to him?"

"No, sir. I'm afraid he's under sedation. The doctor gave him nitroglycerin, and they did a Cardiac catheterization, but he's going to pull through okay."

"What's a Cardiac catheterization?"

The operator went quiet for a moment. I heard her whispering to someone else. A new voice came on the line. She said, "Hello. I'm a nurse here. The Cardiac catheterization is where we put a tube through a blood vessel in the wrist to the heart to open up a clogged artery. We did this for your father and he's doing fine. Honestly, he was lucky to get here so quick. From what I heard, he's lucky there was a pedestrian on the scene to help him out. But he's not out of the woods yet. We're keeping him here overnight and moving him in the morning to Flagstaff General tomorrow. They've got the better conditions to observe him. He's going to need to stay in the hospital for a few days."

I asked, "Has the sheriff been there yet?"

"No one's been here for him. No law enforcement. Not yet."

I thanked her for the information and hung up the phone. I set it down on the table for Kara to pick up. She saw I was done with her phone and walked over to pick it up. I glanced at the parking lot again. I saw a new arrival. A pair of headlights jumped over a dip in the road, slowed, turned into the parking lot. It parked in a space next to the Explorer.

The car was a dark blue Ford Taurus. At first, I suspected the new arrival might be an unmarked police car because the model and the tinted windows and an array of antennas stuck on the back. Plus, the driver handled the car with a careless bravado like a cop.

Maybe Moreno figured out enough about Fry to figure out why he was here? Maybe, he'd informed the US Marshals, and now, they were sending cops to sit on Kara.

If this was a cop, then I was just happy to see him. It made me smile because possibly the cavalry was here. Good thing too, because I was feeling a little tired. Coffee or no coffee, I get sleepy like everyone else. Plus, I was ready to move on, preferably to a motel room with a soft, welcoming bed and a good night's sleep to follow.

I was dead wrong.

10

THE DRIVER of the Taurus turned off his engine and climbed out. He wore a thin leather jacket, a shirt and tie, and blue jeans. He looked like he'd been driving awhile, maybe all night because as soon as he stepped out, he stretched his legs and arms and rubbed his eyes like he was fighting away the sleepiness.

He stretched several times to the right and repeated it to the left, like he was preparing to go on a morning jog. After, he stepped over to the guys in the black Ford Explorer, but something was wrong about his demeanor. He didn't look like a cop who was questioning a couple of suspicious guys staking out a diner. He looked like he knew them. And they knew him because they shut off the Explorer's engine and climbed out. They huddled with the Taurus driver like they were teammates on a sports team, discussing plays from the playbook.

There were two guys in the Explorer—the driver and the passenger. There was no one in the backseat. The two guys from the Explorer were the kind of guys I had seen before—rough and dangerous. They were less than upstanding citizens. That was obvious. They were the kind of guys you saw on a sidewalk who made you spin back around and go the other way.

The Explorer's driver was a big guy, probably as tall as me, but heavier, like twenty-five pounds heavier. I'm two hundred and twenty-five pounds. But this guy was over two hundred and fifty pounds. He had to be. It was all muscle, built into massive arms, shoulders, and a barrel chest. There was a lot of gym hours penciled into his daily schedule. He was so big, his skin looked stretched to the max. The guy probably consumed whole chickens in a single day. He was so big that any blood test he took would've returned results showing huge amounts of steroids in his veins. No question about it.

The Explorer's passenger was a slick-looking guy—slick-backed hair, slick clothes. He wore an expensive suit. Some suit shop somewhere tailored his suit to fit his frame. The guy had a gray beard, cropped close to his face, and a steel look in his eyes, like he was the guy in charge of the three of them. The big guy either worked as muscle for the Explorer's passenger, or he was an actor playing the part of a mafia wise guy. He fit the part perfectly.

Although I had hoped the Taurus guy was a plain-clothes cop, I doubted it now. Not unless he was meeting with two mafia informants, which I doubted.

The Taurus guy looked, walked, and stood like a cop, but he wasn't. I had grown up around cops and worked with all kinds of cops. These were not cops. However, I suspected the Taurus guy was a cop in the past. The only way he was a cop currently was if he was moonlighting with the mob.

The three of them walked up to the diner, slowly and spaced farther apart. The big guy and the Taurus guy scanned the perimeter, noting the exits and any dangers they might encounter. I knew the look. The steel-eyed guy walked between them. He was the leader. No doubt about that either. He walked like a man who paid guys to do his work for him. Once they reached the stairs to the entrance, the big guy stepped up first. He grabbed the door handle, opened it, and stepped back, holding the door open. The door chimed. The steel-eyed guy walked through first. He carried himself like royalty.

The steel-eyed guy stepped all the way into the diner. He passed a lectern, standing at the front with a sign on it that read: *Seat yourself.* The steel-eyed guy gazed around the diner slowly, like he was taking in inventory of everything and everyone. He stopped when his eyes fell on Kara. He homed in on her.

Five seconds later, the big guy entered behind him. His massive bulk barely squeezed through the doorway without scraping his arms on the doorsill. He slipped around the steel-eyed guy and scanned the room, as he had the parking lot. He looked at the people at the counter first, and then, he swung his head over to my direction. His eyes landed on me. He stared at me like he instantly recognized me as his biggest threat in the diner. The big guy's eyes were beady, like two tiny black holes taking up the entirety of small eye sockets. I saw no whites in his eyes. They were all dark and gleaming. There was no real life there. He was devoid of empathy or independent thought. He was obviously a human being, but he was as emotionless as a shark, and probably as deadly.

Kara stared at them. I studied her face to see if she recognized them. But she didn't. Still, there was an uneasiness about her. It was in her demeanor and her eyes. She was one turn-of-the-dial away from terror.

Kara struck me as a fearless woman. Working the grave shift in an all-night diner like this, she's probably gone through it all. She's probably been hit on and harassed by men passing through every day of her life since she entered WITSEC. So, that these three made her look uneasy was really saying something. Since she didn't recognize them, I figured it wasn't that she didn't know them that made her uneasy. It was the fact that she recognized the type, like they could be from the same trouble she left behind six years ago.

I stayed calm, but my muscles were ready to move, ready to react. If one of them pulled a gun, I'd have to be quick. If they all pulled guns, then we might all die. But they didn't pull out any firearms. Not yet.

Kara stood behind the counter and called out to them. She fake-smiled and said, "Hello, guys. Please, seat yourself wherever you like. I'll bring you some menus."

The steel-eyed guy didn't respond. He just gazed left and gazed right. He swung his body to the right and walked to a booth on the opposite corner from me. The big guy followed. They ended up diagonal to me. There was thirty feet between us.

The Taurus guy entered last. He waited outside for a spell, like he was guarding anyone else from entering behind him. He stopped near the lectern and scanned the diner, same as the big guy had. And his eyes stopped directly on me, same as the big guy had. He stared at me like we were sworn enemies.

He barely looked at the truckers, the dishwasher, the cook, or Kara. He followed the others over to the booth but didn't sit with them, not in the booth. Instead, he pulled a chair up from another table and sat in it.

Kara walked over to them with some menus pressed against her stomach. She stopped at the edge of the booth, close to the Taurus guy. She fanned out the menus on the tabletop, reaching across the Taurus guy because he sat in the aisle. The Taurus guy rubbernecked his head back and stared at her ass as she set the menus down.

The steel-eyed guy smiled at her. The big guy did nothing. He just sat at attention like a guard dog waiting for a command.

Kara asked if she could take their drink orders. They said nothing. She gave them more time and left them with menus. The new arrivals never picked them up. They just sat there. The Taurus guy fidgeted in his chair like he was uncomfortable. He pulled out a gun that had been tucked into a clip-on holster on his belt and placed it on the table. I glanced over at it but didn't stare. It's not illegal to open carry in Arizona. And he kept it holstered, which was only slightly reassuring. I didn't want to make eye contact with them, so I stared at my coffee and took another pull from it. The big guy stared at me the whole time.

The gun was a Glock 22, a standard weapon for a lot of police departments. Which made me question if the Taurus guy was a cop again. Then, I remembered the Glock 22 was also a standard for US Marshals. Fry had the same model in his car earlier. Maybe the Taurus guy was a Marshal? Although I doubted it. Several things about him struck me as a guy who wouldn't last in most police departments.

The truckers asked Kara for their checks, separate. They each paid, stood up from the counter, and left at the same time. The front door chimed after them. The new arrivals remained where they were. They talked in hushed tones. The menus remained on the tabletop, undisturbed. A long minute passed, and then, one of the truckers cranked his rig to life and drove away. A few minutes later, the other trucker did the same. I watched as the last truck crawled out of the motel parking lot, turned onto the main strip, and vanished into the highway darkness.

A moment later, the dishwasher came out of the kitchen. He wore a jacket over his dishwasher apron. He said goodbye to the staff. He was done for the night. Kara would just leave any further dirty dishes in a bus tub under the counter to be picked up by the morning dishwasher.

The dynamics had changed. When the three guys entered, there were five people, plus them, making eight. Now, there were only six. Three of us and three of them. Three versus three. If it came to that.

Ceanna's Diner was empty except for Kara, the three guys, the cook, and me.

11

PEOPLE ALWAYS CLAIM that time seems to drag whenever you're waiting around. Take airport layovers and delays. Delayed planes always seem to take forever. The feeling is doubled when you're locked in a dangerous situation with three criminals who want revenge on a federal witness.

The Taurus guy's back was to me, but something told me that didn't mean he had taken his eyes off of me. I glanced over at them and realized he hadn't. He watched me in a window's reflection. Not a great view, but effective enough to know my position in the room. Certainly, he would know if I stood up or made any drastic movements.

So far, they hadn't made a move. Which got me questioning If I was right. Maybe they weren't here for Kara? Then I realized they hadn't made a move because they were waiting for me to finish up and go, leaving Kara, the cook, and the three of them.

I sat, drinking my coffee, acting as if I hadn't a care in the world and no intention of leaving.

Kara came over and asked, "You having more coffee?"

"No, I guess not. I better lay off for a while."

"Really? I thought coffee was your *drug of choice?*"

"It is. But I don't want to overdose. I'm still human."

"Here I was thinking you were some kind of mutant."

I stared at her and said, "Ouch. That hurts."

"I'm only kidding. You get that a lot because you're so big?"

"I'm not that big."

"Bigger than most people."

"That guy over there looks bigger."

Kara glanced over her shoulder at them, casually. She said, "They're kind of scary."

"Have you ever seen them before?"

"No. Never," she said, then she turned back to me. "Hey. You going to stick around here for a while longer?"

"I ain't got no plans."

"Good. I'd like it if you stayed. At least, till they leave."

"Why?" I asked, but I already knew the answer. She feared them. That was obvious. They were scary guys. They'd make a room full of cops uneasy.

Kara said, "They give me bad vibes."

I nodded and said, "In that case, I change my mind on the coffee. You can bring me another. Take your time."

She nodded and walked away. A few minutes later, she returned to me with the coffeepot and a slice of pecan pie, which I had never had outside of the South before.

She set the pie down on the table and refilled my coffee cup. She said, "The pie is on me. Thank you for staying."

"I didn't know there were pecan trees in Arizona."

"Of course. They grow in the south part of the state."

The Taurus guy called out to Kara. He leaned back in his chair, craned his head in our direction, and said, "Get me one of those too, baby. And two coffees."

Kara rolled her eyes back. They didn't see it. She called back to them. She said, "Coming right up."

She brought them coffee and pie. The Taurus guy drank coffee. The big guy drank nothing. The steel-eyed guy had a coffee in front of him but never touched it. Instead, he joined his big friend and also stared at me.

The big guy stopped staring but kept his eyes in my general direction. He stared at the cheap paintings on the walls around my booth. The guy looked bored.

Boredom is a great tactic to deploy against the enemy. Boredom makes the other side weak, complacent. It makes them overconfident. They think they can manage on autopilot, but they can't. When the enemy is complacent, that's the perfect time to strike.

Boredom was going to be my advantage, but I had made a mistake. The mistake I had made was that no man could drink as much coffee as I had in the last several hours and not have to go to the bathroom. Essentially, coffee is primarily water. And water goes straight through any man, and fast.

I figured I had two options—well, really three, if you considered my bladder bursting to be an option. On the one hand, I could get up and go to the bathroom. At which point, they would have the chance to make a move. They could get up, lock the door, draw their weapons, and shoot Kara dead. They could shoot the cook and wait for me to come out of the bathroom and shoot me. After, they could set the place on fire and watch it burn to the ground, destroying any evidence they were ever here. Then they could disappear into the night, down Route 66, never to be heard from again.

My second option was to get up, walk over to them, and make the first move. This would be risky. The one guy had a Glock already out. I'm sure his gun wasn't the only gun in the room. The steel-eyed guy probably had one. The big guy might not have one. I wasn't sure. He looked more like the type who liked to beat his enemies to death with his bare hands. He didn't need a gun to do his job.

I assumed that there were at least two guns, maybe three.

Before I could deliberate my options, my bladder made my choice for me. I scooted out of the booth, kept my hands out in plain view, and asked Kara where the bathroom was.

"Through the kitchen. Near the back door," she said.

I smiled, nodded, and shuffled off quickly through the dining room. I didn't want to give the guys time to make a move or to take advantage of my position. So, I hurried. I passed through a swinging door into the kitchen and stopped on the inside and spun back around. I peeked through an opening between the swinging doors. The three guys stayed seated. They didn't get up to do whatever they were going to do. I waited, stayed peeking out at them. The Taurus guy did what I was hoping he would do. He stood up and nodded at the steel-eyed guy.

He was headed in my direction. He was going to follow me into the kitchen, to the bathroom, and take me out first. He could neutralize me quietly, before Kara and the cook knew. It would make taking them down easier.

I turned, left the swinging doors, and weaved through the kitchen appliances and workstations. There was no one else in the kitchen besides me. The place was clean. Stainless steel ovens and counter tops were all wiped. The floors were swept and mopped.

I passed to the back of the kitchen, past the sinks, past a walk-in fridge, and saw the bathroom. The door was wide open. The light was switched off, but I saw the sink and toilet. There was one bathroom, no men's, and women's restrooms, just the one, shared bathroom.

I stepped inside and studied the door's lock. The door was weak. The lock was a doorknob lock, which was what I was hoping for. A deadbolt wouldn't work because I couldn't lock it and step out. I hoped for a doorknob lock, so that I could lock it, shut it, and pretend I was inside.

I switched the light on, the vent, and ran the water in the sink, leaving it running to make it sound like it was occupied. Then I locked it, shut the door, tried the knob—to make sure it was locked. Next I went to the back door, which was right across from it, opened it, and left it ajar.

Time was running out. So, I looked around for anything I could use as a weapon. First, I looked for cutlery. A sharp kitchen knife would do the job. It would be bloody, but effective. But I wasn't in the food prep area or near the grills. And I heard footsteps, then the swinging doors. There was no time to backtrack to search for a knife. I should've grabbed one when I passed them. Stupid mistake. So, I stepped out back, hoping to find cleaning supplies. A broom handle would make a nice clubbing weapon. It could be used as a Billy Club or as a stabbing weapon, broken in half with a jagged, spear-like end. But there was nothing like that.

All I found outside the back door was a group of empty garbage cans, turned upside down because someone had washed them out recently. Water seeped out onto the concrete from inside the cans. And there was a large, black rubber hose. It was long and thick and strong. It looked strong enough to scale a wall with. It looked durable enough to resist a knife slash. It had no spigot on the end, just a mouth for the water to pour out.

I scooped up the hose, cranked the water up full blast, pinched the end shut—closing off water from getting out—and waited.

12

PRISON RIOTS BREAK out all the time. It's an everyday occurrence all over the world. Prison guards, in most countries, don't carry firearms. They have them at their disposal, but firearms lead to shootings. Too often, they're taken away from the guards and used against them. Dead guards. Dead inmates. Those aren't the kinds of things the public wants to hear about their nearby prisons. A better solution to riot control is the use of water pressure.

High-pressure hoses are often used to subdue rioters. The water's pressure is so great that it can knock full-grown men down on their butts. The water pressure can be so great that it takes two or three guys to hold the hose while it's being sprayed. The same water pressure is often used by firemen to douse burning structures.

Restaurant hoses weren't equipped with the same strength and pressure as fire or prison hoses. That wouldn't make sense. But restaurants use hoses to spray down their floors at night. The pressure needed for this act was less than the pressure needed to fight fires or subdue prisoners, but it was a lot greater than the pressure from an everyday garden hose.

Until this point, I had really nothing to go on but instinct and observation regarding whether these guys were the threat that had caused a retired US Marshal to jump into his car and drive so recklessly in order to save Kara. That changed right there because the Taurus guy told me all I needed to know when he followed me into the kitchen. I waited silently. Then his shoe turned the corner. I pulled the back door tight until it looked completely closed. I left a sliver of a crack so that I could watch him through it. And I stayed quiet.

The Taurus guy snuck through the kitchen, past the ovens and counters. He stopped in front of the bathroom door, leaned in, put a cupped hand against the door, and listened. The faucet water sprayed inside the bathroom. He held his breath, trying to hear if I was in there talking on a phone, or humming to myself—things men did when they're alone in a bathroom. But he heard nothing but the buzzing of the vents and the water running from the tap. He gently tried to turn the knob. It was locked. Satisfied, he let go of the knob, stepped back, brandished his Glock, racked the slide, reared back, and kicked the bathroom door in. The door busted off of one of the hinges. The frame around the lock splintered, and the doorknob lock cracked and dangled from the door. The kick busted the knob. It left the outer knob dented inward. The Taurus guy exploded into the bathroom. He shoved his gun out into empty air and squeezed the trigger. The gunshot blasted and echoed in the cramped space. The bullet shattered the mirror. Glass exploded and crashed into the sink.

The Taurus guy expected to shoot me in the back as I stood at the sink. But I wasn't there. He stared at fragments of mirror that remained on the wall. He saw the top of his head, but over his shoulder, in the reflection, he saw something else. A massive figure stood behind him in the open back doorway. It was me.

The Taurus guy reacted. He pivoted—fast. He spun around and aimed at the back door and fired. But I wasn't there. Again, the gunshot echoed through the tight space and rocked my eardrums. The bullet went out through the back door and shattered the back window of an old, single-cab pickup truck parked behind the diner. The window glass exploded, and glass shards sprayed all over the truck's cabin.

The Taurus guy tried to shoot me twice. Both times, he missed.

The second time, I sidestepped before he aimed. I squeezed the hose tight. The water pressure had been building up. The force multiplied and grew in strength. It was getting hard to keep it back. I half-covered and half-pinched the end with my palm to allow the pressure to build up to the maximum amount.

A few seconds ago, when the Taurus guy stepped to the bathroom door, his back to the back door as he kicked the bathroom door in, I opened the back door and stepped in behind him—swiftly. So, when he turned back to shoot me in the back doorway, I was already out of the line of fire.

He fired. I sidestepped, grabbed a handful of his hair with one hand, squeezed hard, jerked his head up, and shoved the hose straight into his face with the other hand. I let go of my grip around the hose's end and let the water spray out—full force, full pressure. The water sprayed all out, drenching his face all at once.

Spray someone in the face with an explosion of high-pressure water and they'll instantly struggle to breathe. It's the same principle as waterboarding or having extremely cold air blasted in the face.

The Taurus guy gushed and winced, shifting his face from side to side to breathe. That was all he wanted. In a millisecond, it became the most important thing in the world to him. It's a natural thing, on a primal instinct level. We all need to breathe. The moment we feel like we're drowning, the body reacts, overriding everything else. He suddenly felt like he was drowning. And I wasn't going to let up on him.

As the water disoriented him, I clamped down on his gun hand, squeezed hard, and jerked the Glock straight down. He didn't get a chance to fire again, but he fell straight backward, gurgling from the shock of the water spray in his face.

I ripped the Glock from his hands, withdrew the water spraying in his face, tossed the hose aside, and shoved the Glock in his face. The water sprayed erratically on the floor. It streamed into the bathroom.

I pressed the Glock hard into his cheek, put a finger to my lips, and said, "Shhhh."

13

I BUNCHED up a handful of the Taurus guy's shirt and jerked him forward. He went up on his tippytoes. Water soaked his face and shirt. He coughed and spat water out and said, "You got no idea what you just did!"

"What? What did I do?"

"I'm a cop!" he lied.

"No, you're not. You're an assassin. You're here to kill Kara."

His eyes lit up. Surprise spang across his face.

"How...how do you know her name? She told you? Did she hire you?"

I said, "She has no idea about me. What about you? Who sent you?"

"She knows who sent us."

"What were you going to do to her?"

"Nothing, man. We're just going to escort her back home," the Taurus guy said.

"Where's that?"

He paused a beat, like he was thinking if he should answer me or not. So, I gave him incentive. I punched him in the gut, hard. Not enough to kill him, but enough to knock the wind out of him. He already had trouble breathing from nearly being suffocated by the water I shoved into his face.

The Taurus guy heaved forward. I let him go. He fell to his knees and gasped. I stepped back, shoved the Glock back in his face, and said, "Answer me. This isn't a negotiation."

"Okay. Okay," he said, stumbling over his words. "I used to be a cop. Now, I work for the O'Malley's."

"Who?"

"They're an Irish mob family. East Coast."

"Kara is part of an Irish mob family?"

"No. She's a regular chick from North Carolina. Her family are associates of the O'Malley's. That's all. They scratched our backs. Now, we scratch theirs. Like a favor for a favor."

I asked, "What's the plan? You guys come in here and kill everyone?"

"No. Just take her back with us."

"Who's the guy out there? He some kind of big Irish mob boss?"

The Taurus guy didn't answer. I shoved the gun harder into his cheek. He still didn't answer. So, I asked, "You ever been shot?"

His face turned a deep shade of blue, like he was strongly considering the question, which he should have been.

He said, "No! Please!"

"Who's the guy? Your boss?"

He said something, and then, stopped himself. I guessed he was going to deny it, play stupid, but he looked at my face and decided that was a bad idea.

"His name is Carter Shay. He's a midlevel guy. Important, but not that important. He just acts like he's a big dog."

I stayed quiet.

He asked, "What are you then? Some kind of US Marshal? Or bodyguard?"

"Nope. I'm just a guy passing through."

"What? Like a good Samaritan?"

"Something like that. I'm the kind of guy who doesn't like guys like you."

He looked puzzled. He said, "So you don't work for anyone?"

"I'm here to make sure Kara doesn't get hurt."

"What? Like a hired bodyguard?" he asked, and smirked.

I smiled and said, "You shouldn't make fun. See, I don't work for the government. I'm not bound by laws. Right now, I could put a bullet in your head, and no one would know. No one knows I'm here but you. No one here knows anything about me."

He gulped.

"Listen up. I got one question. It's important. You could say it's a matter of life or death—your life or death. Depending on how you answer, you might live—and then again, you might not. Got it? You understand the rules?"

He nodded.

I asked, "You understand the stakes?"

He nodded.

I asked, "How many guns are out there? Is Shay and the big guy both armed?"

"Yes. The other dude is called Little Adam. He doesn't like guns, but he's got one," he said, and smirked again.

I pushed the muzzle harder against his cheek.

He said nothing.

"Okay," I said, and backed off him. I let him go and backed away. He stayed on his knees.

He looked astonished. He asked, "You're letting me go?"

I stayed quiet and looked around the room. I wanted to tie him up with something, then I glanced at the Glock. I could hit him over the head hard enough to put him to sleep. But he made my decision for me, because just then, he got up on his haunches, stood and grabbed something out of his boot. It was something small and shiny. It was a small pistol in an ankle holster.

The Taurus guy drew the backup gun fast and pointed it in my direction. Before he could get me in front of the muzzle, I kicked him dead in the chest, with a heavy foot in a heavy boot. He got one shot off. The bullet whizzed through the space between my lifted-foot and the floor. It slammed into the floor, kicking up a dust of tile.

I reacted and shot him in the chest—once. It was a shot through the heart. The Taurus guy's eyes rolled back in his head. He tumbled backwards. He was dead before he hit the floor. The backup gun skidded out of his hand and across the tile.

Blood gushed out from the bullet hole and onto the tile. Eventually, it seeped into a drain in the middle of the kitchen floor.

I felt a little mad at the guy. He got himself killed. I would've been satisfied restraining him and leaving him for the cops to deal with. But I wasn't going to cry over it.

Four shots were fired. The guy called Shay probably drew his gun on the first one. He and the big guy probably jumped to their feet, alarming the cook and Kara, who probably threw their hands up in the air, as you do when someone points a firearm at you. So far, I had heard no gunshots from the dining room.

When Nelson fired the first shot, Shay and Little Adam probably expected that I was dead. They wouldn't have suspected the first shot. And maybe not the second one. Nelson might've shot me twice. Maybe I didn't go down on the first shot. So, he did a second one, just to make sure I was dead. But the third and fourth shots would've raised eyebrows. Shay and Little Adam would've been suspicious.

I heard the guy called Shay call out. He said, "Nelson, everything okay in there?"

I glanced down at Nelson, like he might respond. He didn't. So, I answered for him. I said, "Yeah. Be right out. Do nothing yet. Wait for me."

Shay said, "Okay." But there was confusion in his voice. Apparently, Nelson and I sounded nothing alike. I wasn't going to make it as an impressionist.

I had to ask them to wait for me because I had urgent business to take care of. Nature called. I went outside and relieved myself of all the coffee. It wasn't the best timing, but *when you gotta go, you gotta go.*

14

I STEPPED BACK into the kitchen through the back door and headed to the dining room, stopped at the swinging doors, and peeked out. Kara and the cook stood outside the counter. Their hands were up, like they were being held at gunpoint, which they were. Shay and Little Adam stood on the other side of them.

Shay had a .38 revolver out and pointed at the ground. He held it down by his side, one-handed. He already showed it to them. And now their backs were to him. He had it down by his side because he felt safe. Nelson had already taken care of the only threat in the diner, so why wouldn't he? Only Nelson was dead, and Shay didn't know it, not yet.

Little Adam had another Glock. He pointed at the cook and Kara from the side.

The angle of Little Adam and Shay put Kara and the cook in my line of fire. If I were on a SWAT team, it's doubtful my team leader would approve what I planned to do. But I wasn't on a SWAT team. It all happened fast. I pushed through the swing doors and into the dining room, making myself known. Everyone stared at me. I smiled at them and shouted, "Kara! Get down!"

She responded instantly, faster than she had when I called her Beth. She saw me, saw the Glock, and saw I pointed it straight at her. She exploded to action and shoved the cook out of the way. She was good under pressure, quick on her feet. The two of them fell to the floor, and I squeezed the trigger—twice.

The first shot hit Shay in the chest, center mass. The second shot went straight through Little Adam's head. It wasn't dead center, but anywhere on the head was devastating for the target. This was no different. A cloud of red mist exploded behind his head. Like Nelson, he was dead before he hit the ground.

Kara reacted fast. She had been in gunfights before. That was obvious. She rolled away from the cook and grabbed at Shay's .38. I stopped her. I said, "No! Leave it!"

She froze, looked back at me, and asked, "Why?"

"Fingerprints. We can't do anything about your prints in the store, but let's keep them off his gun. No reason to complicate things."

She nodded and scrambled to her feet. The cook came up slower. He glanced at me and then at Kara. He had questions in his eyes. But he didn't ask them. He didn't speak at all. I got the impression he knew to stay quiet. The less he knew, the better for him.

I entered the room, threaded past the counter, and stood over Shay, who was still alive, but barely. He wasn't looking good. He held his chest with one hand, trying to stop the bleeding. He clenched the bullet hole tight, but blood gushed between his fingers like water through cracks in a dam. His other hand inched for the .38. I stomped on the dropped weapon and put my weight on it, making it impossible for him to lift it. He tried anyway. With all of his strength, he tugged at the weapon. It didn't budge.

I pointed the Glock at him, stared into his steel-gaze, and said, "You must be Shay?"

He looked up at me, confused. He asked, "Who're you?"

"I'm nobody."

Shay spat up blood.

Kara came up behind me. She put two hands on my bicep, like we had known each other for years. She asked, "Are you going to shoot him?"

"I should."

"Please, don't. He's disarmed now."

I looked at Shay and said, "You're lucky. I ever see you again. I'll kill you. This girl is none of your concern anymore. Got it?"

Shay nodded and said, "There's more."

I lowered the Glock and asked, "More?"

"More of us."

"Where?"

"Here. In town. They're going for the kid," Shay said, and spat, like he was trying to make a deathbed confession. He was warning us, like it was his last chance for redemption, before he crossed over to the other side.

Suddenly, Kara's expression changed to sheer terror. She squeezed my arm and said, "Christopher! My son!"

"Where is he?"

"He's at my house with a babysitter. Oh God! We have to get to him before they do! Please! Help me!"

"I will."

Kara let go of her grip on me and turned and ran toward the kitchen's swinging doors. I stepped back, scooted the .38 away from Shay, and turned to the cook. He still had his hands up in the air, like now he feared I was going to shoot him. I took my foot off the .38 and said, "Pick it up."

The cook lowered his hands reluctantly, knelt, and scooped up the .38. He held it like a hot potato. I said, "He try anything, shoot him. Wait till we leave, then call the cops. Got it?"

The cook nodded.

I tucked the Glock into my waistband and chased after Kara through the swinging doors and past the kitchen and out the back door. She was at the driver side door of an expensive Ford Mustang GT.

I called out to her. I said, "Kara, wait for me."

She opened the driver's side door and hopped in. I ran over and got in on the passenger side. Before I could buckle my seatbelt, she had fired up the car. The engine roared to life. She reversed, backed out of a parking space, and we were off.

15

KARA DROVE like a bat out of hell, threading and plaiting around cars on the road, running traffic lights and stop signs. She tried calling the babysitter's phone through a digital interface in her car. There was no answer, just a dial and a ring and a voicemail.

I said, "We should call the police. They might get there faster."

Kara took a hard left turn off the highway and onto a two-way road. I had to put my hand up on the dash to keep myself from sliding. There were no other headlights on the street. There was no sign of life except for low lights coming off rows of rural houses in the distance.

Kara said, "No police. The men after me are extremely dangerous. And they don't just want me. They want Christopher too. They're well-connected."

"You think they've got the local cops in their pocket?"

"There aren't any local cops. The closest cops are in Ash Fork. They won't get here in time, anyway. Our local cops are sheriff's deputies. They're hardly ever here. They police the whole county. And these guys would've planned on police already. We need to get my son. Then I know a guy I can call. He's a US Marshal."

"You mean Fry?"

Kara glanced at me, and then, back at the dark road ahead. She asked, "How do you know him?"

"He sent me."

"He sent you? Are you a Marshal too?"

"No," I said, and I explained it to her as briefly as possible. I told her I was who I said I was, a drifter. I told her about Fry's driving, his heart attack, he went off in an ambulance, and he asked for my help.

She glanced at me again. It was a quick, sideways glance, like she didn't know what to believe. She said nothing about it. She tried dialing her landline on the car. It was the same as the babysitter's phone—no answer.

She shivered. Her cheeks turned flush. She was frantic.

I said, "Don't worry. We'll get to him first."

It took a little longer before we turned onto her street. The houses were spaced far apart. Mailboxes stood at the end of long driveways. Some houses I couldn't make out. They were too far back from the road or hidden behind clusters of trees.

The road became a dead end up ahead. "Oh, no!" Kara said, and slowed the Mustang to a crawl.

There was a house at the very end of the road. It was off from the road about a hundred yards. The yard comprised well-kept grass and a few big trees scattered about. The land was once used as farmland for raising horses, probably. I figured that because there was an old stable house at the rear that looked unused since the last century. Plus, there was plenty of empty pens and land for horses to run and graze at the back.

The house was a two-story wood farmhouse with big windows and a brick fireplace. A large porch wrapped around the front of the house. It had a porch swing. There were long rows of flower beds around the house, too. The house's lights were on in several windows, but dim.

The reason Kara reacted like she did was there were two vehicles parked in her driveway in front of the house. I'm guessing they didn't belong there. There was a third little car off in the driveway, pulled up to a garage door. It looked more like a babysitter's car than the other two.

The other two vehicles were a truck and a panel van. Both were painted black. And both had their engines idling. Smoke pooled out of the exhaust of the panel van. The truck was reversed and facing the street. No one was inside the cabin. But the panel van faced the house. It had North Carolina plates.

Kara stopped at her mailbox. She said, "That's my house."

"Kill the headlights," I said.

She switched them off and asked, "Now what?"

"Move slow, take us to the house."

She sped up, keeping the Mustang around five to ten miles per hour. At the end of the driveway, she stopped, parking the car nose-to-nose to the truck.

I turned to her. She stared at me. She shivered. I reached out, put my hands on both of her cheeks, and stared at her. I said, "Stay calm. They're not going to hurt him."

"How do you know? He might already be dead."

"He's not. They wouldn't send two vehicles and numerous guys just to kill a kid. Just the same, as they didn't go into the diner to kill you. This is a rendition."

"What?"

"Abduction," I said, and I opened my door, unbuckled my seatbelt, and got out of the car.

"Wait," Kara said, and she leaned across the console and popped open the glovebox. She reached in and pulled out a snub-nosed .38 Smith and Wesson, not unlike Shay's .38. She grabbed it and reached it out to me. "Take this."

I waved it off and pulled Nelson's Glock out of my waistband, showed it to her, and said, "You keep it. I got plenty here. Is the babysitter and Christopher the only two that are supposed to be in the house?"

Kara nodded.

"What's the babysitter look like?"

"She's eighteen, blonde, and around my height. She probably weighs a buck twenty."

I nodded. She could've stopped at *she's a teenager*. I doubt these guys brought anyone with them who fit that description.

Kara said, "Let me come with you."

"No. You stay with the car. We may need a fast getaway. Turn the car around, face the street, and get ready to roll. Honk the horn if anyone else pulls up. And try not to shoot unless you need to."

I shut the door and headed toward the house. I crept, staying low, but moved fast. Stealth was on my side, but time wasn't. First, I stopped at the truck and then the panel van. I checked to make sure they were empty, and I killed the engines on both, and, on both, I swiped the keys. I didn't want them getting out of the house and getting away in their vehicles.

It wasn't until I was at the side of the house, near the babysitter's car and the garage door, that I noticed a side entrance. It was wide open. I had the Glock out, pointed at the doorway. I burst through the open doorway and came into the garage. The door was a side door to the garage. Inside, the room was cold. There was an old junker, missing parts, like Kara liked to work on it. Also, there was a motorcycle missing parts. She must've liked to work on automotive.

I moved through the garage to another open door. This one led to the kitchen. I peeked in and saw no one. There were multiple scuff marks on the floor, like from boot prints. I scanned the kitchen with the Glock, saw no one. I heard noise from another room. It sounded like a television. There was low pistol fire and horses galloping and Native American calls, like an old western movie.

Above me, the ceiling squeaked. Someone stepped on the second level floorboards above me. I continued through the kitchen and stopped at another doorway. Only this one didn't have a door on it. It led to an open foyer, near the front door.

That part of the house was half opened up. There was a family room with furniture, shelves with books, plants, and the fireplace. From where I stood, the farthest wall was twenty-five feet. On that wall hung a large flatscreen television, where I saw cowboys on horseback shooting it out with cartoonish depictions of Native Americans—hooting and hollering. The movie was an ancient classic, filmed in black and white but later colorized. The gun smoke came out of the gun barrels like cap guns.

The floors were dark hardwood and old—maybe turn of the century, the last century. There were rugs strategically placed about. Some were longer than church wall tapestries. Others were short.

The foyer had the highest ceiling, with a large chandelier hanging up high above. The front door was dead bolted shut, which meant the intruders came in the way I came in. How had they got in? I had no idea. I didn't stop to check if locks were picked.

The house looked lit up from the street, but actually, the place was pretty dark. The chandelier was off. Same went for the lights over the living room. But there were standing lamps switched on, making the living room cozy. It was all setup for a babysitter and a little boy to lie around and watch an old western on the television. Which might've been what was going on before the intruders showed up because the babysitter faced the television like she had been watching it.

She was sprawled out on a sofa. She was to the side of the television. Her eyes were wide open, staring at the television, and lifeless. There was a bullet hole in the center of her forehead. But she wasn't alone in the room. There was a lone man standing there, facing her. He hovered over her corpse. His head was tilted downward. He stared at her, disturbingly, like he was gawking over her. And he held a gun down by his side.

I felt anger in my bones. Off to the right, there was a staircase that led up to the second floor. I heard more than one set of floorboards squeak above me. There were a couple of guys up there. They were stomping around and making a lot of noise. Down the hall, I heard another guy. He nearly saw me because he stepped out of one room and kicked in the door of another. The second door was across the hall from the room he barged out of. They were searching for something, or someone, probably the kid. He was hiding somewhere. The guy downstairs in the rooms was ransacking the room. It must've been a bedroom because I heard him overturn a bed.

He shouted back to the guy standing over the dead babysitter. He said, "Ron? What are you doing out there?"

I dipped back into the kitchen and stepped out of sight. The one called Ron flipped around and called back. He said, "I'm blocking the exits. You keep looking."

So far, I counted four of them. The kid was hiding somewhere. Therefore, he would stay quiet in a hiding place. So, I can discard him as one of the two making noises upstairs, indicating there are four guys.

If I was going to take these guys out, I needed to stay silent as long as possible. In the corner of my eye, I saw the solution. There was a wood block with an assortment of kitchen knives sheathed in it. I reached over, grabbed the handle of one, and pulled out a chef's knife. I kept the Glock in my dominant hand, but wielded the knife in the other.

I peeked back around the corner, saw Ron returned to standing over the dead babysitter. He stared at her like

Michael Myers might do. But I was the one with the big chef's knife.

I crept past the hall opening, across the foyer, and into the living room. The cowboys had escaped the *savages* and were now shooting it out with each other in some kind of double cross. One of them died on screen, clutching a bag of stolen money. It might've been a lot of money, but it was only five hundred dollars. People died for less. But not Ron. He was going to die because of what he did.

Quietly, I darted across the living room, past the staircase, and between the furniture. I kept my boots on the rugs as much as possible. I got behind him and he heard me. He probably felt me standing there, towering over him. He spun around, expecting to see his comrade, but he didn't. He saw me.

There was a demented look on his face, which reflected the demented brain in his head. We made eye contact. He stared at me, opened his mouth to speak. But he gasped instead. I stabbed the blade upward, under his chin, hard as I could with my weaker hand. With his mouth wide open, part of the blade appeared. One second it appeared through his tongue. And the next the point stabbed through the roof of his mouth. Beyond that, I'm not sure how far into his brain the blade went.

The guy stared at me for one long second, until the life in his eyes faded away. I didn't bother trying to pull the blade out. I let go of the handle. The guy dropped to the floor. I knelt fast and wiped the handle with the collar of his shirt. I try not to leave fingerprints when I don't need to. The last thing I wanted was to be attached to a crime scene. Why run the risk?

Ron had the same sentiment in mind before he invaded Kara's house and killed her babysitter because he wore gloves. I pulled them off him and put them on my hands. They were a tight squeeze, but I made it work. I wasn't going to need them that long, anyway.

Ron also had something else of use. He had an HK Tactical with a suppressor on it. Looking at the guy, I doubted he was ever in the military. He looked more like a reject. But the choice of weapon was good. The Heckler and Koch Tactical is a fine handgun. It's a .45 caliber, making it great for damage, but the offset is a smaller magazine capacity. I pocketed Nelson's Glock and ejected the HK Tactical's magazine. There were eight bullets in the magazine, with two slots empty. The magazine held ten rounds. One of the bullets was in the chamber. The other was embedded in the babysitter's forehead.

I reinserted the magazine and left Ron to rot and threaded back through the furniture. I stopped at the fire, picked up a fire poker with my inferior hand, and carried it to the hallway. I checked the hallway with the HK Tactical before entering. The other guy was ransacking the rest of a downstairs bedroom. He called out to Ron. He said, "Ron, come help me." Then, he called out to the kid. "Where are you? You little brat!"

I walked down the hall. The floorboards squeaked under my weight. The guy in the room said, "Ron, check the next room."

I stopped at the edge of the doorframe and glanced in. The guy's back was to me, but the way he had tossed a bed frame and mattress over, he had some cover on the other side. I stepped past the door quietly.

The guy in the room said, "Ron? Did you hear me? Get busy, so we can get out of here."

Of course, Ron didn't answer. The guy in the room became suspicious. It was in his voice. He said, "Ron?"

He stopped searching and came toward the door. The hallway was dimly lit from lights in the living room and the kitchen. But it was dark on my side. I stayed in the shadows, back against the same wall as the open door. The guy in the room started coming out into the hall. I held the gun right-handed. The fire poker was in my left. The bar was across my chest.

The guy in the room stopped inside the doorway and called out again. The eerie silence bothered him. He said, "Ron? You better not be horsing around!"

Just then a gun barrel appeared in the doorway and the tip of a shoe and the bridge of the guy's nose. The second his face breached the doorway, I cracked him with the fire poker. I swung it backhanded and hard. The bar slammed into the guy's mouth. Several of his front teeth shattered on impact into dozens of chips. He dropped his gun. A scream nearly emerged out of his mouth, but the shock of it bought me an extra second. I used that second to backhand him again, full-on in the throat. The blow crushed his voice box. He grabbed at his face and throat and fell backwards, landing on a pile of Kara's stuff he had tossed all over the place.

I stepped into the doorway, stopped over him, and pointed the HK Tactical at him. I raised the fire poker again. The guy floundered on the ground like a fish out of water. He was in immense pain. That was obvious.

I shoved the gun in his face. His eyeballs widened and slowed his squirming. He couldn't stop completely. He was in too much pain for that. I asked, "How many guys in the house?"

The guy tried to speak, but couldn't. Blood gushed out of his mouth, over the broken teeth that remained intact. He held up one of his hands and showed me four fingers.

I looked into his eyes and asked, "Four?"

He nodded.

I was done with him. So, I shot him twice in the chest fast. *Bang! Bang!* The bullet casings spat out of the gun and bounced off the hardwood floor. The noise was audible in the stillness.

The guy stopped flailing around. He was dead.

I moved on. I checked the rest of the downstairs, calling out for the boy in whispered tones. I said, "Christopher? Christopher?"

No answer.

"I'm with your mom. Where are you?"

No answer. Just then, I heard him, because the two guys upstairs found him. He was screaming, like he was struggling to escape them. One of them had flipped over a set of cabinets, found him hiding under it.

There was no need for me to go upstairs, so I went back to the end of the hallway. I rushed over to Ron and put the fire poker back into its slot on a poker stand. It clinked. I grabbed the bottom of Ron's pants sleeve and dragged him out of the living room and down the hall, left him there. I returned to the foyer, turned the corner, and entered the living room. I heard the kid screaming and crying upstairs, as well as the footfalls of the two guys who grabbed him. The floorboards squeaked as loud as any hundred-year-old farmhouse's floorboards would.

I dashed through the living room, weaved around another sofa, and squeezed myself back down a tight alley between the back of the staircase and a closet door. I waited. Seconds later, the two other guys came down the stairs. The last one carried Christopher, who pounded on the guy's shoulders with his little fists, trying to escape. The kid was full of fight, which I liked.

They reached the bottom step and entered the living room. The front guy spread out toward the foyer. He called out to Ron and the other guy to come out.

There was no answer.

He said, "Hey, guys. We got the kid. Come on! Let's go!"

The front guy went to the front door, unlocked the deadbolt, and pulled the door open. Cold wind gusted past him. I felt it on my face all the way across the room.

The back guy entered the living room and followed the front guy to the foyer. Terror and panic stretched across Christopher's face. The front guy spun around after opening the door. He called out to the dead guys again.

"Guys? We got him. Let's go!" he repeated, only this time he stopped dead in his tracks. He saw Ron and the other guy dead and slumped over the hallway floor like two sacks of potatoes.

He went for a gun stuffed into the front of his waistband. Before he got it out, I stepped out of the alley and into the living room, behind them.

The front guy saw me, jerked his gun out of his pants, fumbling with it like an idiot. I shot him twice in the chest, like his dead friend. I missed the second shot. It hit him in the gut, toppling him over, and backwards through the open front door. He landed out on the porch.

The bullet casings had ejected out of the HK Tactical like before. And, like before, they bounced off the floorboards. The sound echoed.

The back guy spun around with Christopher in his arm. He had a gun, but like the front guy, it wasn't in his hand. It stuck out of his front pocket.

Both the back guy and Christopher stared at me. The kid was no longer screaming or struggling.

I pointed the gun at the back guy. He couldn't beat me with his gun. I was already pointing mine at him. I had him dead-to-rights. His weapon was essentially holstered. He couldn't quick-draw it and expect to beat me. No one's that fast.

He could put both hands around the kid's throat, use him as a bargaining chip, and force me to drop the HK Tactical. That's what I was worried about.

But the guy didn't do that. He stared at me, a little scared and a lot dumbfounded. He lowered Christopher to the ground and stepped back and put his hands up.

I looked at the kid and said, "You okay?"

He put his hands up too, like he didn't know what to do.

I said, "Your mom is in the driveway. Go to her."

Christopher said, "They killed Lauren."

"I know."

Christopher said, "She was my friend."

I nodded and said, "Go to your mom."

He nodded and turned and ran out the front door. But first, he kicked the back guy in the shin, which made me chuckle. *I like this kid already.*

Christopher hopped over the dead guy lying on his porch and ran down the steps. Kara got out of the Mustang and met him in the driveway. They hugged.

The back guy stared at me. He said, "Don't kill me!"

I stayed quiet.

He said, "I can tell you who hired us."

"I don't care."

His face turned ghostly white because he had no leverage. He said, "Come on. You're not going to shoot an unarmed man, right?"

I stared at him and said, "I've done it before."

"Please!"

I said, "Look over my shoulder."

He looked over my shoulder into the living room. On the television screen, the main star of the movie kissed the leading lady and told her goodbye. Then, he got on his horse and rode off into the sunset. Credits rolled.

I said, "See that girl."

The guy nodded but said nothing.

I said, "She was unarmed. Innocent."

"Please don't shoot me!"

I said, "You're not unarmed. You got a gun right there in your pocket."

"But your gun is pointed at me."

I lowered the HK Tactical and ejected the magazine. It clattered to the floor. Then I turned the weapon and racked the slide. The last bullet, the chambered bullet, ejected out of the gun and clunked off a small, nearby table. It clunked once more on the floor.

The guy's eyes narrowed. I tossed the HK Tactical back into the living room and said, "Now it's not."

The old western's music played during the rolling credits. It was that generic, old western music, the kind played during the part where two cowboys gun-duel on the street. Their weapons are both holstered. They each tap the hilt of their guns before drawing on each other.

The guy stared at me. He moved his hand slowly up toward his pocketed weapon. In my best Clint Eastwood impression, I asked, "What are you waiting for, punk?"

As I figured he would, the guy went overdramatic. It was a combination of the cowboy music and the situation. He got confused, thought he was in an old gunslinger movie. He waited for me to inch my hand to the Glock in my waistband. But I didn't.

I didn't *inch* it at all. I grabbed it on the word *punk* and shot him.

The guy wasn't entirely dumb. He died with his gun in hand. And he cleared his pocket, but that was all. He never got his finger on the trigger. Never got the weapon even pointed in my direction.

I shot him through the chest like his friends, but only once. Red mist exploded into the air. The guy was dead seconds after he hit the floor.

I walked out of the house and took the Glock with me.

Kara and Christopher were in her car by the time I made it to the driveway. She had her window rolled down. She said, "Come on. We better get out of here."

I pocketed the Glock, tore off Ron's gloves, and tossed them out into the yard on my walk over to them. I didn't want Christopher associating me with it. First impressions are important. I'd rather him think of me as saving his life and not just killing a bunch of bad guys.

The moonlight shone white in the sky. A beam flashed across Kara's face. She looked luminous in it.

The nearest neighbors were coming out of their homes. Porch lights switched on across the street. They heard the gunshots that weren't silenced.

I stepped around the car, stopped next to the driver's side, put a hand on the door pillar, and bent over and looked into Kara's eyes. I said, "You guys should stay here and wait for the police."

Kara tilted her head. Disappointment came over her eyes. She said, "I told you. We can't trust them."

"I doubt the local cops are in these guys' pockets. I mean maybe they got someone somewhere."

"I can't risk it," she said, and glanced back at her son. He was in the backseat, strapped into a seatbelt. He stared at me. He had big, blue eyes and blond hair. He looked like her, all but the hair color. He was her whole world. That was obvious.

She looked back at me, took one hand off the steering wheel, and placed it on my forearm. She said, "Come with us."

I glanced up. The neighbors were all the way out in their driveways now. A couple of them were at their mailboxes. Smartphones came out. Some of them were pointed in our direction. They were filming us. Luckily, they were too far away to get the details of my face. This thought urged me to get away. I don't like being detained. And I just killed four guys, plus two at Ceanna's Diner. Even though the killings were justified, the cops won't care about that. Not at first. In my experience, they'll arrest me first thing and sort it out later. So, I said, "Okay."

I got in the passenger seat, closed the door, and Kara peeled out of the driveway. Minutes later, we were down the street. Thirty minutes after that, we checked into a motel in Ash Fork for the night because we needed to stay near Fry.

We would need his help.

16

We stayed in a motel off the main highway, in two rooms, one for me and one for Kara and her son. The rooms were single beds. So, they shared a bed in one room. And I took the bed in the other. We slept through the night. There were no questions. And there were no answers given. I figured they'd been through it. They should get some rest for the night.

The next morning, I got up early and showered with only hot water because the motel didn't provide a single serving of soap or body wash, unless my room was just overlooked or ran out. After I was showered and dressed, I left my room, put my ear to Kara's door, and listened to see if they were up yet. They weren't.

I left them there to sleep and walked down the stretch of the motel and checked around. I saw no prying eyes. No surveillance. No sign that we were in any danger of being found by whoever sent the guys from last night.

I exited the motel's lot and went down the street, looking for coffee. I settled on a fast-food joint, next to a thrift store, which made me decide to detour into the thrift store first. Inside, I shopped around and bought three pairs of clothes. Kara was still in her waitress uniform and Christopher had nothing but the clothes on his back. They never got to pack before we left Kara's house. I realized they'd need new clothes.

Sizing Kara up was easy because I had stared at her all night at the diner. Christopher was harder, not his size but what he might be interested in. I was easy.

I looked for a while before picking out clothes for the three of us. It was tempting to buy Kara several outfits that I saw, but only because I wanted to see her in them. Judging by her style, she probably would've loved some of them. There were a lot of low-cut tops that ignited my imagination. But I wasn't trying to get her noticed. Subtle was the goal. Protecting her meant keeping a low profile. It was going to be hard enough to keep random men's attention off her. The last thing I needed to do was buy her clothing that was anything more than boring.

I ended up buying everyone boring old casual clothing. I got Kara a long sleeve designer t-shirt and a plain sweater and black jeans. I got Christopher blue jeans and a designer t-shirt with a comic book hero on it. I didn't know who. It was one of those with the word *man* in the title, like Spider-man or Batman.

For myself, I bought black everything—a shirt, sweater, jeans, and boots, which I wore out of the store, ditching my old clothes in a bin set up for charity drop-offs. *Pay it forward* had always been a good motto to live by. The only item I had on before that I kept was a jacket. I paid for everything and carried it out in huge shopping bags with the store's logo on both sides. Then, I stopped in at the fast-food joint, picked up breakfast in a greasy bag and a couple of coffees shoved into a cardboard carrying tray, and soda for the kid.

I carried everything back across a few blocks to the motel.

An hour had passed since I left. I figured they'd be up by then. So, I knocked on their door. I glanced up at the sun and then down at shadows on the ground. I figured it was around eight in the morning.

Christopher opened the door. He was awake, but Kara was still in bed, still asleep. It was obvious because she snored. It wasn't a loud, obnoxious thing, but a subtle buzz, like a honeybee in your ear.

She lay on the bed in her uniform top, but her skirt and panty hose were off. They were draped over a chair in the room with her jacket. Her purse was on a table. The covers were mostly off her. She slept in her underwear. I saw her legs. I didn't stare, but it was hard not to look.

The room had a little wall-mounted television. It was on. Christopher watched cartoons on it. The volume was low, as to not wake his mom. He seemed to know the drill, like this was just another Saturday morning for him.

Christopher was tiny compared to me. He reminded me of that kid in *Home Alone*. He was a little younger and a little smaller, but had similar features and hair. I imagined a passerby would take one look at the two of us together and think he was staring at the kid from *Home Alone* talking to the Rock, only I looked nothing like the Rock. At least, not in terms of looks. We only resembled each other in stature and size.

I looked down at him and said, "I got you guys breakfast and some new clothes."

He released the doorknob, like it was too hard to keep holding onto something just above him for a long period. He said, "Oh, cool. Come in."

I entered the room and stopped in the doorway. I said, "Maybe I should wait outside until your mom wakes up?"

"It's okay."

"Are you sure?"

The kid said, "Yeah. Come in."

I glanced at Kara. She slept peacefully, except for the low snoring. I said, "Why don't we go eat your breakfast in my room? You can turn your cartoons on in there. Let her sleep a little longer. She might need it."

The kid said, "Okay. Let me get my shoes on."

I looked down. He was standing in his socks. He wore all the rest of his clothes, just not his jacket or his shoes. Then I realized he never grabbed a jacket from his house. Maybe he had one in his mom's car? Most moms keep spare stuff like that for their kids. Mine did. I asked, "You got a jacket?"

He turned, stepped into the room near his shoes, and plopped himself down on the floor. He picked up his shoes and fiddled with them, trying to get them back on. He said, "No. I left it in my room at our house."

I glanced down into the shopping bag. I hadn't got him a coat, and it was chilly out. He'd need it. I said, "After breakfast, I'll take you to get a new one."

He looked up at me, smiled, and asked, "Can I pick it out?"

"Of course."

His smile turned big. Then he returned to putting his shoes on. He finally got them on his feet and socks, but stopped with the laces on both pairs undone.

I watched him. He stared at them like he faced a real dilemma, like Albert Einstein trying to solve the world's greatest math problem. I asked, "Do you know how to tie your laces?"

He glanced at the bed, like he was seeing if his mom was listening. She was still asleep. Then, he looked up at me and said, "I keep forgetting."

I set the shopping bags down on the carpet, walked into the room, and set the breakfast down on the table. I got down on my haunches over him. I said, "Okay. I can show you."

"Really? That would be great, mister."

I realized I hadn't introduced myself to him. I put my hand out to him, palm up, and said, "My name is Jack Widow."

He looked at my open hand and slid his tiny paw into it. We shook. He said, "I'm Christopher Reece, only that's not my real name."

"It's nice to meet you Christopher Reece."

"That's not my real name."

"What's your real name?"

"It's Christopher," he said, and then he glanced at his mom's side of the bed again, making sure she wasn't listening. "My mom told me we changed my real last name because we're in Witness Protection."

The kid was giving away the whole farm. So, I said, "I don't think you're supposed to tell that to strangers."

"You're not a stranger. You're Mr. Widow. My mom told me we could trust you," Christopher said, and we stopped shaking.

I nodded and said, "Okay. Let's get these shoes on."

I showed him how to tie them the best way I knew how. I took the laces of one shoe and tied them slowly. I added an old rhyme to it. I said, "Bunny ears, bunny ears, playing by a tree. Criss-crossed the tree, trying to catch me. Bunny ears, Bunny ears, jumped into the hole, popped out the other side beautiful and bold."

He looked at me and asked, "Where did you learn that?"

"My momma taught me when I was little."

"You have a momma?"

"I did. Once."

"Where is she?"

"She's moved on now."

"Moved on?"

Uh oh! I thought. Was I about to teach this kid about death? Great!

I said, "She's gone."

"You mean like to heaven?"

"Yeah. She went to heaven," I agreed. I didn't know what else to say, and I wanted to get off the subject. I wasn't about to argue with a six-year-old the complexities of humanity's belief in different religions and afterlife questions.

After I showed him how to tie the shoe with the kids' rhyme, I asked him to do the other one. He went slowly with it. Repeating the rhyme word-for-word, line-by-line, until there was a knot and a tied shoe. Then we got up and left the room. I carried the breakfast, but left the shopping bags with their new clothes.

We ate breakfast and talked a long while. Christopher's legs dangled off a chair as he ate over the table. I did the same and sat across from him. Afterward, I drank my coffee until it was gone, and then, like a greedy jerk, I drank Kara's too. I convinced myself that I could just buy her a new one later on.

Christopher turned on the television to cartoons but never watched them. He was more interested in me. I told him things that I was comfortable telling a developing mind.

Eventually, there was a loud knock at my door. I got up and peeked out the window to see who it was before I opened it. It was Kara.

I opened the door, and she stood there wide awake, no pants on, and worried. She said, "Where is he?"

I opened the door all the way and stepped aside. She saw Christopher and her level of worry dialed down to zero. She entered my room and went over to him and hugged him tight and kissed him on the forehead. He squirmed and pulled away from her. He said, "Mom, I'm okay. Mr. Widow was just telling me about his time in the army."

She glanced at me and said, "He is? That's cool, but I don't think we need to be talking about the army. You're too young for that stuff."

"Navy," I corrected them, but they didn't respond.

Kara saw the remains of wrapping paper from the kid's breakfast and looked at me. She said, "You got him breakfast? That's so nice. Thank you."

"I got some for all of us. Yours is in the bag. It's cold by now."

"That's okay. Thank you. I could use some coffee," she said and glanced at the two paper coffee cups on the table. She reached for one. "Is one of these mine?"

She lifted the cup and felt it was empty.

I said, "They're both empty. I drank them both. Sorry."

"That's okay," Kara said, and looked down at her legs. "Oh shit. I better get some pants on."

"I got you some clothes."

"Is that what's in those shopping bags?"

"Yes. I picked you guys out some stuff to wear. I think I got your size right."

Kara looked at her son and cupped his ears with her hands in what my own mother used to call *earmuffs*, a motherly tactic used all over the world to block out sounds and bad words from ruining a child's innocence.

She said, "I might have to return whatever top you got me. Don't get offended. I know I look skinny, but I'm big. You know? Up top."

I nodded and said nothing.

She removed the earmuffs from her son and said, "Okay. I'm going to take a shower. I'll be back. You two behave."

Before she left, the kid stopped her and said, "Mr. Widow is going to buy me a new jacket."

"He is?"

I said, "I forgot when I bought the clothes. I'll take him over there while you're in the shower. We'll be back by the time you get out."

Kara stared at me, then at her son.

I asked, "Is that okay?"

She looked at me. I could see she struggled to trust me. It was all over her face. I realized because of her situation she probably struggled to trust everyone she had met in the last six years.

"Yes. Of course," she said and smiled. She looked at the kid. "Christopher, you do as Mr. Widow says."

He stayed quiet.

She repeated her instructions but added, "Got it?"

He said, "Yes, ma'am."

"And what do you do if you have to cross the street?"

Christopher lowered his shoulders and said, "Hold Mr. Widow's hand."

"Okay. Good," Kara said. She walked to the door, stopped, and looked up at me. She put a hand on my bicep, like she'd done the night before in the diner. "Thank you for everything."

She got up on her tippy-toes and kissed me on the cheek. Then, she left the room to go shower.

I killed the last of the coffee that was intended for Kara and took the kid back to the thrift store, where we spent forty-five minutes sifting through kids' jackets.

I promised him one, but he swindled me for two.

BACK AT THE MOTEL, we returned to my room. Christopher took his new jackets and went over to his mom's room. He brought her the breakfast I got her and thirty minutes later, they knocked on my door. Kara was dressed in the clothes I got for her. Turned out she was right. The clothes were the right size, including her top, but it was tight around the upper area. I should've gone up a size for her. She wore it, anyway, saying she didn't mind if I glanced at her more than I already was.

We sat in my room. Christopher watched cartoons on the television. Kara and I sat on the bed, talking about our next move.

I used Kara's phone to make a phone call to the emergency room in Cedar Springs, to inquire about Fry's condition. I pretended to be his son, seeking information on my father. They told me he was stable, but *still not out of the woods*, and that he'd been moved to an ambulance and transported to the hospital in Ash Fork, where I already was. They said he was sent there for further viewing and would have to stay bed-rested in the hospital for a few days.

I informed Kara of the news and asked to borrow her car. I needed to see him first thing. She agreed and loaned me her car. I got directions for the hospital from her phone and told her I'd be gone an hour tops. I told her if I wasn't back by noon, then they should think of an alternate plan. In case I was detained by police. It was entirely possible some cop investigating the diner and the dead guys at her house might get a description of me from either the cook or either of the paramedics I rode in with last night.

At the hospital, I parked Kara's car in the lot, near the road, making it easier for a mad dash over the curb and onto the highway, in case I needed to get away fast.

The hospital was a long and low one-story building. It was half-brick, half-stucco. The stucco was painted pink. There were large bay windows, tinted to reflect nearly everything, like one-way mirrors. I saw myself in them as I approached the entrance. The cops could've been standing on the other side of the glass, weapons drawn, waiting for me. The hospital's front automatic doors sucked open, and I was met with no one, no cops.

The foyer of the hospital opened to a large waiting room with a woman behind a desk. She wore scrubs. There were people seated in the lobby, but none of them struck me as a plainclothes officer waiting around to see who might turn up. So, I went to the woman at the desk and asked about Fry. She gave me a room number. There was no check-in, no record of visitors.

I followed a blue painted line on the floor down a corridor, past the emergency room entrance, and the ICU and various medical departments, until I reached the main rooms with patients.

Fry was at the end of the hall. He shared a room with another man, ten years older than Fry. The guy was joking around with Fry. There was laughter and talk about sponge baths. I entered the room, and both men went quiet.

Fry stared at me with recognition in his eyes. I walked into the room, walked up to the side of Fry's bed, and asked, "Remember me?"

Fry narrowed his eyes, like he was trying hard to remember me, but couldn't quite place me. He said, "No."

"I'm the guy you nearly ran over with your car last night."

Nothing.

I said, "I called the ambulance for you."

Fry's eyes went big. He remembered me. He said, "John Capone?"

I nodded and glanced at the other guy.

Fry looked at him and said, "This is Joe. He's okay."

Joe said, "I'm here for a stroke. But I can see you two need privacy."

Joe sat up in his bed and grabbed a curtain and pulled it shut to give the illusion of privacy. A heart monitor machine beeped and sped up as he did the whole effort.

I turned back to Fry and said, "I'm also the guy who saved your witness from a bunch of professional killers."

"You're John Capone?"

I nodded and said, "The name is Widow. Jack Widow."

"I figured that. A guy named John Capone would be taunted his whole life, asked if he was related to Al Capone."

"It's a combination of John Dillinger and Capone. I'm doing a historical mobster thing now."

"What?"

"Never mind. Just let me in on what's going on?"

"First, I gotta ask is she alright? I wanted to call her, but the staff took away my phone and haven't returned it to me yet. And I forgot her number. It's stored in my phone. I'm old now. It's harder to recall things like people's numbers."

"Kara is safe. She's with her kid."

"Where are they?"

"Nearby."

Fry said, "Good. Thank you for helping me when you did, Widow. I appreciate it. I know Kara does as well."

"Okay. But now it's time for answers. I think I'm entitled to know the truth. Plus, I need to know what I'm up against here."

"How many professional killers did you encounter?"

I glanced over at the privacy sheet. Joe wasn't making any noise. I put up two hands and seven fingers, five fingers on one hand and two on the other.

"Wow! How did you get away from so many?"

"They're dead."

Fry stared at me in disbelief. He asked, "Is that true? All of them?"

"Yes."

"By yourself?"

"Kara helped."

"I'm sorry. I knew they were sending someone, but I didn't know seven. You could've been killed."

"I managed."

"You're right. You're entitled to the truth," Fry said, and hauled himself up all the way to a seated position. He rested his back against a pillow. "You ever heard of The Phantom Sons?"

"No. What is that, a rock band?"

"No. Although they do like rock and roll music, I'm sure. It's a motorcycle gang out of North Carolina."

I arched an eyebrow and stared at him and said, "A motorcycle gang? Like Hell's Angels?"

"Something like that. But motorcycle gangs nowadays aren't what you think. Now they're like organized crime. They run all kinds of schemes. They're organized like a corporation that rides Harleys. But they're a criminal empire. Make no mistake about that, Widow. They run drugs and guns and girls. They're involved in political assassinations and terrorism. Anything that makes them an awful lot of money. They do dirty work for major criminal families, like the Italians or the Irish mob."

I said, "Some of the guys from last night were Irish."

"Really?"

"One guy was named Shay."

Fry stared at me, fear on his face this time. He said, "Did you kill him?"

"He's the only one I left alive. But he wasn't in good shape. And if you didn't see him at the emergency room in Cedar Springs or here, then he might not have made it."

"That's not good. The Irish will take that personally. They probably sent them to grab Kara because they're closer. Shay is based out of Las Vegas."

I asked, "So what's Kara got to do with the Phantom Menace?"

"Phantom Sons. *The Phantom Menace* is a Star Wars movie. My grandson makes me watch it with him."

"Whatever. Why do they want Kara so bad?"

"The Phantom Sons are a motorcycle club. That's what they like to be called. Not gangs. They are very tribal. All of them are like that. They have rituals and ceremonies and allegiances and a sense of honor."

"Honor? They sent four large thugs to kidnap a six-year-old boy and they murdered a teenage babysitter."

Fry said, "I'm sorry to hear that. But yes, they have a sense of honor. It's situational honor."

I stayed quiet.

Fry said, "The Sons were founded by a guy named Butch Sabo. Ever heard of him?"

"Nope."

"Think Whitey Bulger but worse."

I had heard of Bulger before. He was a notorious gangster out of Boston who murdered a lot of people—personally. He was also an FBI informant, until he ran from charges. He remained at large for sixteen years, but was eventually caught. He died in prison.

Fry said, "Sabo was the father of The Phantom Sons—the founder. He ran it like an emperor. He murdered informants and anyone who crossed the Sons. They've got a ritual for everything. And they got one for traitors and snitches."

"You said *was*. He *was* the founder."

"He's dead now. Killed by a car bomb. Supposedly, it was by a rival gang, or any number of enemies he made of a long career. No one really knows. The feds never solved it. They weren't in a big hurry to catch the guy who did them a favor, anyway."

"So, what was Kara? She witnessed something?"

"Kara witnessed a lot of things. She was his daughter. Her real name is Kara Sabo."

"Oh. So, if Butch is dead, what do they want with Kara?"

"Yeah. It gets worse. The new leader is Butch's son-in-law, a guy called Mike Berghorn. He's a ruthless, suave leader. A real cool customer. He's as deadly as Butch, only more civil. But still he's not to be underestimated."

"Son-in-law?"

"That's right. He's Kara's husband. Christopher is his son. A son he never met. Kara was pregnant when she came to us."

I stayed quiet.

Fry said, "There was an attempt on her life once. She was in WITSEC, the official way. But somewhere there's a breach in the WITSEC pipeline and they sent guys after her. Berghorn wants his kid back. Like I said, they're tribal. He'll want to raise the kid to be just like him and one day take over. Plus, he'll want to kill her in some twisted public ceremony."

"Public?"

"In front of the inner circle. Those are the members in the club that are a part of all criminal aspects. They're like brothers. They believe in blood being thicker than water. And they will kill anyone who steps out of line. And Kara Sabo stepped way out when she came to us pregnant and willing to give up evidence and details about her father. He died shortly after she ran. But Berghorn will carry on his rituals."

"I see. So, what do we do now?"

Fry started looking weak. He slumped back down in his bed. His heartbeat monitor weakened its beats. He yawned a deep, heavy yawn, and then he said, "I need you to watch over her a little longer. Can you do that? Can you be her protector?"

I nodded.

He said, "I need to hear it."

"Without question. I'll protect them."

"Good. I need a little more time to recover. They said I had a mild heart attack. They want me to stay here for a few days."

"We're holed up in a motel right now. But that's not a good place."

"I agree. You should take them somewhere else for a few days."

"Where?"

Fry thought for a moment, and then, he said, "I know a guy who will help us. His name's J. D. Coger. He's reclusive, but a good man. He's my former partner. He'll know all about Sabo. He met her before. He's retired now. Lives in San Diego on a boat. Be careful, he doesn't like strangers, but he'll do this for us. I'd call him, but I don't have a number. I don't think he even has a phone. When he left the agency, he wanted nothing more to do with us, even me. I kept up with him though."

And he told me where to find Coger exactly. Then Fry took another deep yawn and said he was feeling weak. He mentioned it was the meds they gave him. A minute later, he was fast asleep, but first he said one last thing. He said, "Widow, trust no one outside of our circle. Including the Marshals. Somewhere there's a rat."

I tucked him in with his hospital covers and left the room.

17

I LEFT the hospital room and back out down the hallway, reversing the path of the blue line on the floor. I passed the various medical departments and the ICU and the emergency room entrance. Eventually, I came back out into the lobby and passed the reception desk, with the same lady behind it. She nodded at me as I walked out.

The automatic doors sucked open, and I passed through undisturbed until I reached the sidewalk outside. Then I heard a voice behind me. Someone was calling to me.

"Excuse me, sir. Wait up."

I continued walking, but again, someone called out to me. I stopped on the walkway ten yards outside the hospital entrance and spun around. A tall, thin man speed-walked toward me. He was well-built, tough. His height was around six feet two inches, but he wore boots with two-inch heels. So, he would've been six feet tops. He had dark hair, thick with grey speckled throughout, but mostly on the sides. His face was shaved, and he dressed neatly, like a guy trying to look professional. Only he wasn't in my choice of clothing. He wore a Texas suit, a cheap, grey tailored suit with a white cowboy hat. The hat was large enough to be used as an umbrella or to sneak a metal file into a prison.

The guy was talking to me. He had to be. There was no one else leaving the hospital at that exact moment. He walked straight up to me, put a hand out for me to shake, and said, "My name is Brandon Campbell. I'm with the US Marshal's Service."

I ignored his hand and asked, "Got a badge?"

I stood there, hands by my sides, but I already ran scenarios in my head of how to dispatch the man if he turned into a threat. The first ten ways were to take him out, but not kill him. The other ten ways were to kill him. I did none of them because the guy calmly lowered his offered shaking hand and reached into his coat inside pocket, and came out with a black, leather billfold. I saw an over the shoulder gun holster rig as his coat flapped open. I only got a glimpse of the firearm's hilt, but it appeared to be the same as Fry's Glock 22 that fell out onto his car's floorboards last night, after he ran into the tree.

The guy whipped his badge at me and flipped it closed, like we were finished with that part. I said, "Can you hold it open for me?"

"Sure. Sorry. Most people don't actually stare that hard at it."

The guy whipped it open again. This time he held it there. I stared at it, but kept one eye over the leather at him to make sure he didn't make any sudden moves. I was pretty sure that no one followed us from Cedar Springs, but all they might have to do was stick a guy like him here at the hospital and wait to see who visits Fry.

But the badge was real. It was a gold star, and it had his picture and name on an ID behind a plastic screen.

He asked, "Okay. Satisfied?"

"Looks real," I said.

He closed the billfold and reinserted it back into his coat pocket. I saw the gun again. It was definitely the same Glock 22, which was also the same one I had left in the center console of Kara's Mustang. But I couldn't get to it fast enough if he drew on me. All I could do was stare at the car, parked in the end of the lot, while the guy shot me dead. If he drew on me, but he didn't.

He said, "Like I said, the name's Campbell and I've got some questions for you."

"For me? Why?"

"Were you visiting with Fry?"

I stayed quiet.

He said, "You were. I know that. Why don't you come with me?"

"Where to?"

He looked around. We stood on the walkway and there were people coming in and out of the hospital. He said, "Let's go to the parking lot. We can talk in my car."

I wondered if he meant I sit in the back of an unmarked police car, where the rear doors only open from the outside, while he sat in the front. I said, "No thanks."

He glanced at the pedestrians coming out of the hospital at that exact moment. He said, "I just want a word in private."

Curious about what he had to say, I said, "Tell you what. Buy me a coffee in the cafeteria and I'll hear you out there."

Plus, it might be a good idea to get him out of the parking lot. I hoped he hadn't seen what car I drove in with and that he wouldn't see me leave in it. The last thing I wanted was for him to have Kara's plates.

Five minutes later, we sat at a table at the other end of the hospital. There was a cafeteria with outside access. We sat near the window. Campbell removed his cowboy hat and placed it gently on the tabletop like it was the most important possession he owned.

A waitress came by and took our orders, which was coffee for both. She returned a minute later with two piping hot coffees in Styrofoam cups without lids. She asked, "Anything else for you guys?"

Campbell fiddled with the table setup, which was lacking, and he said, "Bring a spoon and sugar and creamer for my friend here."

"No thanks," I said.

"You sure? You don't want sugar? Cream? I'm going to use up what's here."

"Don't need it. Black is fine for me," I said and smiled at the waitress. She left us.

Campbell's face looked disappointed that I didn't take the offer of sugar, creamer, and a spoon. I didn't take them for two reasons. First, I didn't want to leave anything on the table or trash that he could swipe and pull prints or DNA off. Not that my DNA would turn up anything. My prints would lead him down a NCIS bureaucratic rabbit hole. The second reason is I drink coffee black.

Campbell looked at me squarely and asked, "So, who are you?"

"Who do you think I am?"

He said nothing. I sipped the coffee, a standoff. After a long minute of him opening sugar packets, five of them, and pouring them into his coffee, and then mixing in two creamers and stirring it all at the end, he finally spoke. He said, "Lying to a federal agent is a crime, you know?"

"Hardly. And I've not lied to you."

"Not answering me is lying by omission."

"So, arrest me. Try to explain that to a judge."

"I could arrest you. You might not get charged with anything, but in the state of Arizona I could arrest you and detain you for forty-eight hours."

"You can't do anything. You'd have to have local police do it."

"I could do it. There's a cop on property here. There always is near a hospital."

I stayed quiet.

Campbell said, "Why don't you tell me your name?"

I stayed quiet, took a pull from my coffee.

He said, "Come on. You're not helping Fry."

I said, "Who do you think I am?"

"You're not John Capone."

"I didn't say I was."

"Isn't that the name you gave to 911 dispatch?"

"Sounds like you already got your answers."

He stared at me a long while, through two more pulls of my coffee. He never touched his, even after all that effort to get it the way he liked.

"So, let me tell you what I know, Mr. Capone," Campbell said. "I've got a morgue full of dead bodies from a tiny shit-hole twenty-five miles west of here. I've got a decorated but retired US Marshal in a hospital bed from the same town. And I've got witnesses who claim to have seen a large unidentified male at all three scenes. Plus, I've got a missing citizen of that shit-hole town. I'm told the large male may have abducted her."

"Sounds like you gotta bunch of hearsay."

"Are you not the one who found Fry?"

"I found him. You already know that. Why else would I be here? I came to check on him, make sure he's alive. And that's it."

Campbell glanced at my cup and said, "So, you're denying knowledge of the other events I mentioned?"

I shrugged and said, "The old guy had a heart attack while driving. He nearly ran me over and I called 911, sure."

"You still didn't deny the other stuff."

I shrugged.

He asked, "If you're not involved, then why did you come to Ash Fork? The paramedics said they dropped you off in Cedar Springs. They said you walked away, headed in the diner's direction I'm referring to. If you're not running from something, then why leave?"

"Like you said. It's a shit-hole," I said, and smiled and added nothing else.

Finally, Campbell relented his campaign to get me to admit to anything. He went quiet a little while. I finished my coffee but didn't wait for him to finish his. I was done. I stood up, and he said, "Wait, let me just..."

He stood up too and reached into his pocket, pulled out his wallet, flipped it open so I saw the badge again. Then, he pulled out a business card. He reversed it in his hand and returned the badge and wallet to his jacket. He handed me the business card. I took it and glanced at it. It had his name, information, and the official seal of the US Marshal's Service on it. It was the same as Fry's, only no mention of the word: *retired,* on it.

He said, "Call me if you think of anything else."

I pocketed the card and stayed quiet. He lifted his cowboy hat and put it on. I stood over a trash can and finished my coffee in front of him. He watched closely, then I took it with me and left. He appeared visibly frustrated by this. Another missed opportunity for fingerprints and DNA.

18

IN THE PARKING LOT, I saw Kara's Mustang still parked where I left it. Her keys were in my pocket. I was tempted to get in it and drive back to her. I figured Campbell was still at the cafeteria, paying the check, or maybe he did that already, but he'd still be too far behind me to watch me. I was almost positive that he hadn't seen what vehicle I arrived in. He might identify which one I left in, which would give him a leg up because he could run the plates, get Kara's fake last name, and identify her as the waitress who I supposedly abducted.

Campbell may not be watching the parking lot, but that didn't mean he wasn't alone. There could've been someone else there. Someone he left behind, who could be watching me. I glanced around the lot. There were plenty of parked cars with tinted windows. Any of them could hide another Marshal or any other law enforcement.

So, I walked past the parked Mustang, left the keys in my pocket, and crossed the street. On the opposite side of the street, there was a bus stop. I stopped near a bench and studied a bus route display on a map. It hung from a plastic apparatus, along with other information about the local metro system. The next bus was thirty minutes out, so I sat on the bench and waited.

Campbell never came back out of the hospital, not while I sat at the bus stop.

* * *

EVENTUALLY, a bus arrived nearly on time, and I boarded. The route it followed was nowhere near the motel. So, I had to get off and swap buses and ride back in the same direction I left from. I rode and changed buses for ninety minutes before I was sure no one followed me.

I got off the bus at a stop in the same shopping center that I bought breakfast and clothes for Kara and Christopher earlier. By this time, it was nearly lunch. So, I bought another round of fast food for us and went back to the motel, again checking that I wasn't followed. And I wasn't.

Kara met me at her door. She looked scared and worried. She said, "Thank God you're here. I thought something happened."

"I had some dead weight to shake off."

I entered the room. Kara stayed in the doorway, staring at the parking lot. Christopher jumped up when he saw I was carrying more bags of food. He ran over to me from the bed. His shoes were off again. They piled in the room's corner, next to Kara's shoes, which were set down neatly.

Christopher asked, "What did you get me? A Happy Friend Meal?"

"A what?" I asked.

"You know, like the meal for kids, with the toy?" he said, and he rattled off some obscure action figure toy franchise that I never heard of and forgot the name of seconds later.

I said, "Sorry, I got us all some cheeseburgers and fries."

Suddenly, his shoulders dropped like his entire world was destroyed. But he didn't complain, and minutes later he forgot all about his disappointment. French fries and globs of ketchup seemed to make him forget all about it.

Before that, his mother stood in the doorway, still studying the lot. She stepped out onto the walkway, barefoot, and traversed from side to side, like a water sprinkler in a suburban yard spraying water from the twelve to six on a dial, and then, resetting to start all over again.

I said, "Don't worry, your car is fine."

"Where is it?"

"I had to leave it at the hospital. There was another US Marshal there."

"Not just Fry?"

"No. There was a guy named Campbell. Ever heard of him?"

"No. But if Fry trusts him, then maybe we can too?"

I shook my head and said, "No. He wasn't with Fry. He approached me after I left Fry. I think he was there, staking out the hospital to see who might show up and visit Fry. He asked me about the..."

I stopped because I almost said *dead guys*, but I glanced at Christopher and didn't say it. Instead, he looked up at me and asked, "Earmuffs?"

"No need. Just eat your lunch," I said, and turned back to Kara. "He asked about last night. But he knows nothing. Not really. He definitely doesn't know who you really are."

"Can we trust him, though?"

"No. Fry said to trust no one. He told me all about your situation. The Phantom Sons."

A look of terror came over her face at the very mention of their name. She said, "I was going to tell you, anyway. You deserve the truth."

She looked over my shoulder at Christopher. He was already tearing into a cheeseburger. But there was still some fries and ketchup left for him to mix it up with.

Kara walked over to him at the table. She tussled his hair and bent down and kissed him on the head. He blurted, "Mom!"

She said, "Stay here. Don't leave this room."

"Where're you going?"

"Mr. Widow and I are going to eat our lunch next door. We got adult stuff to talk about."

Christopher stared at me over a half-eaten cheeseburger and a dab of ketchup on his lips. He looked back at his mom and said, "Are you two going to kiss?"

"Shh. That's not your concern. Eat your lunch and watch cartoons. I'll be back," she said, stood up, snagged the fast-food bag off the table with what was left of the lunch, and came over to me. She grabbed my hand, not the whole hand. She just took a couple of fingers and guided me out the door and into my own room.

We sat at the table in my room, took out the fast food, and ate our own. I brought up Marshal Campbell, just to get a confirmation that she didn't know him. She didn't.

I told her Fry warned me to trust no one. She confirmed he always told her that, too.

While we ate, she unfolded the story for me. She confirmed her father, Butch, and the motorcycle club, The Phantom Sons, and that she was technically married to the new leader of The Phantom Sons.

Kara stopped eating about halfway through. She put the rest of her cheeseburger down, half-wrapped in paper, and she said, "Butch pawned me off. My mother died when I was young. I don't remember it. Butch raised me like one of the girls that came in off the street. I grew up with them. Patterned myself around their culture. That's why I got these tattoos and style."

She raised her shirt and showed me a large one-piece tattoo across her abdomen. The design on it, I presumed it covered far more than I was seeing. She lowered her shirt and said, "Butch was terrible to me. He barely treated me like I was worthless. Anyway, he pawned me to marry his number one up-and-coming guy, Michael Berghorn."

She slowed just then, and a single tear welled up in her eye. She said, "He's Christopher's biological father. Christopher's never met his father. And I don't want him to. Not ever. Those guys are animals, Widow. I saw them murder and maim and all kinds of crazy outlaw stuff."

I put down the rest of my cheeseburger in its wrapper and scooted my chair closer to hers. I put my hand out and wiped the tear off her face. I said, "I'm not going to let anything happen to you or him. Nothing's going to happen. Not on my watch. I'll protect you both."

She reached up, as my hand brushed the tear off her cheek, and she grabbed it, held it. She put her face on it, rubbing her face along my palm, and whispered, "I know you will. I knew it last night. It's so obvious. You're the most genuine person I've met since Fry."

I stayed quiet, just listening to her, just touching her.

She said, "So what now?"

"I think the best thing to do is get you both somewhere safe, which means somewhere they won't go. Got anywhere you can stay that no one knows about?"

"I have no one else."

"Fry mentioned one place. One guy he said we could trust. His old partner."

She said, "I remember him—vaguely. He left the case before long. Nothing to do with me. If Fry said we can trust him, then he's our best bet."

"Let's finish our lunch. I've got to catch another bus, so I can get your car," I said. We finished up our burgers and fries and held hands a little longer. Then, I left them at the motel. They were going to pack up. They didn't have much. But, unlike me, they had yesterday's clothes. Already, I could feel the burden of extra things to carry.

I got on another bus and rode a more direct route to the hospital. Kara's Mustang was still parked at the end of the lot, near the street. It was right where I left it. I checked the lot again, to make sure there was nobody left watching the lot for me to return. There was no one. Campbell was gone. I entered the hospital and visited Fry in his room again. He was still weak, but awake. I told him the plan. He accepted it and told me to call him in a few days. He could take over for me and I'd be on my way.

After, I left Fry in his hospital bed to recover. I got in the Mustang, fired it up, and picked up Kara and Christopher. They were ready by the time I got to the motel. We checked out of our rooms and got on the same Route 66 patch of road where Fry almost ran me over. We drove on past it, through the afternoon.

We headed to San Diego.

19

WE DROVE through the afternoon and into the evening. The sky faded to pink as the December sun set over the Pacific Ocean. The sunset seemed longer than it actually was, like it was being stretched over the horizon.

We took the interstate most of the way and turned off and followed the Google Maps app on Kara's phone. She drove. Her phone was held up on a mount on her dashboard. It made it easy for her to glance at her phone and drive at the same time.

As the sky darkened, we found a rural road in northern San Diego County, which led us past quiet industrial parks. Google Maps moved us further along to a dingy, gloomy street that ended at a long turnoff. The turnoff turned out to be a driveway. The concrete ended and turned to gravel at the mouth of it. There was overgrown brush and trees canvassing over the road, which cast long, dark shadows, making the road dark no matter what time of day it was.

We stopped in front at the mouth of the drive.

There were broken, dilapidated signs posted on both sides of the drive. They read things like: *Private Property, Turn Back,* and *Will Shoot On Sight.* But the first sign we saw was a large metal sign pushed back off the road. It hung high on a pole near the trees. It read: *Coger's Harbor.*

Christopher leaned against the window and read the signs and sounded out the words. He was still at that age where he was tweaking and improving his reading.

I said, "Coger. This must be the right place."

Kara said, "It looks abandoned."

"It looks like he doesn't like visitors."

"Maybe we should turn back. That's what the sign says. We might be better off just on our own."

"We can't go back. I'm going to need help to protect you."

"Fry will be out in a few days. He can take us then. You'll be free to leave and forget us."

I turned, looked at her, and said, "I'm not leaving you. But I need freedom of movement. I may need to do things to improve your situation."

"What things?"

I stayed quiet.

Christopher leaned forward from the backseat, popping his head between Kara and I in the front. He leaned over the center console. He asked, "Mr. Widow, what does *onslaught* mean?"

Kara asked, "What? Where did you see that?"

Christopher said, "The sign said: *Will Shoot Onslaught?*

I turned my head and gazed at him through my peripheral and said, "It didn't say *onslaught*. It said: *on sight*. It just means upon seeing."

Christopher turned to Kara, panic in his face, and asked, "Mom, are we going to get shot if we're seen?"

I hope not, I thought.

"No, honey. Sit back. Put your seatbelt back on!"

Christopher did as Kara ordered, like a dutiful son. Then, she glanced at me and asked, "Are we going forward?"

"We can't turn back now."

She nodded and drove on. Gravel *popped* and *crunched* under the Mustang's tires. The drive winded and twisted and looped around. We drove over acres of wooded land, until we came out into a huge clearing. We'd reached the end of the country. Right in front of us, there was an old busted up and forgotten harbor and a couple of buildings and the Pacific Ocean. The waves were calm. The moon was large in the sky. It reflected off the dark water.

The harbor was more like a marina than a harbor. It was too small for tankers and yachts, but big enough for sailboats or small schooners or small shrimp boats. And that was it.

The base of the marina was a large concrete lot, with two boat launch ramps separated by fifty yards of parking. The boat slips came off three-pronged catwalks that jetted out like the head of a trident. The prongs were built with wood, like long private piers. There were ten boat slots on each side of the prongs, making for a maximum capacity of sixty boat slots.

There were some boats using up slots. Each prong had boats here and there. None of them were crowded by direct neighbors. They were all spaced out. Some boats were old and broken down, like they had been docked and forgotten ten years in the past. Some of them looked attended to. And one of them, on the far end of the last prong, had lights on.

The boats rocked and swayed in the calm sea.

The parking lot was pretty big. I figured it could hold a hundred cars, bigger than the lot at Kara's diner but smaller than the hospital's parking lot in Ash Fork. There was an old truck parked in one space, nearest to the third prong. It was an old Chevy. It was white, but more from the original paint fading away than from choice.

There were vapor lights high on poles throughout the complex. Some shined. Some didn't. Some were broken out, like the bulbs exploded and no one changed them out. Some of them were just burnt out and still not changed.

There were three buildings. The furthest one was a small, one-story house. The stucco was old. The paint was peeling in places. One of the windows was boarded up. But there was dim light on in the house, like someone lived there. The second building was a public toilet. It was small, like an outhouse. It had two open doorways. There were no doors that I could see. Each doorway had a toilet sign on the wall next to it. One was for men, the other for women. The third building was a utility shed.

Kara asked, "Where do you think he is?"

"Let's try the house."

Kara eased the Mustang into the parking lot and over toward the parked truck. The Mustang's headlights washed over the lot and across the swaying boats and the old Chevy's chrome bumper reflecting at us.

She pulled up close to the truck and slid into a parking space next to it. She asked, "Now what?"

"Stay here. I'll look for him," I said. I popped open the passenger door and slid out and stopped and turned back. "If this goes sideways, you better take off."

Kara stayed quiet. I glanced back at Christopher. He gritted his teeth and looked worried.

I closed the door and turned to the house. There were a lot of long, dark shadows stretched across the gravel. Some patches were so dark goblins could've hidden in them, waiting for me to step close enough before they grabbed me and jerked me in.

I walked toward the house, my hands open, palms up, and I called out. I said, "Mr. Coger? Are you here?"

There was no answer.

"Coger? Patton Fry sent us. We're friendly."

No answer.

I stepped closer to the house. Suddenly, there was a noise and movement. Something ran at me, but not from the house. It was snarling like a hungry, feral beast. It came running at me from down the third prong on the trident. From the last boat, the one lit up. The creature was shadowy in the darkness. It was hard to see what it was. But it made a sound that was universally recognized. It barked.

The animal came running out of the darkness to the end of the pier, my end. It leapt off the last plank of wood and ran straight at me. I took an athletic pose. I loved dogs, but I'm not willing to get shredded to death by one. I braced myself to punch or kick or whatever I needed to do to disable the dog long enough for me to jump back in the Mustang.

As it came closer to me, it crossed into the light from the nearest pole. I saw it. It was an enormous dog. It had pointed ears and huge teeth and a black face. It was a German Shepherd. It was black and tan, but more black than tan. The teeth sparkled white in the vapor light. The animal snarled and growled and barked. It had death in its eyes, like a shark.

I readied myself, but at the last second the animal stopped dead in its tracks because there was a bigger threat. Twenty yards behind it, on the third prong of the marina, about halfway back to the boat the dog exited, there was a man standing there. He shouted out a German word and fired a shell up into the air from a pump-action shotgun. The weapon was black with a pistol grip. The gunshot *boomed* and echoed through the stillness. The snarling German Shepherd stopped and stared at me. He had deep brown eyes that were closer to a wolf's than a dog's. The dog had stopped, but was still close enough to leap at me and tear my face off.

The Mustang's engine ran idle. Exhaust pooled from the rear pipes. I held my hands up horizontally with my shoulders. The dog growled and breathed heavily. White clouds of breath puffed out of his mouth and evaporated into the air. The guy with the shotgun walked down the pier toward us. He pumped the shotgun and pointed it in my direction. He shouted, "Don't think I can't hit you from here! I can."

I stayed quiet.

The guy with the shotgun continued approaching us. He made it to the end of the pier and across the concrete and stopped ten feet behind his dog, near the Chevy's back tire. He looked me up and down, then glanced over at the Mustang. He said, "You make any moves I don't like; Scout here will attack, and he goes for the groin. If you catch my drift."

I stayed quiet, glanced at the dog. It growled again like it was on command.

The guy with the shotgun was shadowed by the darkness, but I saw he was about five foot eleven. He had wild, bushy grey hair on his head. And something was over his face, but I couldn't make it out. He spoke with a commanding voice, not yelling, not over shouting. It was just the right aggressive tone, like a trained cop.

He said, "You tell that little lady in there to not make any moves for a gun either or I'll shoot her."

I bent down at the waist. The dog snarled but didn't attack. My groin was safe for the moment. I looked into the window and raised my voice, so Kara heard me through the glass. I said, "Don't provoke him."

She nodded at me.

The guy with the shotgun asked, "Are you guys lost? If so, the way you want to go is back the way you came."

I said, "We're not lost."

"Then state your business."

"We're looking for Coger."

"What you want with him?"

"We're looking for J.D. Coger, former US Marshal."

"What would he want to see you for?" the guy asked.

"Patton Fry sent us."

The guy stepped closer, into the light. The thing on his face was an eye patch over his right eye. He walked a little stiffly. He wobbled a little, and I knew why. The guy was a little drunk. I smelled whisky from here.

He said, "Patton Fry? I've not heard that name in like five years. He sent you to see me for what?"

I motioned toward the Mustang with my head, kept my hands up in plain view, and said, "Because we need your help. He said you'd help me protect this woman and her kid."

The guy leaned back, lowering his head back and to the left like he was trying to see into the Mustang. He said, "Who are they?"

"This is Kara and Christopher. She's Butch Sabo's kid."

The guy returned to a straight position and stared at me. He lowered the shotgun and said, "Sabo. That's Kara?"

"Yes."

The guy said, "I'm Coger. This is Scout. What's your name?"

"I'm Jack Widow."

"You a cop?" he asked, and looked me over again.

"Do I look like a cop?" I asked, regretting it because the guy still had his hands on a shotgun, which he wouldn't need because the dog called Scout was strong enough to take me down on its own.

"You her boyfriend or something?"

"No. I'm just a guy who wants to help."

Coger said nothing.

I added, "Invite us in. We'll explain it all."

Coger lowered the shotgun all the way, held it one handed, and barked an order at Scout in German, which must've translated to: *At ease, soldier,* because Scout sat and lowered his ears and turned like a reverse werewolf cycle from a vicious guard dog to a friendly pooch. Coger said, "Tell them to park and follow me."

20

WE BOARDED A TWENTY-FIVE-FOOT CABIN CRUISER. Out of all the boats docked in Coger's marina, it was the smallest and dingiest. It was old but well-kept, and it floated. The boat swayed gently in the last slip. We gathered belowdeck in the salon. Christopher and Kara sat around a dinette, while Coger served them crawfish that he was already preparing in the galley. Apparently, he was boiling loads of crawfish for himself. He said that he and Scout ate it all up in a couple of days. Which meant that Coger boiled it and peeled it and put the meat from the tails in a dog bowl just for Scout.

Tomorrow, he'd planned to boil the rest of it. But now that he had guests, he boiled it all up. I offered to help him, but he told me I looked awkward standing in the galley with my head tilted below the ceiling. My head didn't actually touch the ceiling. I stood six foot four inches, but the ceiling wasn't much higher. I kept feeling like I would hit it. The head tilt was just an involuntary precaution.

Christopher had never had crawfish before. Kara had to help him peel it. He made a lot of commentaries that started with how gross it looked to his fear that he would get a live one, to finally, loving it. They ate boiled crawfish and corn on the cob.

I started out not hungry, but the smell of it lured me in. I finished a large bowl of it on my own. Coger and I started off on the wrong foot because he pointed a shotgun at me. I rarely befriend guys who point firearms at me. But he made a pot of coffee and served it to me. It was the best coffee I'd had in months. And we became instant friends.

Scout laid on the floor at Coger's feet, but never took his eyes off me. Every time I stood up, he stood up. If I sat back down, he laid back down. I guessed he saw me as the only question mark for him to worry about. He was a good dog. If I had a house of my own, I'd get a dog like him.

While Coger boiled more crawfish and corn, we explained the whole story to him. I told him about myself and how I got involved with Fry. We told him about Kara's situation, which he seemed to know about already. He told us he was Fry's partner way back when Butch Sabo got on the Marshal Service's radar. Kara vaguely remembered meeting him. This was his first-time meeting Christopher, who was obsessed with Coger's eye patch.

He asked about it once, but Kara corrected him. And he didn't mention it again. Coger didn't explain it. It was possibly an injury in the line of duty. I didn't ask about it either.

Coger seemed to have a few marbles loose, but he was okay. He'd be a good protector for them if I needed to leave. He told us he and Fry maintained a mutual respect for each other. That's how he put it. He didn't say they were friends, just that they respected each other. I got the impression there was some unresolved issue between them. It was none of my business, so I didn't ask about that either.

After dinner, Coger took us and Scout off the boat and onto the pier. He walked us down the pier and over to the first prong on the trident, and without the shotgun. He took us to the end of that one, where there was a forty-foot sailboat. It was the nicest boat in the marina.

He and I stood on the pier in front of it. Christopher spared no time and jumped on deck. He said, "Cool! Mom, look at this boat!"

She followed him on deck and said, "Christopher, get back here!"

Coger held his hands up, waved them about, and with a huge smile on his face and a chuckle in his throat, he said, "It's okay. This is the guest boat. You guys sleep on board this one tonight."

I looked at the boat. It was a nice sailboat. I said, "Are you sure? That looks expensive."

Coger turned back to me, smiled, and said, "Sure. Mine is too small for all of us. And my house is a mess. I hardly go in there. It's more like a storage shed for me. Below deck, you'll find this has got plenty of space to sleep and there's food stocked in the fridge and a shower with hot running water. You need me to show you everything?"

"No. I got it."

"I figured you being a salty dog from the Navy you'd know your way around a boat."

I stayed quiet.

From below deck, Christopher shouted, "Mom, this one has a TV!"

Kara said, "Don't touch it."

I turned to Coger and asked, "Is this even your boat?"

"No. But the owner's not coming by anytime soon."

"How do you know?"

"He's in prison. But he pays his rent ten years in advance. A lot of my clients like their privacy. That's why they dock their boats with me. I tell them as long as they leave me out of their business and they pay on time, I ask no questions."

"When did he go to prison?"

Coger stopped and looked up at the sky, like the answer was in the moon. He said, "About eight years ago. Maybe ten, but he ain't coming back anytime soon. I keep things clean and stocked for the boat because he paid me extra to do so."

"Okay."

Christopher shouted out something else that I couldn't make out. But Scout seemed to hear him. His ears went up, and he leapt off the pier onto the sailboat. The next sound we heard sounded like Scout licking the kids face frantically.

Kara called out. She said, "Mr. Coger, can you get your dog back?"

Coger whistled and seconds later Scout was back at his feet like the dinner bell had been rung. Christopher and Kara appeared above deck. Christopher wiped his face and spat like the dog licked him so hard it disheveled his face.

Kara said, "It's very nice of you to take us in like this. We'll try to be gone soon."

Coger petted Scout's head. The dog's tongue dangled out of his mouth. It was as long as my hand. Coger said, "No way. You guys stay as long as you need. Don't rush. You're safe here. We can wait for Fry to get out before you make other arrangements."

I stuck my hand out to him, a handshake offering, and said, "Thank you."

He shook my hand, using a hard grip, like we were having a thumb war. He said, "Don't mention it, salty dog."

We shook hands and stopped, and I said, "You keep calling me that. You ever in the service?"

"Aye, I was. But I was never a squid," Coger said and smiled.

"You were a jarhead?"

"Of course I was. The only real branch is the Corps."

I shook my head and said, "Semper Fi."

He replied, "Ooh Rah!"

We stayed there on the first prong of the trident, watching Kara chase her son around the deck. Scout stared up at Coger with huge eyes, like he was begging to play with the kid. Coger said, "Go on, boy."

The dog sprinted and leapt back on deck. The three of them played for a long time. We stayed there watching. We could've been a family.

Finally, Coger asked, "You like scotch?"

"Not really."

"What do you drink?"

"Coffee."

"What liquor you drink?"

"I don't. I'm not much of a drinker."

Coger said, "Geez, I never met a sailor who didn't like the bottle."

"I drink beer occasionally."

"Okay, why don't you all board and shower. You all look like you could use it. There's a good shower in the head. And there're clothes in the closet for the woman. They should fit her. The owner had various girlfriends that joined him onboard, and they were various sizes. There's also some kids' clothing in the drawers. His son was close to the same age and size. But for you, there's nothing there that will fit you, I'm afraid," he said and glanced at an old Timex watch on his wrist. He looked. "Meet me at my boat at twenty hundred hours."

"Sure. What are we doing?"

"It's a surprise. Bring the kid and the girlfriend."

"She's not my girlfriend."

He said nothing to that. He just whistled and Scout came running and hopped off the sailboat. The two of them walked back down the first prong in the trident, side-by-side, like two animals that were in sync, and nothing would divide them. Not ever.

* * *

I GATHERED up Kara and Christopher and told them of Coger's request. She wanted to know what he wanted us for. And I told her I didn't know. But there would be scotch. She was unsure if they should join me and Coger. In the end, she figured it was mandatory since he was doing us a huge favor.

I showered first, and then Christopher. He was like a little man-in-training. He showered with no help, which amazed me because I couldn't remember taking showers that young. I think I still took baths until I was nine or ten years old. Our showers took twenty-five minutes. Mine was only eleven minutes. It was always eleven minutes, unless I wasn't alone.

Kara showered last. She was not a quick showerer. She was in there for forty-five minutes. By the time she came out, Christopher and I were both asleep in the salon. The television was still on. He turned it to an all-cartoon station. I fell asleep on the larger sofa. My feet hung off the end. Christopher fell asleep on the floor.

I woke up to Kara nearly ninety minutes since the time she went to take a shower. She spent forty-five minutes showering and the same dressing. She wore an outfit that could only be described as *racy*. She was in tight red pants. I mean tight. There was little left up to the imagination. There were curves I missed before. The pants had zippers here and there that served no purpose. It was the type of thing you'd find on a rocker chick back in the eighties. She wore a tiny white top with a lot showing on the bottom and the top. It was under a short black leather biker jacket. She had black shoes and a choker around her neck to boot. It wasn't the kind of outfit I'd call *wholesome*, but I certainly wasn't objecting to it.

I sat up and couldn't help but stare at her. I gave her a look from top-to-bottom and then back up again.

She did a turnaround for me and asked, "What do you think?"

Christopher planted his face into his hands. He turned a shade of red and said, "Mom, you're embarrassing me!"

She looked at me and repeated, "What do you think?"

"I think you look amazing. Not what I expected, but amazing."

She spun around again to give me a look at the back. Amazing wasn't the right word for it. She looked spectacular. If I ever needed a partner to rob a bank with, to act as a distraction, she was perfect. If she walked into a bank wearing that outfit, I could walk right in and out the back with all the money and no one would notice.

Christopher asked, "Mom! Why did you pick these clothes?"

She said, "Actually, these were the most conservative clothes I could find. I think the owner's previous girlfriends were hookers."

I said, "Well, you look good."

"I can tell you approve because your jaw is still hanging open."

I must've blushed and turned a red similar to Christopher because he pointed at me and giggled.

I ignored him and said, "You look almost like a different woman, but in a good way."

"I used to be a biker chick. Remember? This is basically how I dressed."

I nodded. There wasn't much more for me to add. So, I stayed quiet.

We met Coger and Scout at his boat, where we boarded, and Coger fired up the engine. The surprise was a nighttime excursion. He had me untie the docking line, and we were off.

Coger's boat was old, but the motors on it worked like a charm. He had spliced parts together from different junked motors. It ran great.

We took to open water within minutes. He stayed at the helm with Christopher and Scout at his side. Coger explained to Christopher about the controls, to which Christopher's only interest seemed to be to *go faster*.

Christopher spent half the journey out to sea studying the controls and the other half playing tug-of-war with Scout and an old, triple-knotted rope. It was one of Scout's favorite chew toys. You could tell because there were loose threads all over it and dried dog slobber.

Kara and I sat in the back of the cockpit, watching the waves. The wind blew hard as the boat picked up speed. Waves broke outward. The ocean sprayed mists of water behind us. The sea was pretty calm, making cruising on it pretty pleasant. The further out we went, the more stars blanketed the night sky. Kara kept her eyes on it all, like she'd never been out on a boat before. She kept her hands stuffed between her thighs. Her hair whipped in the wind, but she didn't seem uncomfortable by it.

I sat across from her. I called out to her over the roar of the motors and gusts of wind. I asked, "Are you cold?"

She smiled at me and said, "A little. I should've dressed warmer."

I started to take off my coat to give it to her. I got one hand out of the sleeve. But she put a hand up, stopped me, and said, "No. Then you'll be cold. Why don't you come sit by me? Our body heat will keep us warm."

I slipped my coat back on and got up and dumped myself down beside her. There were six inches between us. She put a hand on my thigh and guided me closer, to close the gap. I did as ordered and got really close to her. She reached the other hand across me and put it on my abdomen. She squeezed herself close to me and lowered her head onto my chest. I draped my arm around her. No choice. There was nowhere else for it to go.

She was right. The body heat warmed us up quickly, faster than a campfire. We couldn't get any warmer if we were sitting in jet fuel.

We stayed quiet for a long time. Until Christopher glanced back at us. Then Kara pulled her head up and moved slightly away. She stayed touching me. She just inched away a little, like she didn't want her son seeing us like that.

He looked forward again and didn't look back at us. Scout eyeballed me constantly. There was a lot of mistrust in his eyes, like I was the threat to watch.

Kara asked, "How fast do you think we're going?"

I glanced out into the darkness at the water racing by us and said, "We're going about twenty-five knots."

"Which is how fast? In English."

I looked down at her. I stared into her eyes. They were deep, deep blue. I could get lost in them. I said, "It's like thirty miles, maybe."

Coger yelled back at us over the wind. He said, "It's twenty-nine miles per hour, sailor."

There was a big smile on his face. There was a big smile on Christopher's face. We all smiled, even Scout.

We spent another thirty minutes cruising around, enjoying the ride, enjoying each other's warm body heat. Coger took us out a ways and turned back. Once we were back closer to shore, he took us south toward San Diego and Coronado Island. At one point, he shouted at me, "Hey, sailor. This place look familiar?"

I didn't answer, but we were nearing NBSD, or Naval Base San Diego, a major US Navy base. It's also home to BUD/S or Navy SEAL training. I didn't mention any of that.

We stopped at one point. Coger switched off the motors and anchored the boat. He took Christopher on a tour of the boat, but mostly kept him and Scout at the bow. It looked like he was showing Christopher the stars, then showing him knots in a length of rope. There was a hatch at the bow. He lifted it and showed something to Christopher. I had no idea what. It could've been fishing gear or engine parts. Whatever it was, the kid was having the time of his life. That was obvious.

Kara and I stayed quiet. We stayed there, holding each other, staring at the ocean and the stars.

Finally, she looked up at me and said, "Christopher's never seen me with a man who's stuck around. I don't want him to get attached to you."

I said, "That's random."

"I'm sorry. I just see how he looks at you and I can see it's different from before."

"Different?"

"I mean, I can see him growing attached to you so fast. Even in the last forty-eight hours."

I stayed quiet.

She said, "I have grown attached to you already. I never had a man protect me like this before."

"I'm just doing the right thing."

"Is that all this is? You feel sorry for us?"

"That's not what I mean. I'm doing this because it's right."

"Are you a Boy Scout?"

I shook my head and smiled.

She asked, "Are you only helping us because it's the right thing?"

I stayed quiet.

She asked, "Is there more to it?"

"I want to help. It's an insatiable need to help. I can't help it. But also, I want to. I like you and Christopher."

She smiled and glanced at the boat's bow, at her son to see if he wasn't looking at us. He wasn't. She reached a hand up, brushed my stubble with it, and hauled herself up and kissed me. Her tongue was soft and wet. She tasted like strawberries. I kissed her back—full-force, full-throttle, full-speed. I didn't hold back. I couldn't hold back. Not anymore. Not with her.

She grabbed my hand and pulled it down across her cheek, across her neck, brushing hair off her face, and down. She pulled my hand down over her breasts and down her stomach. Her skin was warm and soft. She guided me down over her pants. We kissed and stayed that way for a long, exhilarating moment. She was thrilling. She was dangerous, in a good way, in the best way. I felt like I was dancing on a knife's edge.

We were at the edge of the world. Nothing else mattered.

And then, the moment ended because Scout barked at us. He was right there, staring at me, like he was protective of her now because he had already bonded with Christopher.

Kara pulled away and composed herself, and smiled at me. She said, "I don't want to get hurt. I don't want my son to get hurt."

I whispered, "I'll never let that happen."

She said nothing else because right then, Christopher was back and showing his mother something. It was a waterproof flashlight. The beam was on. It waved into the air, casting a spotlight high above us.

Christopher said, "Mom! Mom! Come check it out!"

Kara pulled away from me and stood up and went to her son. He stood near the gunwale, holding onto a bar that ran along the boat, so he didn't fall off the side. The waterproof flashlight was in one hand and the bar was in the other.

Kara said, "Be careful now!"

"I am! Come check it out!"

"I'm coming," Kara said, and glanced back at me once.

Coger came around the starboard side and climbed into the cockpit. He ventured down belowdeck. A moment later, I heard clinging and clattering like he was tossing around pots and pans. I stayed there for a second, watching Kara climb along the port side of the boat to the bow. Her son led her up there. Scout followed them. I was surprised he stayed with Christopher over following his master.

Traitor, I thought and smiled. German Shepherds are fiercely loyal to their masters and widely misunderstood. It's a dog that looks terrifying, and, in all honesty, it is terrifying. But it also loves unconditionally. And they love children, a lot faster than they do grown men. That's almost always automatic. Scout took to Christopher almost like they were long-lost friends.

Coger called to me from belowdeck. He said, "Widow? Come down here. Join me."

I joined Coger belowdeck in the galley. He had poured himself a glass of scotch, neat, and opened a bottle of Bud for me. He handed me the beer, and we sat across from each other on opposite sofas.

He took a drink, and I followed suit. We talked about our circumstances. He recounted his and Fry's friendship and how personally Fry took the Sabo case.

He said, "Sabo was a bad guy. The worst of the worst. I've met a lot of monsters in my career, but he was the worst. At first, we had Kara in WITSEC. Under normal parameters. But Sabo tracked her down somehow. They killed three agents trying to get to her. Fry blamed himself. He took Kara into an off-the-books layer of protection that we rarely talk about. The public knows nothing about it."

"Another layer of protection?"

"Yeah, the program has no name. The world's getting larger. The internet and technology have made us all closer than ever. And the population is growing."

"What're you saying?"

Coger took another deep swig of his scotch and said, "It's harder to hide a witness. Harder than ever. In the good ole days, we just changed their names, gave them new identities, gave them new driver's licenses, social security numbers, and so on and so forth. But nowadays, everyone's got all your information at the touch of a button."

I drank a gulp of beer and said, "Or the swipe of a finger on a phone screen?"

"Yes. Exactly. A man like Sabo is powerful enough to find her wherever she goes."

"I thought Sabo was dead?"

Coger shrugged and said, "Dead or not, The Phantom Sons won't care. They won't forget her. You'll have to protect her for the rest of your life if you get involved."

"I'm already involved."

He drank another pull from his scotch and looked at the opening up to the night sky and the stars above. He said, "The new leader of the Sons will keep coming."

"What do you suggest?"

"I think it's time to take the fight to him. Maybe."

I drank more beer, looked him in the eyes, and said, "I'll call Fry when we return to shore."

He nodded. We drank more until Christopher called me up to the deck. He shouted in a lot of excitement. Scout barked aggressively, but playfully. Kara called us too, but her voice was drowned out under her son's shouts and Scout's barks.

Coger and I set our drinks down and surfaced. The three of them were at the bow, all the way to the tip. Kara and Christopher turned to us and beckoned us to join them. They were huddled close together because of the cold wind. I grabbed at a railing and hauled myself along the gunwale and made it to the bow. Coger was directly behind me. We got to them. Scout barked continuously at something out in the water.

I asked, "What is it?"

Christopher pointed over the bow and into the water, about ten yards off the boat. I came up behind them, stopped inches behind Kara. She reached back, grabbed my hand, and pulled me behind her until I was touching her. Coger joined Scout and petted him. Christopher was over excited. He pointed and hopped up and down. He shouted, "Look, Mr. Widow! Look!"

I looked.

A huge dorsal fin breached the waves. It must've been two yards high. The creature attached to it breached the surface of the ocean. Seconds later, a huge splash of water blew into the air, joined with the sound of breathing, like something large took a breath.

The creature's breath was followed by another massive creature. Then there was another and another.

It was a pod of killer whales.

An hour later, we were back on shore. Coger shot the rest of his scotch and asked if I would drive the boat back. I obliged, which meant that Christopher stayed next to me the whole time, begging to use the throttle and asking questions about everything. I was certain that Coger already answered all the same questions. And I realized why Coger wanted me to drive us back to the marina. He was tired of answering questions. Still, I'd say he was pretty patient, for a recluse.

Being the driver of the boat also meant that Scout stayed next to me as well. He never growled or snarled or barked at me. But he stayed tense. He was a good guard dog.

Onshore, we said our goodnights and parted ways. Coger and Scout stayed on his boat, although Scout looked torn about who he'd go with—his lifelong master or the kid he just met.

Kara and Christopher took the berth, or bedroom, belowdeck. And I slept on deck. The drug dealer's sailboat had large, comfy sofas on deck. It wasn't a problem.

Before I crashed, I used Kara's phone to call Fry's hospital room again. There was no answer.

Around midnight, I heard someone stirring belowdeck. I opened my eyes. The clouds above moved slowly and loomed. There was plenty of starlight. The stars twinkled. The moon was big in the sky. The ocean swaying filled the air with a calm, serene sound. I sat up to listen to see who was stirring below. I didn't want the kid to come up here and then go wandering alone.

A figure emerged from the stairs leading belowdeck. It was Kara. She climbed up and came over to me. She wasn't in the racy clothes anymore. She changed into something else. It was sleeping attire. But as she neared me, I saw it was only a silk gown. There was only one piece. It was like a sheet-thin robe. I saw her naked silhouette in the moonlight.

I reached my hands up to her and said, "You must be cold?"

"Then warm me up," she said, and she slid into my arms. We laid back together. She kissed me. The boat swayed.

She ran her hands over my clothed body. She whispered to me, "Let me take your clothes off."

I did as ordered. And we made love—right there, in the darkness, and the starlight, and the moonlight. The boat swayed. We swayed harder.

21

A COUPLE OF DAYS PASSED. The five of us, including Coger and Scout, carried on like everything was normal, like this was our new life. It was refreshing for me. I was happy for a spell. I felt at home with Kara and Christopher. The only point of contention among us was Scout and me. He still didn't trust me. Not a hundred percent. He spent most of his time chasing Christopher around on the grounds. Kara walked with them from one end of Coger's property to the other. She mentioned to him a few times he should hire a landscaper to cut the over-grown grass. He just snarled at the comment.

Kara enlisted Christopher and me to help clean Coger's boat for him. It was fun and Coger was grateful.

Over the course of those days, Coger took Christopher fishing twice. Both times early in the morning. Over the course of those days, Kara and I made love every chance we got. We took showers together. We slept out under the stars together. And we did it all without Christopher knowing. It helped that Coger spent so much time with the kid.

Today, I woke up and borrowed Kara's phone and stepped out onto the dock to call Fry again. And again, I got no answer. Not from his phone. And the receptionist at the hospital wouldn't put me through.

Coger saw me standing alone. He and Scout approached me from his prong of the trident. He walked up to me and stopped. Scout stopped right at his feet.

He asked, "Still can't get him on the phone?"

"No."

"That means nothing. The man had a heart attack."

"He told me he'd be out in a few days."

"Fry's a tough SOB, but he's not a doctor. Give him some more time."

I stayed quiet.

He asked, "What?"

"I thought about what you said. The other night. We can't wait here forever. I'm going to drive back there. It's a five-hour drive. I'll be back tonight. I need to know what's the next step. We can't watch over her like this forever."

"Okay."

"You don't agree?"

Coger said, "I think you can stay longer. If you wanted to."

"It's not that I want to leave. I need to protect them. I can't do it like this. Watching over our shoulders, constantly wondering when the other shoe is going to drop. If they found her in her new life, they'll find her here too. Plus, I want to put eyes on Fry, make sure he's okay."

Coger looked away toward Kara and Christopher. They were hanging out on the sailboat, talking and laughing, like mothers and sons do. Like I did with my own mother a lifetime ago. Scout kept his eyes on me. Coger turned back and said, "Whatever you want to do."

"You don't think I should go? You were for it a couple of nights ago."

"I just never had people around that I wanted to stay around. Not in a long, long time."

Just then, I felt for him. He was a recluse. He was alone. And it was all by choice. We had a lot in common. I supposed. The difference was I wasn't lonely. He was.

Coger, a bit choked up, said, "I can take them out on the boat for the day. The kid'll love it. It'll keep them safe and occupied till you get back."

I nodded.

He added, "You need to take my truck?"

I glanced at his truck and said, "No thanks. I'll tell Kara before I go. I can take her Mustang. It'll be faster. I'll be back by nightfall."

Coger glanced at his Timex and said, "You better get going."

I nodded and left him there. I walked up the first prong of the trident to the sailboat. I pulled Kara away and told her my plan. She agreed and hugged me tight. I hugged her back. She whispered, "Come back to me in one piece."

"I will. I promise."

I gave her the phone back for the car keys, but she told me to keep the phone. If they needed me, they could call me directly on it. So I pocketed the phone.

Kara hugged me again. She kissed me before letting me go. I told Christopher goodbye. He ran off the boat and hugged at my waist, the highest he could reach on me. I hugged him back and told him I'd see him tonight.

I left them both there, standing on the pier, near the sailboat. The morning sun shone in their eyes as they watched me walk back down the pier to the parking lot. They both cupped a hand over their eyes to shield them from the sunlight.

At Kara's Mustang, Coger and Scout waited to tell me to come back safely and not to worry, only Scout barked at me as I left. It was like he was telling me not to go.

I returned to the Mustang, opened the driver's door, and pulled out the Glock 22 I had commandeered from Nelson, back at Ceanna's diner, and placed it in the center console. I got in, shut the door, fired up the engine, and buckled the seatbelt across my chest. I took one last look at Coger, Scout, Christopher, and Kara before leaving.

Before I pulled away, Coger told me he didn't have a phone. But not to worry. They'd be out on the boat, anyway. No one would get to them on the open water.

I drove back down the winding path to the San Diego roads.

* * *

THE DRIVE from San Diego back to Ash Fork, Arizona was uneventful. I stopped once to fill Kara's tank up and grabbed myself two large coffees from the gas station. I finished them both off before I got back to the hospital.

I pulled into the same lot as before and parked far away, as I had before. I got out and locked the doors. A bus pulled up and stopped at the same bus stop I used just a few days ago. No one was there to board, but the bus stopped anyway and waited.

I walked through the lot and entered the hospital. The same automatic doors sucked open as I stepped on a black rubber mat. I scanned the lobby, looking out for Campbell. He wasn't there. At least, I didn't see him anywhere.

There was a man behind the reception counter this time. He asked if I needed help, but I shook my head and walked right past the desk. I followed the same blue line I had before all the way back to Fry's room.

The door was closed this time. I pushed it open and entered his room. The first thing I noticed was that Joe's bed was empty. But Fry was right there, lying in his, watching sports on a television that was mounted to the wall behind me. He'd improved by leaps and bounds from the last time I laid eyes on him.

He stared at me and sat up. He said, "Widow? Everything okay?"

I went further into the room, rounded his bed, and pulled up a chair. I sat and said, "Yeah. We're worried about you. I've been calling you, but you never answer."

"Sorry about that. The hospital staff swears they *lost* my phone," he said, and used air quotes around the word *lost*, insinuating that he didn't believe them.

"You think they're lying to you?"

"I do. There's a damn US Marshal lingering around. I think he had them block me from receiving calls."

"Campbell?"

Fry nodded and asked, "You met him?"

"In the parking lot. The last time I was here. He tried to get information from me."

"Did he succeed?"

"No. I didn't even let him see me drive away. I took the bus to throw him off my tracks. I told him I was just checking on you. He might've bought it."

"He's been in here every day, asking me questions."

"About Kara?"

"Yeah. He knows I have her hidden."

"How does he know about her?"

Fry shrugged and said, "I don't know. The Service might do some poking around. I mean there is a string of dead bad guys you left in your wake."

"Better them than Kara."

"How is she?"

"She and Christopher are good."

"You left them with Coger?"

I nodded.

He asked, "What you think about him?"

"He's a character."

"He's a hard-ass, but he'll die to protect her. I'd trust my life to him."

I glanced at Joe's bed and asked, "Your roommate get out already?"

Fry's face turned a little sad. He said, "No. He moved on."

"I'm sorry to hear that."

"It's okay. Let's not pretend like he was my old friend or something. Just a nice guy."

"Where's Campbell now?"

"I don't know. He was here a few hours ago, and then he left. He never came back."

I stayed quiet.

Fry said, "Widow, I gotta thank you for looking after Kara and her kid for me."

I nodded.

He said, "Once I get out of here and get my phone back, I'll make some calls to guys in the Service I trust. We'll get them moved somewhere else."

"Coger explained to me the deeper layers of WITSEC. He said because of changing technologies, you guys now have layers that go beyond the official program."

"That's right. And it gets worse every year. Technology moves at lightspeed these days."

We stayed quiet for a long moment. The television played a baseball game, showing the highlights of another game.

Fry said, "Just hold on to Kara and the kid at Coger's a little longer. They're talking about releasing me tomorrow."

"You sure Campbell isn't forcing them to keep you longer than necessary?"

"If he is or if he isn't, I'm out of here tomorrow. I'll get up and walk out in this hospital gown with my ass hanging out and all if they won't give me my clothes back."

We chuckled.

I said, "Okay. Sounds good. Think I'll grab a coffee. There's decent coffee at a cafeteria on the other side of the hospital. You want me to bring you anything?"

Fry said, "Coffee sounds good."

I went through the hospital back to the same cafeteria that Campbell and I had coffee at the other day, bought two coffees, and returned to Fry's room. I handed his coffee to him, and we sat there, drinking coffee, and talking about if the Mets would ever have a chance at any World Series.

I stuck around to keep Fry company for about an hour before I told him goodbye. I memorized his hospital room's direct phone number. And I wrote Kara's phone number down for him. So now he could call us directly from the hospital phone if he had to. And I left. I drove back to San Diego. Back to Kara.

The trip back was as boring as the trip there. But at least I could confirm Fry was alive and recovering. Plus, now we had a plan. My job from now on was to keep them safe until they can start a new life all over again.

Even though the drive back was boring, it gave me plenty of time to think. I imagined it must be hard on Kara, being a single mother, and having to look over her shoulder all the time at when might be the moment that Berghorn finds her. And Christopher must be in a constant state of confusion.

I made good time back to San Diego. I stopped once, filled the tank up again, and grabbed a couple of coffees for the road. By the time I reached San Diego County, I was out of coffee.

Driving over the interstates and across the county was a little intense due to traffic. It slowed me down. San Diego traffic wasn't the same as Los Angeles traffic, but it wasn't fun either. It slowed me down about an hour.

I made it to Coger's warning signs at the end of the winding, private driveway at dark.

Something was wrong. I saw it from earlier, but I wasn't sure it came from Coger's until I reached the end of his drive.

High above the trees, coming from the water, coming from Coger's marina, there was smoke. Black smoke plumed and billowed over the trees.

22

THE MUSTANG'S ENGINE IDLED. Smoke billowed above the trees from Coger's marina. I stared onward, into the darkness of Coger's drive. I put the Mustang's gear in park and got out and looked ahead and behind me. No one was around.

Coger's marina was not only behind a few acres of trees, but also his private drive started in an industrial park. The sun was down, and evening darkness had set in. The industrial park was a graveyard after hours. The workers had already all gone home, leaving no one around to notice the smoke and call the fire department. Therefore, they weren't coming. Not yet.

I walked around the Mustang's hood and studied the gravel and the mud at the beginning of Coger's private drive. There were multiple tire tracks heading into the complex. I counted three vehicles in and three vehicles out. At least, that's the way it looked. I couldn't be sure. There weren't enough mud tracks to be sure. Plus, I wasn't that good of a tracker. The SEALs taught me a lot, but that was twenty-plus years in the past now. I don't use tracking skills too often. Like any former military fighter will tell you: *you use it or lose it.*

I got back into the Mustang, buzzed the car windows down, and drove onto the grounds. I killed the headlights and drove two-thirds of the way back down the track, past the winding loops, and thick trees. Toward the end of the track, I pulled off the side of the road and turned the car off. I took up the Glock and the car keys and stepped out. I pocketed the keys and Kara's phone, but not the Glock. I held it out and darted into the woods. The wind blew hard. It howled through the trees. The smoke grew thicker as I neared the parking lot. Large plumes of black smoke lingered in the air, making visibility low.

The old SEAL instincts took over. I didn't know who I was dealing with or how they found us, but I knew someone had been here. Some of them might *still* be there. If three vehicles came in full, that could number a dozen men, or more. Although I counted them leaving, they could've left some guys behind. Maybe they were upset about Shay? Fry had said Shay was part of the Irish mob. Maybe they grabbed Kara and Christopher and Coger, but were disappointed when they didn't find me here. So, they left behind a kill team, waiting in the darkness and shadows and smoke for me to return. My primal brain told me to expect the worst. So, I stayed in the trees all the way back to the edge of the marina's parking lot.

The worst case was if I was dealing with special forces professionals, a team of trained killers, who'd set an ambush for me. And now, they were here, in the woods, just waiting for me to show my face. But there was no one in the woods. At least, if there were, they were better than me. I studied all angles, before stepping out into the open. I saw no one, no trace of anyone.

At the edge of the parking lot, I stepped out into the darkness. Coger's parking lot had vapor lights high on poles, but even half of them didn't work. And the ones that did were dim enough that a forklift could hide in the shadows cast around them. The problem was the vapor lights made little difference because half the parking lot was filled with lingering black smoke. The firelight helped, but in this smoke, all it did was brighten everything to a bright orange hue.

I came out of the trees behind the utility shed and the bathrooms. The firelight cast huge shadows behind them. I ran to the shed and stayed in the shadows. I snuck up between the buildings, Glock out, ready to return fire to whoever might be there. At the bathroom's corner, I stopped and peeked around it.

The fire came from Coger's cabin cruiser. It was engulfed in flames. The whole boat burned and raged in a fire big enough to be part of an ancient pagan ceremony. Smoke billowed and ballooned into the air, blocking out most of the starlight above. The air was filled with the smell of gasoline.

I looked around and saw nothing else. No one was around. The other boats in the marina were untouched. I leapt out and headed toward the third prong in the trident. I crossed carefully in front of Coger's house, thinking someone would leap out and shoot me. But no one did. The small house was quiet. I ran the length of the pier to Coger's boat. The hull was the only thing not burning, not yet.

I lowered the Glock and looked into the flames. The heat was incredible. Standing so close to it, I could hardly breathe. I tried to see if there was any way for me to board without burning to death. There wasn't. I looked into the entrance to the cabin. Black smoke roared out of it. Everything was on fire.

"Coger?" I shouted into the flames and smoke.

No answer.

"Coger?"

Nothing.

Even if he was alive in there, I wouldn't have been able to save him, not without being burnt to toast. The smoke was so thick it hurt my lungs. I backed away just to breathe. I coughed.

Suddenly, I heard something. It was the crackle of a radio. I dropped to a crouch on the third prong of the trident and glanced in the radio crackle's direction. It came from a boat in one of the slips on the second prong of the trident. The boat was another cabin cruiser, but far superior to Coger's personal one. This one was a thirty-five-footer, painted black. There was no name on the stern. There was something strange about it, like it didn't belong. I closed my eyes and recounted what Coger's marina looked like eleven hours ago, when I left this morning. I saw the boats docked in their slips, scattered haphazardly, in no particular order. I saw Coger's cabin cruiser, the sailboat, and the others. This one wasn't there. It was a new arrival.

Just then, I heard something I had completely forgotten about —Scout. Muffled barking and scratching filled the silence. I spun to my left and looked back down the pier, into the black smoke, and tried to see beyond it. The barking came from the bathrooms.

My first day here I had noticed the two public bathrooms and thought there were no doors. But there were doors. They were strung open with duct tape. It was a rig that Coger made just to leave them open all the time. It was part of public regulations. Even though Coger had signs plastered at the mouth of his private drive that dissuaded visitors, technically, Coger's marina was open to the public. Anyone could request business with him. He was a functioning marina. This meant that he was susceptible to regulations just like everybody else. And California had the most regulations of any state in the Union. Therefore, he had to maintain public bathrooms. So, he had them and cleaned them and stocked them and never shut the doors. But one of the doors was closed. The men's bathroom door was closed. And Scout was locked inside. He was quiet before. Maybe he had been drugged? Or just didn't smell me yet. Now he barked and pawed at the door. It was muffled, but he was a loud dog.

I didn't know why he'd been quiet. But I knew why he barked. A guy stood right in front of the door. He was dressed in black —black boots, black pants, black shirt and jacket, and a black ball cap. He held a sub-machine gun with a suppressor on the end and a fat scope on top. The weapon was strapped around him. And he aimed it in my direction.

I turned my head and glanced at the pier. There were two other guys creeping toward me. The pier's planks creaked under their footsteps. Both men looked the same as the first.

The guy standing near the public bathrooms had intended to shoot me while my head was turned toward their boat. He aimed through the sub-machine's scope at me. But he didn't shoot me because Scout's noise startled him. He fired, jerking the weapon upwards. The bullets sprayed into the air over my head. He missed. Out in the open, with the flames roaring behind me, the gunshots were pretty quiet, but still audible. Suppressors don't silence gunfire like in the movies. Silenced gunfire can be heard in any environment. Out in the open, it sounded like a cinder block being dropped off a roof. You heard the *crackle* and the break, but it wasn't anything to bat an eye at, not like actual gunfire, which is deafening in close quarters, and not much better out in the open.

The other two guys walked the pier and saw that I noticed them and started charging me. They raised their weapons, the same sub-machine guns with the same fat scope and suppressors as the first guy.

They fired. Both were shots from the hip because they were running straight at me. Shooting stances while running are hard to do because of balance. SEALs can do it, but these guys were no SEALs. They looked more like cosplay wannabes. Not that they were terrible. They got the drop on Coger and Scout, which is saying something. They were decent. But I was better.

Still, bullets don't bounce off me. So I reacted. I saw the two guys charging. They shot their guns in my direction, but between us was twenty yards of distance and sweeping plumes of smoke and darkness. Plus, Scout's violent barking rattled them too.

There was nowhere for me to go. I couldn't go backward because the third prong ended at Coger's burning boat. Forward was no good because I'd be running into a hail of bullets. So I dove off the dock and into the water. I moved fast.

No choice. I lost the Glock. But I dodged incoming fire. I counted it as a win.

I had been out of the SEALs for years now, but I still could hold my breath for six minutes and I could swim. Maybe not as good as when I was a young man, but good enough. I dove outward, forecasting my direction, a misdirect. Once I was underwater, I reversed course and swam toward them. I swam hard but calmly. I didn't want to make waves, giving away my position.

The two guys on the pier fired blindly into the water. I heard the ripples. The bullets came close. They were at my feet. I kept swimming. I swam until I was underneath the pier. The fire raged on about three yards in front of me. I felt the heat from here. The water was hot below the cabin cruiser's hull.

I stopped and looked around for my dropped gun. Glock makes a damn fine gun. It'll fire when wet. The hot water stung my eyes. Normally, Pacific water is pretty dark and cold, but the fire illuminated the ocean below me and heated it up. The water below Coger's marina was deep. This far out from shore, it dropped a hundred feet or more. I couldn't tell because I couldn't see the bottom, not even the fire lit it up that far down. All I saw was murky darkness below my feet.

I gave up on finding the Glock and swam to the surface. I breached the water silently. I was underneath the pier. I heard the first guy. He ran down the third prong of the trident to join his companions. I listened. They spoke to each other, standing directly over me. And they spoke with Irish accents. Scout continued to bark and claw at that bathroom door.

The Irish guys stopped firing blindly into the water.

One guy asked, "Do you see him?"

Another said, "No."

"I think we got him."

The first guy said, "We better be sure. Shay wants a picture of his body."

Shay, the guy I left alive at the diner, was helping Berghorn track down and abduct Kara and Christopher. *I should've killed him when I had the chance*, I thought.

Another one asked, "What do we do?"

They went quiet for a long moment, and then, the first one said, "We got a spotlight on the boat."

"I'll get it. You guys stay here. We can cover both perspectives," the last guy said, and he ran down the pier, to go up the second prong back to their boat. The boards creaked and echoed underneath the pier as the guy ran.

There was no chance that I would recover the Glock. And it was only a matter of time for them to figure out where I went. They seemed dumb, but not dumb enough to never figure it out.

I turned and swam while the last guy ran above me. His heavy footfalls masked my splashing. At the end of the third prong of the trident, I waited till he was on the parking lot's gravel and running toward the second prong. Then, I went the other way and came up out of the water behind Coger's house. I crouched and crept through the smoke and shadows until I was at the back door.

With his shotgun and Scout and all this land between him and civilization, Coger didn't strike me as the kind of guy who needed to lock his doors. I hoped that was true. I came up out of the water. My clothes were soaked and clung to me. I wasn't cold, though. The raging fire heated the air up pretty good. I got to the back of the house with no problem and tried the back door. It was unlocked. The door creaked open, but there was too much outside noise to worry about that.

I entered. It was cluttered. There were open boxes stacked on top of closed boxes. Coger was a hoarder. The house was dimly lit by an automatic lamp, set to a timer, in the living room. Plus, firelight came in through the kitchen window. I threaded my way through boxes and old furniture. I passed a hallway that probably led to bedrooms and made my way into the kitchen. I stayed out of the window's view and searched everywhere for a weapon. I figured Coger had to have more than just a shotgun.

It didn't take long to find a cache of firearms. Right there, mounted on a wall, was the same shotgun. It was placed neatly across hooks. Above it, there were various hunting rifles. Most were bolt-action, which would be too slow for my purposes. I skipped them and grabbed the shotgun and checked it. It was empty. I searched a cabinet below the mounted guns and found boxes of shotgun shells of all types. I grabbed the magnum shells. Because why not?

I loaded the weapon and stuffed more shells into my pockets. I stepped to the back door, opened it, and went out to do my work.

The first guy was onboard their boat. He wielded a spotlight, mounted on the bow. He pointed it into the water, where they thought I was. He swept the light across the water. It was a pretty good light. Even from the side of the house, I saw pretty deep.

The two guys nearest me, on the third prong, scanned the water frantically for me. They looked desperate like if they didn't get that picture of my dead body, Shay would kill them next.

I looked around, planning my move. I needed to get closer to them to be effective with a pump-action shotgun. Magnum shells would do a lot of damage, but the range was too far. I didn't want a shootout with these guys. Dumb or not, they had the advantage of firepower and numbers. If I was going to get them, it would have to be with shock and awe. I needed a distraction. I needed help.

So, I turned to the parking lot and scanned it for an idea. I saw nothing but Coger's truck and the lights on the poles. Anything past Coger's truck was pretty hazy because of the smoke.

Then Scout barked again. I reared back and ran across the back of Coger's house. I came up between the trees and the utility shed, stopped, and walked along the side of the bathroom. Scout barked and clawed at the door frantically, violently. He was out for blood.

The door opened inward, but if it had opened outward, he would've knocked it open already. The door shook violently against the frame. It was like they'd locked a monster inside the men's room and not a domesticated dog.

I stepped around the front of the bathroom, stopped in front of the door. Suddenly, a fear came over me. Scout didn't like me. He'd made that clear. He didn't trust me. What if he attacked me? That was a risk I was willing to take.

I pushed open the door. Scout leapt out. He looked at me and snarled. His eyes were glossed over and bloodshot. He wobbled and swayed a bit. The hair on his back stood straight up. There was a dart sticking out of his back. Now I knew how they got past him. They used tranquilizers. They probably used them on Kara and Christopher. That's how they bested Coger. They approached from the driveway. Three vehicles roared up it and entered the parking lot. That set Scout into a frenzy. And Shay's three guys came by boat. They invaded the marina with a force filling four vehicles, not three. Some of them were armed with tranquilizer guns. They shot Scout, dragged him into the bathroom, and locked him inside. They must've shot Coger and knocked him out, too. Then, Kara and Christopher would've gone along with them at gunpoint. Kara wasn't going to fight back against a small platoon of scary guys with guns. She wouldn't risk getting Christopher shot.

Scout growled at me. I reached my hand out slowly and let him smell it. He stopped growling, but kept his teeth showing. I petted him softly, reached back, and yanked out the dart. He yelped quietly, but then, he saw the dart and sniffed me. I tossed the dart into the smoke and glanced up at the marina. The three guys were still searching for me with the spotlight. I didn't know any of Coger's German commands, so I pointed at the guy on the boat behind the spotlight.

Scout looked in that direction and snarled. I said, "Kill him!"

Without hesitation, he took off running, like he was on a mission, like the Terminator. Scout ran through the parking lot, through the smoke, and up the second prong of the trident toward the spotlight. I followed suit and darted up the third prong of the trident, toward the other two.

On the second prong, Scout ran and barked and snarled. The first guy heard him. Scout's paws stomped on the pier's boards. They creaked and howled under his weight. He was fast. I couldn't outrun him. No way.

I slowed my pace halfway to the other two guys. I didn't want them to hear me approach. But they heard Scout. They turned their attention from the beam of light in the water to the snarling German Shepherd on the second prong.

The first guy twisted the spotlight. The beam went up from the water and landed on Scout. But the dog kept charging at full speed. The first guy aimed his sub-machine gun at the fast-moving mass and fired. The gun purred and the planks along the pier splintered and exploded from bullet impacts.

Scout didn't stop. he didn't flinch. The first guy kept firing. He screamed in terror. I heard it over his gun's purring. His screams were chilling. There was real fear in his voice. The closer Scout got, the more terrified the guy got. Finally, his gun stopped purring because it *clicked* empty. The guy screamed as Scout leapt at him, tearing into the guy's legs and, probably, his femoral artery.

The two guys in front of me watched in horror. The closest one said, "Let's go." And he tapped his buddy on the shoulder. They turned to run down the pier and over to help their friend, but they didn't make it.

I shot the first one from two yards away. The magnum round blew a hole through his gut the size of a cannonball. Red mist exploded into the air. Blood and guts sprayed out the exit wound and covered his friend's face. The guy I shot flew off the pier, dead before he hit the water. Ocean water splashed back up on the pier.

The other guy stared at me in disbelief.

We both heard the last screams of the first guy. Scout bit and tore and shredded at the guy. His screams dulled down to just the sounds of a dog shredding something to bits.

The last guy stared at me. His eyes flicked from me to the spotlight, where his friend was probably dead. His eyes flicked back to me, then down to his sub-machine gun.

I pumped the action on the shotgun. The empty shell casing clattered across the pier's planks and bounced into the water. The guy stared at the end of the shotgun's barrel. It still smoked from the last shot.

I pointed it at his center mass and said, "Go for it. I dare you."

He released the sub-machine gun, and it fell and dangled off the strap around his chest. He raised his hands in surrender.

Just then, we heard a phone ringing. It rang from across the water. It rang from the dead shredded guy's pocket. He glanced in that direction.

I asked, "Is that the boss calling?"

He looked at me and said, "Probably."

We waited. I stayed quiet, just aimed down Coger's shotgun's sights at the last guy. He trembled, staring at the end of the barrel, at the fading gun smoke.

A long, silent moment went by. The only noises we heard was the crackle of the fiery boat behind him, the dead guy's ringing phone, and Scout's chomping.

Finally, the guy asked, "What now?"

The phone stopped ringing. A second later, right on cue, the phone in his pocket rang. He glanced down at his pocket and back at me, like he was waiting for orders. I stepped closer to him, kept the shotgun trained on him. I leaned in and grabbed the sub-machine gun. I clicked the button to release the magazine and stepped back. I said, "Slip it off of you, slow. If your finger comes close to the trigger, I'll kill you."

He nodded and slowly removed the weapon. He held it out in front of him by the strap, and asked, "Now, what?"

"Drop it there."

He dropped it. There was a sidearm holstered in a pancake holster on his belt, right side. He was right-handed. I said, "Now, pinch the butt of your sidearm with two fingers on your left hand. Same rules apply."

He maintained eye contact with me and pinched the sidearm with his left-hand fingers and pulled it out of the holster. I said, "Toss it."

He tossed the gun. It splashed in the water. The phone in his pocket kept ringing. I said, "Answer it."

He fished the phone out of his pocket and answered it.

I said, "On speaker."

He said, "He's FaceTiming me."

"Answer it."

He answered it. He looked at his phone's screen. The screen lit up his face. Sweat streamed across his brow. I wasn't sure if it was from the heat of the fire or the fear of death.

He said, "Hello."

Shay's voice spoke on the other end. He sounded diminished, like he was in pain, recovering in a hospital bed from when I shot him. He said, "Michael, where the hell is everybody? Why didn't Sean answer?"

Michael glanced up at me, waiting for instructions.

Shay asked, "What're you staring at? Who's there?"

I said, "Tell him."

Michael said, "It's a guy with a gun. He's pointing it at me."

"What? Who is it?"

"I don't know. Just some guy."

Shay asked, "Where's the others? Where's Sean and Franklin?"

I said, "Tell him."

"They're dead. He killed them."

Shay said, "Turn the phone around. I want to see this asshole!"

Before Michael turned the phone around, I shot him. The shotgun *boomed* in the stillness. The magnum blew Michael's head clean off. I don't mean it blew a hole in his head. I mean it blew it clean off. His head exploded in a red mist of blood and flesh and brain. It merged with the black smoke from the fire and vanished in it.

The rest of his body stood there for a long second, still holding the phone, until finally the headless corpse collapsed onto the pier, like a pound of dead meat. The phone clattered away and stopped near the edge of the pier. I stepped over to it and picked it up. Blood covered the screen and the camera lens.

Shay said, "Sweet Mary Mother of Jesus!"

I used my soaking sleeve to wipe the screen and camera off. Then I held the phone up and stared at Shay.

His voice trembled as he spoke. He said, "You!"

I stayed quiet.

He said, "You shot an unarmed man in cold blood. I thought you were some sort of hero. Some sort of Boy Scout."

I said, "I let you live. I regret that now. So, I made sure not to repeat that mistake."

He said, "I'll never tell you where they are. The girl and that kid are as good as dead."

"I wouldn't concern yourself with them."

"Oh yeah? Why's that?"

"I'd be more concerned about what's going to happen to you," I said, and pumped the action, again ejecting an empty shell casing, and replacing it with a new one.

Before he could respond, I clicked off the call and pocketed the phone. I still had Kara's phone in my pocket, but I was pretty sure it was ruined because of the swim I took. So I figured I better hold on to it.

I left the headless corpse and turned and walked back toward the parking lot. The second guy's dead body floated in the water. The hole in his gut was filled with water. I made it back to the parking lot and over to Coger's truck. I passed it and headed to the first prong on the trident. I wanted to search the sailboat in case they left Coger onboard. Maybe they'd hit him with a dart too. So far, it looked like they took him with them. If they had shot him, I'd have seen his body.

Huge plumes of smoke covered the parking lot. I could barely see five yards in front of me. I made it to the first prong on the trident and looked at the sailboat. It swayed gently, like nothing was happening. I ran back up the pier and reached it and scanned it with the shotgun just in case. But there was no sign of anyone else around. I boarded the sailboat, searched everywhere, above deck and belowdeck. Both Kara and Christopher were gone, which I knew.

The clothes I bought Kara were still there on the bed. Christopher's jacket was still there.

I called out for Coger. There was no answer.

Where the hell are you? I thought.

I stood on the bow, looked across the horizon, and then, across Coger's marina. I looked at his little house, the outhouse bathrooms, and the utility shed. Then I scanned the parking lot. I cupped my hands together and shouted for him.

"Coger?"

Nothing.

Then I looked back to the parking lot and at the end of the driveway. I saw someone standing in the lot. Smoke billowed around him. I can't believe I missed him before. Someone stood beyond the parking lot. The black smoke plumes wafted through the air, making it harder to make out if the person standing there was a man or a woman.

I ran back down the first prong and stepped on the parking lot's gravel. I pointed the shotgun at the figure. I walked toward it. Scout heard me and stopped chomping down on whatever was left of the first guy and ran toward me from the second prong. He joined me in the parking lot. I feared he'd attack me next, but he didn't. Instead, he walked with me, like we were two SEALs on patrol.

At first, I pointed the shotgun at the figure and called out to it.

"Hey!"

No answer.

"Hey!"

No response.

Scout and I eased through the parking lot and through the smoke and approached it. At first, I thought maybe it was Christopher because of the figure's short height. It stood about four and a half feet tall. Christopher still had a few years before he shot up tall enough to even reach that. Besides, they took him with them. He was just as valuable as Kara was— maybe more so.

I called out to the short figure again, keeping the shotgun locked on it. I said, "Hey!"

No answer.

The figure didn't move. It stood absolutely still. As I got closer, I saw the figure was short, but also incredibly skinny, like a skeleton.

When I crossed half the parking lot, Scout picked up a scent. He pointed his head toward the skinny figure. His ears pointed straight up in the air. The hair on his back lowered, and he sniffed the air and took off running. He ran straight into the smoke, toward the skinny figure, and vanished.

"Scout?" I called after him, but it was no use. He was gone. I lost sight of him. I followed behind him, weapon ready to kill the guy if it was one of them.

Suddenly, Scout stopped snarling and made a different sound. He whimpered. It was unlike any animal whimper I'd ever heard. He whimpered like he stepped into a bear trap, like his foot was caught in the powerful metal teeth. But he wasn't in a bear trap. It was worse.

I ran toward him, through the last of the smoke. When I cleared it, I saw why he whimpered.

Scout stood at the edge of Coger's parking lot, pawing at a face he knew well. He whimpered fiercely, sadly, heartbreakingly at what he saw. Stuck on a pike in the ground, there was Coger's severed head. The stump under his chin, where his neck used to be, was jabbed onto an iron rod. Blood crusted around the hole. The ground beneath the head was soaked with his blood. His one good eye was wide open. The eye patch was still there. It glimmered black under a vapor light. His mouth hung open. The tongue was pale blue. It dangled out, lifeless.

His body was nowhere to be found. It was burnt up in the fiery boat or dumped in the ocean.

* * *

I walked away from Scout. He stayed with what was left of his master and whimpered. I walked back to the truck and took out the dead guy's phone. I tapped on the screen to call

Fry's hospital room. The screen came up with a request to use facial recognition to open the phone. But I couldn't do that because the phone's owner's face was gone with his head. I walked back to the boat they came in to search the first guy for his phone. That was a no-go because Scout left too little of the guy to even know which chunk of meat was a face. And the only other guy's phone was ruined from the water as it was in his pocket and he was dead, floating in the ocean.

Coger had no cell phone, but maybe there was a landline in the house. So, I returned to it and there was a landline. It was in the kitchen on the wall. There was a handwritten memo beneath it. It was from Coger to himself. It read: *Be Nice!*

Coger was an unfortunate casualty in this. I hoped that whoever killed him and displayed his head like that was one of the three guys I already dealt with.

I scooped the phone out of its cradle and dialed Fry's hospital room from memory, not the reception desk. This time it rang and rang, and he answered it. He said, "Hello?"

I said, "Fry, it's Widow."

"Widow? You made it back okay?"

"Coger's dead."

Silence on the phone.

Fry's voice cracked up. He asked, "What? How?"

They found us while I was gone. Three of them were Irish mob. They wanted revenge for Shay and his men I killed.

"Shay's men? Are you sure?"

"I saw him on the one of their phones. He's in a hospital bed. Could be there."

Fry said, "No way. I double and triple checked. The staff here has no idea where he is."

"He was gut-shot. He's gotta be somewhere."

"The Irish mob is well-connected. They probably choppered him somewhere expensive. He could be back in Las Vegas by now. But he's not here."

"You sure? You could be in danger."

Fry said, "I'm sure. It's a small hospital. Besides, I'd already be dead if he knew where I was. But what about Kara?"

"Gone. They took her. Christopher too."

"Of course. They won't hurt him. Berghorn wants him alive. Kara is a different story. They'll take her back and do something awful to her in a public ceremony."

I squeezed the phone. Rage pumped through my veins. I asked, "How did they find us?"

"They must be tracking Kara's phone or her car, somehow. You'd better ditch both."

"The phone is broken, anyway. I took a swim. The car I can ditch. But I'm going to need wheels," I said, and glanced at a set of keys hanging from a nail on the wall above the counter. They were Coger's truck keys. "Never mind. I think I got that covered."

Fry asked, "How did Coger die?"

"You don't want to know."

Silence.

Fry said, "Please? I want to know."

"They chopped off his head and stuck it on a pike."

Silence for a beat.

Fry said, "Oh no! That's horrible!"

"They didn't kill his dog though."

"Dog?"

"Yeah, he has a German Shepherd. Great dog."

"What will you do with him?"

"He's coming with me, I guess. Can't leave him behind. That wouldn't be right."

Fry paused and said, "Widow, they'll pay for this."

I glanced out the window at the burning cabin cruiser. It was sinking now. The hull had caught fire and was breaking apart. I could hear it crackle and splinter from there. I said, "I know they will. Three of them already have."

"Why aren't the cops there? Was there gunfire?"

"They used suppressors. Plus, Coger's marina is out a long way from civilization. But they set his boat on fire. And it's been burning a long time. Someone's bound to call it in."

Fry said, "You gotta get out of there before the cops arrive."

"What about Kara? Where are they?"

Fry said, "We know they're taking her back to North Carolina to face The Phantom Sons. They can't board a plane with her and the kid, not at gunpoint. Too big of a risk. They'll drive her cross-country. No choice. Which buys us some time. But we need to move fast. If she gets back to North Carolina, they'll torture and kill her. The Sons take betrayal seriously. They've got a brutal kill ritual for it. She'll be killed, no matter who her father used to be. You need to come back here and pick me up. Pronto."

I said, "Fry, stay alive. I need you. Kara and Christopher need you."

"You too," he said, and clicked off the call.

I went to the fridge to check out what Coger had in it. There was a half-empty case of bottled waters and some cooked chicken in a Ziploc. I grabbed both and scooped the keys off the ring. I opened up the truck and tossed the water in the back. I put the chicken on the front seat. The driver's side door creaked open, which must've meant something to Scout because he came running. I heard his footfalls and turned and watched him. He sprinted through the smoke and across the lot. He reached me and lunged like a lion taking down a kill. But he flew right past me and landed on the front seat. He moved to the passenger side and took a seat in a worn dip in the seat. His butt fit perfectly into it because it was his seat. That was obvious. He was coming with me whether or not I liked it. He sat up and stared at me. There were real tears in his eyes.

"Good boy," I said and hopped into the truck. Just then, I heard sirens. But they weren't coming from the driveway. I looked up and saw flashing blue and red lights coming from a boat approaching the marina. It was the US Coast Guard. They were coming because of the smoke or because someone reported all the shotgun blasts. Either way, we weren't sticking around to greet them.

I cranked the truck until it sputtered to life. I shut the door, reversed the truck, and sped away, back down the driveway, past Kara's Mustang, past the loops, and back to San Diego's freeways.

23

Fry dressed in the same clothes that he wore when I first met him. Somehow, he got the hospital to return them with his gun and phone. He wasn't sure why they kept his belongings from him. But he suspected Campbell had something to with it. The US Marshal Service wasn't happy about the pile of bodies. Campbell threatened him with investigations.

This was my third time seeing Fry in the same day. And I realized he got no visitors. No kids. No wife. I didn't ask him about it. As it might be a sore topic. But I'd seen it before. A career law enforcement agent married to their job, with too many irons in the fire to get a life. I'd been that guy before —once.

I entered the hospital to help Fry carry anything he needed help with. It turned out he didn't need any help. The hospital fought with him for several minutes on discharging him. The doctor tried to get him to stay, but he refused. In the end, they had to let him out. He signed some papers stating that he was no longer under their care and he wouldn't hold them legally liable if something were to happen to him from this point forward. They made him exit the hospital in a wheelchair, standard procedure. So, an orderly wheeled him out. At the outside entrance, he stood up, and we walked to Coger's truck.

I asked, "Where to first?"

"Airport. Let's get on a plane."

"Can we get a flight out this time of night?" I asked, because from San Diego to Ash Fork was just over five hours to drive. Therefore, I'd left Coger's marina five hours ago, when it was already after dark. I didn't know what airport we'd have to fly out of, but it could be a couple of hours away by car.

"I already got us a flight. We fly out of Flagstaff Pullman Airport," Fry said, and paused a beat to look at his watch. "But we've gotta leave now if we're going to make it. It's a long drive for them."

"It's a thirty-six-hour drive from Coger's marina to North Carolina. They grabbed Kara and Christopher before I got back, which means they've got at least a ten-hour head start."

Fry nodded. I stopped and glanced around the hospital parking lot.

Fry asked, "What you looking for? Did you forget where you parked?"

"I'm checking to see if Campbell is around. He caught me out here the other day. I don't want him tailing us or getting our plates and having Arizona State Patrol keeping an eye out for us.

"Don't worry. He's not watching for us. He left hours ago."

We walked through the lot to Coger's truck. I had left the windows rolled down for Scout. Fry froze in place when he saw Scout pop up in the driver's side window. The dog snarled at him and grinned, showing his massive sharp teeth.

Fry said, "That's Coger's dog?"

"That's him. His name is Scout."

"Widow, that dog is terrifying. I can't ride with him."

"Why not? Doesn't the Marshal Service have police dogs?"

He said, "Sure, but they're trained by professionals. They're not bloodthirsty animals that might bite my face off."

"Relax. Coger was a professional. Scout's a good dog. I vouch for him."

Just then, Scout snarled again, but he did little else. I said, "See, if he didn't like you, he'd have attacked you already."

"What are we going to do with him?"

I looked at Scout, stepped up to the driver's side door of Coger's truck, and, for the first time, Scout let me pet him. I scratched under his chin. He acted like he loved it. I said, "Scout comes with us. It's not a debate."

"How're we going to get him on the plane? I think dogs like him need to be in a crate and shipped like cargo."

I petted Scout behind the ears and said, "He's not cargo. He goes with us. Use your US Marshal credentials to make it happen."

Fry said nothing. He just shrugged. I stepped to the back of the truck, reached into the truck bed, and opened a bottle of water. I asked, "You want one?"

"No. I guess we can try it when we get there. But the dog rides in the back. I'm not sitting upfront with him."

I nodded, opened the water bottle, and drank a bunch of it. Then I opened the door. Scout jumped out and sat. I looked at him and asked, "You thirsty, boy?"

Scout barked.

I poured the rest of the water bottle slowly onto the ground. He lapped it up midstream and drank the rest of the water. I walked back to the tailgate and let it down. I pointed at the truck bed, hoping Scout knew what to do. And he did. He barked once, then jumped into the back. I closed the tailgate and pet him again. He licked my face.

I said, "Okay. I guess he can ride in the back then. Let's go."

Fry opened the passenger door and stopped because Coger's shotgun was on the floorboard. I said, "I'll get that."

I grabbed the shotgun and moved the whole front bench forward to stuff the shotgun behind the seats. Behind the seat, I found Scout's leash, but also something else. I lifted it up and showed it to Coger. It was a dog harness. It had a long patch Velcroed onto it that read: *Certified Service Animal*. I held it up to Fry and said, "He's a service dog."

Fry paused a beat and said, "That makes sense. Coger lost an eye and suffered from PTSD. Back from his military days. Of course, he'd get a service dog."

"Don't service dogs fly on the plane?"

"I think so. We can try."

I looked at Scout and said, "Who'd guess you were a trained service dog?"

He barked at me once.

Fry asked, "Does he know any commands?"

I shrugged and said, "Coger gave him commands, but they're all in German. I got no idea what they are."

"We can take him then. So, let's go."

I nodded, put the harness back, and hopped in the truck. Fry followed suit. I cranked the truck back to life, and we headed out.

The drive took fifty-one minutes. We parked Coger's truck in long-term parking, left the shotgun, and put Scout's harness and leash on him. He sat for it calmly like it was his favorite thing in the world. Suddenly, he was on his best behavior. Boarding the plane with him was easy. In fact, Fry got more grief for trying to bring his former service weapon onboard than we did getting Scout on the plane.

Because I had Scout, they bumped me to First Class so I could be closer to the plane's exit, a perk of being disabled. I wasn't disabled and Scout wasn't my service dog. They gave us no grief about that because of Fry's credentials. And he was able to bring his gun.

Scout was a little uneasy during takeoff. Once we were at cruising altitudes, he closed his eyes and fell asleep at my feet. I guessed this was why they bumped us up to First Class.

Scout was a large breed, and I was a big man. Between the two of us, me sitting in an economy seat and Scout in the footwell would've been very uncomfortable.

I laid my head back and closed my eyes. Scout and I slept until we landed.

24

WE WOKE up in Hartsfield-Jackson Atlanta International Airport early in the morning, before most of the world woke up, and exited the plane and waited in the terminal for a two-hour layover. I grabbed a coffee from a Starbucks at three times the price it was worth. Fry sat with me at a table for two. He drank a decaf coffee. I suspected it was because he had a heart attack four days ago. Not sure he should even drink decaf, but I understood needing that coffee fix. It was a risk worth taking.

Scout rested at my feet like I was the only thing left in his life. He was desperate not to lose me, too. That was obvious. He went from distrusting me to trusting me completely.

I pulled the lid off my coffee, set it on the table, and took a sip from the Starbucks to-go cup. After, I looked at Fry and asked, "What's the plan? We can't just storm their compound with just the two of us and rescue Kara and Christopher. That's a suicide mission."

"I got an idea. First, we catch our connecting flight," Fry said, and he glanced at his watch, which made me think of Coger's old Timex. "Once we get to Charlotte, we'll need wheels and supplies."

"What kind of supplies?"

"We'll need weapons. I got my service weapon, but you'll need a gun. They won't believe you don't carry a gun."

I asked, "Who won't believe?"

Fry ignored the question and said, "And we need a motorcycle." He paused and looked me up and down. "And we'll need new clothes for you. Those aren't going to work. Not if you're going to play the part."

"What part? What're you planning?"

Fry didn't answer that either, like he knew I'd reject it if he told me. The whole thing had me nervous already. He glanced at his watch and said, "Fifteen minutes till we board again. I'm going to go to the john first." He gulped down the rest of his coffee, got up, and left for the men's bathroom.

Fifteen minutes later, we were back on another plane, headed to Charlotte, North Carolina.

* * *

AN HOUR and ten minutes later, our Boeing 717's wheels touched down on the runway at 18C, and fifteen minutes after that, we stood in queue to rent a car.

Back on the plane, Fry had said, "I've got a crazy idea that just might work." And he explained it to me. It was crazy. I reminded him of that fact over and over. He's crazy to think it'll work. But I had no better ideas. We couldn't go to the cops. We couldn't use the US Marshals, not knowing who to trust. The jury was still out on Campbell. The FBI was our best bet, but they've known about The Phantom Sons for decades and have done nothing. Democratic essentials tied their hands, like warrants and rights and the Bill of Rights—specifically, the Second, Third, Fourth, and Fifth Amendments to the Constitution.

The FBI take the Bill of Rights pretty seriously. Especially since they swear an oath to uphold it and all that. So we were on our own for now.

Fry rented a car. The rental company was strained because of high demand. Plus, we rented without a reservation. So the only car we could get was a tiny, lime green Chevy Spark. I'd never heard of it before. Or I'd heard of it and completely forgot it. And for good reason. The car was tiny. It looked like a lima bean on wheels.

The color I couldn't care less about, but the leg room was abysmal for a guy like me. Plus, the ceiling was right on the top of my head. Fry was shorter than me, but he had a middle-aged man's body. He was a little loose in the midsection, making the car an uncomfortable proposition for both of us. In theory, Scout would have the best car ride because he could have the entire backseat to himself. However, that wasn't his plan.

He kept trying to climb over the center console and sit on my lap in the passenger seat. I ended up sitting with him in the backseat just so he would stay back there. At least I could push the passenger seat all the way forward. But my knees were still crammed into the back of the seat.

Once we were situated, Fry backed out of the rental lot and a question dawned on me. I asked, "Hey. Should you be driving?"

"Sure. Why wouldn't I be?"

"Because you just suffered a heart attack. And it was while driving. You nearly ran me over."

Fry said, "Quit whining. You're alive, right?"

I stayed quiet.

Once we left the airport, Fry turned onto a street and followed it for ten minutes, until he was acclimated to where we were.

I asked, "You've been to Charlotte before?"

"Of course. Back when I worked this case, I came through here a lot. And on other occasions."

"What other occasions?"

Fry slowed and stopped at a red traffic light. He keyed a location into his phone and a map with play-by-play directions popped up, showing him where to go to reach the place he was taking me before we launched a two-man-and-a-dog rescue operation. Then he glanced over at me and said, "I used to be sweet on a girl around here."

"Really?"

"Yep."

"What happened to her?"

"She's around."

We drove awhile until we were in a seedy part of town. At least, it looked that way at first. But the buildings were nice, and the streets were well kept. It's just that it was filled with people wearing all black, like it was the darker side of town. There were people walking around in full black makeup and leather clothes. I realized it was where the alternative people hung out.

We pulled into a parking lot of a shopping mall. There was one shop peeled off from the rest in its own square building in the parking lot. Various drill and machine shop sounds emitted from an open garage door with three small bays. It was a mechanic shop, but not just any mechanic shop. It was a bike shop. Several mechanics in blue coveralls, with the bike shop's name plastered on the back, walked around. They carried various mechanic tools and worked in small teams on different motorcycles. Some motorcycles looked expensive. Others looked cheap.

We parked, left Scout in the car with the windows cracked. He stayed put and didn't protest. Which surprised me. I didn't think he'd let me out of his sight. He was a well-trained dog. I regretted not learning Coger's commands for him. But that was a story for another day.

We walked past the garage part of the bike shop to the front side, which was a biker's clothing store. We entered and everyone stopped and stared at us, from the workers to the customers—everyone.

Fry said, "They don't like outsiders I guess."

"They're not staring at me. They're staring at you."

"Me? Why? Half the customers in here are white guys my age. You know? The weekend warrior types," he whispered to me.

"They're not staring at you because you're an older white guy. They're staring at you because you look like a cop."

Fry glanced down at his clothes and said, "Me?"

"Yes. It's so obvious."

"But my gun is concealed."

"They don't care about the gun. Everyone in here is packing a concealed gun. It's just the way you look. The way you carry yourself. You ooze police. You might as well be wearing one of those badges hanging from a chain around your neck with a reflective orange crossing guard vest."

Fry said, "Okay. Good to know. I'm not cut out for undercover work. But you are."

I stayed quiet.

A young girl with nose piercings—plural—approached us and asked if she could help us find something. Fry told her I needed a makeover to make me look like I was part of a motorcycle gang. She looked me up and down and said, "That's possible."

Then, she took me into the store, to the men's big and tall section, and we went shopping. Fry gave her a credit card and told her I just needed one outfit, but price was no object. Then, he left the store, partially to ease the tension with the rest of the people in there and partially to make some phone calls.

The girl took me around and fitted me for various outfits that I wouldn't wear in a million years, unless I was dressing up for Halloween as a biker. She picked stuff out for me and stuffed me into a fitting room. The problem was the clothes didn't fit me. They had plenty of big and tall items, but they were made for large guys with larger waists. It was the weekend warrior types Fry referred to. I stood tall at six feet four inches, but my weight was all in my muscles. My waist was thin for a big guy. Which the girl made a comment about. I replied I walked a lot —lots of cardio.

An hour and a dozen outfits later, we had something acceptable. She kept trying to put me in leather and I kept trying to reduce the leather components of the outfit. I ended up in a pair of what she called *retro stitching motorcycle jeans* and a tight, short-sleeved t-shirt with the word *Outlaw* printed on it above a skull with wings. She rolled the sleeves up over my biceps, making it look like my muscles would rip the shirt to pieces if I flexed. She claimed it was to show off my sleeve tattoos. Which I guessed was plausible for a biker. I got black leather boots, a black leather belt to match, various pieces of jewelry with skulls and ravens on them, and a pair of flashy sunglasses, something I guessed would fit in among bikers. The last item was a black leather motorcycle jacket.

After I approved it all, she took me to the register to ring it all up on Fry's card. I wore all the clothing after transferring my passport, bank card, and foldable toothbrush into my pocket. So, she had to pull off the tags and scan them. She also had to unlock the store security tags on the clothes with some kind of plastic key.

Right then, Fry walked in like he was waiting for us to get to the last stage—the ring-up stage. He was on the phone. He clicked off his call as he threaded through customers and clothing racks.

The girl rang everything up, but he stopped her at the jacket. He said, "No. Not the jacket. Just everything else."

I said, "Fry, bikers wear leather jackets."

"I know, but not this one. We'll get you a realistic one. Don't worry."

I shrugged, and the girl continued ringing in everything but the jacket. She folded it into a bulky leather pile and set it aside.

Fry pocketed his phone and looked me up and down. He nodded slightly and said, "Not bad. You look the part. We might pull this off."

"Who were you talking to?"

"You'll see," he said. "Where's your old clothes? Want to stuff them into the trunk?"

"I don't need them anymore."

"What? You're just going to keep these?"

"I only keep one pair of clothes at a time. Want me to pay you back for these?"

He said, "No. Keep them. But why do you only keep one pair at a time?"

"I don't like to carry things I don't need."

"So, where do you keep your things?"

"I'm wearing them."

"I mean, like your stuff? Where's your belongings?"

I shrugged and said, "Nowhere. This is all my stuff."

Fry looked at me sideways. But he asked no more questions. The girl finished ringing everything up and told Fry the total. His jaw dropped. He said, "Whoa. That's expensive."

She asked, "So, you still want it all?'

"Yeah. Charge it."

She swiped his card. The computer thought for a long moment, like it might decline. But it didn't. She printed a receipt and handed it to Fry. He folded it up and pocketed it. Then we walked back out the door to the parking lot. I said, "You can have all this stuff when we're done. Return it and get your money back."

He said nothing to that. We got back in the Chevy and drove off.

* * *

We stopped for gas, and I bought Scout some beef jerky sticks, which he devoured. I got a coffee, and we left. Fry took me through to the other side of town, where we pulled into an industrial complex. It was warehouses and large office parks. Some were clearly marked with company names. Some weren't. I'd heard of some of them. Others were a mystery.

We turned down a service drive, and Fry said, "This is it."

We drove through and stopped at a security hutch. It wasn't military, but I had no idea what it was. The guard at the gate wore all black. Two others stood guard with sidearms holstered. They had ID badges dangling from shirt pockets with their names, photos, and badge numbers. But there was no specification who they worked for. None of them had any identifying logos or anything.

Fry gave the guard his retired service card. The guy ran his information through an app on his phone. He handed the ID card back and waved us through a chain-link gate.

Fry drove through it at a slow speed.

I asked, "What's this place?"

"It's a federal salvage lockup."

"A what?"

"This is where forgotten things go to be more forgotten."

I glanced at him blankly. But I understood the moment we rounded a bend. Past a large, unmarked warehouse, we saw football fields filled with vehicles of all kinds. They were behind more chain-link fences. There were no guard hutches, just the fences with open gates. We could drive in any of them freely.

There were rows of sedans, sports cars, SUVs, trucks, limos, big rigs, trailers, horse trailers, farm equipment, and boats. There were even private jets parked way out by a hangar made of corrugated steel. It was large and round. It looked like a metal bubble rising out of the earth.

Fry saw me looking at it and said, "There used to be a 747 in there. Not sure if it's still there or not."

"What is all this?"

"These are federally seized vehicles and equipment. This is the hub of the region. All this stuff is seized in federal cases.

Some of it is collected as evidence, and then, once it's past its usefulness, it's stored here. The government keeps it for federal use."

"This stuff is all from FBI cases?"

"Not just the Bureau. It's from all the alphabet agencies. FBI, ATF, DEA—they supply the most expensive assets. Drug dealers buy the most lavish stuff."

"What're we doing here?"

Fry stayed quiet and stared out the windshield, looking for something. Then he said, "There she is."

His face lit up. He turned a little red. I petted Scout and moved his head out of the way. He was breathing on me. I leaned forward, between the front seats, and stared at who Fry was speaking about. He slowed the Spark and pulled into one of the gates.

There was an unmarked police car parked there. The engine idled. There was a woman in a grey pantsuit and a white scarf leaning against the hood. She had long black hair, peppered with white streaks. She looked to be younger than Fry, but not far off the mark. The big difference between them wasn't age. It was health. She was more fit and athletic than he was. She was of Hispanic descent, but mixed with European. She had blue eyes and olive skin. She was thin and tall. Not tall like me, but taller than Fry. Part of that was she wore shoes with two-inch heels. She was attractive. There was a gun under her coat. It was holstered in a shoulder rig.

I asked, "Who's that?"

Fry didn't answer. We pulled up alongside her. She walked around to Fry. He buzzed the window down. She leaned in and they kissed on the lips. It was a quick, friendly kiss, like they were old friends.

She said, "You look like shit."

"It's been a rough few days."

She nodded and turned her attention to me and Scout in the backseat.

Scout turned to her and snarled. I said, "Stop."

He stopped.

She asked, "So, you're Jack Widow?"

I said, "Yes, ma'am."

"Follow me," she said, and backed away from Fry's window. She returned to her car and got in and turned it around and drove off. We followed her past more parked, confiscated vehicles until we reached the back of the lot. And I saw exactly why we were there.

There were rows of confiscated motorcycles.

We parked and got out. Scout hopped out as well, uninvited. The woman parked her car next us and joined us at the trunk. She stopped in front of me and reached a hand out, let Scout sniff her, which he did, like a pat down. He instantly approved of her, which made me think it was just me he had taken an aversion to for several days.

Fry said, "Widow, this is FBI Special Agent Tamara Callesy. This is Widow and Scout, his new sidekick."

Callesy put her hand out for me to shake, which I did. I said, "It's a pleasure to meet you, ma'am."

"No ma'am. Just call me Tamara, okay?"

"Okay, Tamara."

She took her hand back and said, "So, you two are up to no good. That's my first impression."

Fry said, "Tamara, it's about—"

She put her hands up and closed her eyes tight. She said, "No. I'd rather not know. The less I know the better."

Fry said, "If anyone asks, I'll tell them I tricked you."

"No one better ask!" she said, and gave him a look that told me all I needed to know about their dynamic. She was the mystery girl that Fry mentioned earlier. They had once been lovers. Two professionals in law enforcement, working side-by-side, it happens. All the time. Maybe they'd been more than friends with benefits. Maybe they'd been an item.

Callesy said, "Okay. So, here're the bikes we got."

Fry looked at me and said, "Pick one."

I stared at him, and then at the bikes. I said, "I know nothing about motorcycles."

"You don't need to know anything about them. You just have to sell it."

Callesy said, "I thought you said he's a biker?"

Fry said, "He is. Look at him."

She looked me up and down and then said, "No offense, Widow, but you look like a lost puppy."

Fry said, "You just gotta look like you belong. That's all."

I shrugged and walked over to the bikes. I inspected them one by one. There were foreign motorcycles, the type I've heard people call *crotch rockets* because they were fast, and riders bent forward on them. I knew those weren't the kinds that would show up at a motorcycle club's front door. So, I crossed them off the list. Then, I saw a beautiful motorcycle. I sat on it and grabbed the handles, like I was a rider.

Callesy looked at her phone, where she had a document pulled up with an inventory list for each motorcycle. She said, "No. Nope. Not that one."

Fry asked, "Why not? He looks good on that one."

Callesy read from the document on her phone. She said, "It says here that's an ARCH KRGT-1 motorcycle."

Fry said, "So? Sounds like a good bike."

She said, "It's made by the motorcycle company owned by Keanu Reeves."

I asked, "The actor? I liked him in that *Matrix* movie."

Fry looked dumbfounded. He'd never heard of Keanu Reeves or *The Matrix*.

Callesy said, "It's worth $85,000."

I got off instantly. No way was I going to be responsible for a bike that expensive. Callesy pointed at another motorcycle, while reading from her inventory document. She said, "That's a Harley-Davidson FXDL - Dyna Low Rider."

I asked, "How much is it worth?"

"It's good. You can take that one."

Fry said, "Hop on. Try it out."

I got on it. The motorcycle was all black with polished chrome pipes. I pretended like I was riding it. Fry and Callesy stared at me. I asked, "How does it look?"

Callesy asked, "You ever rode a motorcycle before?"

"I rode dirt bikes as a kid."

She shook her head and stepped over to me, explained the various parts and how to operate it. I heard all of it. I caught most of it. And I understood some of it.

Fry said, "It's missing something. Did you bring what I asked for?"

Callesy turned back to him and nodded. She stepped away from my crash course in how to operate the damn thing. She walked to her car, took out her key fob, and popped the trunk. She went to it, opened it, and reached in. Then she came back out with a big, black leather motorcycle jacket. She stepped out and held it up in the sunlight. She stretched it out as far as her arms could reach. We could see it from shoulder to shoulder. She flipped it and showed us the back. It had all the trappings one would expect on a motorcycle jacket. Only this one was worn to a degree. And it had a giant crest on the back and tapes and patches, just like a Navy uniform.

There were long, prominent symbols sewn into the back like a family crest. Callesy said, "It's the Vikings crest. The previous owner was a member of The Vikings Motorcycle Club out of Alabama."

The jacket had a bonus of three finger-sized holes in the back.

Fry said, "It's got holes in it."

I said, "They look like bullet holes."

Callesy said, "They are bullet holes. The previous owner was shot in the back by a rival gang."

I stared at the holes. The sunlight beamed through them. Threads were hanging out. I felt a kinship with the jacket instantly because I'd been shot in the back once. I had three bullet wound scars back there. It was a long time ago. I wore a Kevlar vest. The tips of the bullets got through and left the three wounds. It looked like I'd been shot three times. And it felt like it, too. But I was alive, and this guy wasn't.

"Okay, try it on," Fry said.

I got off the bike, walked to Callesy, and took the jacket. I stared at the bullet holes, slipped a finger through one of them. Then, I slipped the jacket on. It fit pretty well. Not like a glove, but plausible.

Fry and Callesy stared at me. I spun around slowly in front of them and asked, "What do you guys think?"

Fry said, "Get on the bike."

Callesy said, "Wait!"

I waited. She returned to her trunk and took out two more items. The first was a blue generic government folder with documents inside. She handed the documents over to Fry and said, "You'll need these. It's copies of all we got on The Vikings. I hope it's helpful."

The second item she grabbed out of her trunk was a round, black object. It looked like half a bowling ball. She turned to me and walked over. She held up a motorcycle half helmet. It was all black with little Aztec drawings all over it. She handed it to me and said, "North Carolina has helmet laws. You'll need this too."

I took the helmet, put it on, and got on the bike. Fry and Callesy stared at me. I asked, "Well?"

Callesy said, "Now you look like one of them."

Fry said, "It's uncanny. You could pass for one. Definitely."

"Wait," Callesy said. She walked over to me and took her scarf off. She reached over my head and bound the scarf and tucked it into my coat neatly. "It's a lot colder driving the interstate at high speeds on a motorcycle than it is in a car. You're going to need this, or you'll catch cold."

"Thank you, ma'am," I said.

She flashed a smile at me. I could see why Fry liked her so much. She was generous, smart, and glowed when she smiled.

Before we left, Callesy and Fry hugged and got close. She stared into his eyes and said, "I need this stuff back unharmed. Understand?"

"Got it," he said, and kissed her, walking a tightrope between friendly and more than friends. They stopped and he came over to me. She got into her unmarked FBI car, started it up, backed out, and left us there.

I said, "That looked like more than friends to me."

"It's a long story."

He looked at the motorcycle and asked, "You going to be able to ride that?"

"What choice do I got?"

"We're headed to Gasper. It's a small town in the Blue Ridge Mountains. It's a two-hour drive from here. Better learn on the way. Make it look natural."

I nodded, got on the bike, and fired it up. It cranked to life like it had only just been parked. I looked at the gauges. It had a full tank, which was good. I revved the throttle, and the engine roared loudly. It sounded like the kind of motorcycle a major motorcycle club would respect. I had to shout over the loud rumble. I asked, "This going to work?"

"It should at least get you in. But listen, don't let them see you without your shirt. These clubs have their logos tattooed on their backs. The Vikings have the same. If The Phantom Sons see you without The Vikings tattoo, they'll know instantly you're a phony."

I nodded and glanced at Scout. He stared at me. I said, "Go with him, boy."

Scout cocked his head and barked. I wasn't sure if he had a clue what I was saying. Fry petted him and led him back to the Chevy. They both got in. Fry buzzed the passenger window down so Scout could stick his head out. He stared at me.

Fry started the Chevy, reversed it, and stopped alongside me. I was with the bike next to the passenger side, petting Scout's head. Fry called to me from across the seat. He said, "Follow us. I'll lead you there. If we get separated, call my phone. You know the number?"

"I remember it."

Fry led the way back out of the secret federal salvage yards. I followed gracelessly on the motorcycle. The first stop we made was for lunch at a chain restaurant. We sat on the patio with Scout at our feet in his service dog harness. We ordered for the three of us. Scout ate an entire chicken breast. And the cooks brought him out a bone. He chewed on it while Fry and I went over all the documents about the Vikings. I tried to memorize everything I could.

Two hours later, we headed to Gasper, to The Phantom Sons' compound, to rescue Kara and Christopher.

25

We drove Interstate 85 West out of Charlotte, until we forked off on to Highway 321 North. Then we merged onto Interstate 40 until we were on the outskirts of a very remote town in the Blue Ridge Mountains called Gasper. We had no problems on the ride there, except one close call with a North Carolina State Highway Patrol car that tailed me for twenty minutes, like the cop was running my plates and sizing me up. I didn't even think to check the bike's plates. What were the odds that the FBI would keep them current? It turned out they didn't keep them current, not the original plates. Instead, Callesy had secret government plates put on all the bikes in her inventory list by a guy who worked at the secret federal salvation yards. The plates appeared to be regular plates. An internet search would return a name and address. But the plates were really unofficial government plates.

When we'd stopped for gas, I asked Fry about them. And he told me. That information made me like Callesy almost as much as Fry did.

I told him she was a keeper. He reiterated it was *complicated*. And I let it go.

The drive to Gasper took us two hours and ten minutes with a gas station break. Riding the motorcycle was slow going at first, but I got the hang of it after a while. By the time we reached Gasper, I was good enough to be passable. Learning to ride a Harley wasn't rocket science. But I wasn't going to pop any wheelies on it. If you can pop a wheelie on it? I didn't think it was impossible. But it definitely wasn't probable.

Gasper was a town in the valley between several mountains in the Blue Ridge range. The weather in the town was cold and windy, but not snowing. The mountains had snow caps, though. There were falling leaves everywhere. It was a scenic little town. I'd guess the population was under a thousand people. There were all the staples of a small American town. Everything was gothic but craftsmen. There were hardly any large department stores. Everything was local owned, mom-and-pop businesses. There was one of everything—one bank, one grocery store, one police station, one fire station, and one church. The church was the most interesting part. It was built on a hill, above the town. There was a graveyard behind it. Beyond the church, down a long empty road, there was The Phantom Sons' clubhouse. It was built on several acres of land. There was a gate with guards posted at it.

Before we entered Gasper, Fry pulled over. I followed, and we met on the side of the road. He gave me a gun out of the trunk. It was a M9 Beretta. He told me that Callesy gave it to him, off the books, and without me seeing it. He didn't want me to witness her hand it over. The M9 wasn't for my protection so much as it was part of the cover story. I was supposed to an out-of-town biker. No one would believe that I came to another gang's territory unarmed. Then, he gave me a burner phone he picked up at the gas station and told me his number was already programmed in it, as well as the address for The Phantom Sons' compound—which was on the other side of the town, about five miles past the last town business.

He warned me that because of the long road to it, they'd know I was coming before I got to the front gate. Then, we discussed the plan to infiltrate the clubhouse. Fry also pulled some more strings to have my cover story verified by phone. As he explained it to me, there were three guys who could verify me as one of their own. Two of them would never lie about something like that, but one of them was an informant. His handlers were DEA. Fry knew a guy who knew a guy, kind of thing. And he called all his favors in from a guy who owed him. The informant was told to wait for a phone call. Normally, this would've all been set up far in advance, but this was short notice. So the informant couldn't promise anything. When I showed up at The Phantom Sons' front gates, and they called a number to verify my story, there were two-to-one odds that they'd get the wrong guy on the phone, and I'd be eating a bullet.

I wasn't happy to hear this, but what choice did I have? Fry reassured me that the odds weren't that bad because our guy was looking for a phone call. He'd be watching the only number that they would call to do a verification. As long as the guy wasn't out to lunch, I'd survive it. My preference was to avoid them making the phone call. So, I'd try to think of something. Maybe a peace offering?

We went over it all one last time. We'd already gone over it several times as we began crafting it on the plane ride from Atlanta. I was supposed to ride straight up to the front gate, state my business, and request accommodations, just for a day or two.

The idea was that I'm on a Pilgrimage, which The Phantom Sons should respect. They'll be suspicious. But, as long as they buy it, they'll respect it. A Pilgrimage was a universal motorcycle club ritual, where an agent of the club heads somewhere outside his region. Often this was to pay tribute to an elder, who was imprisoned somewhere, or to go to his funeral. Often club members will visit an important elder who was locked up behind bars. There's a strong sense of tribalism and family in motorcycle gangs, Fry had explained to me. I was learning a lot.

Here's where we got a little lucky because The Vikings had an elder doing life in prison in New York. But he recently died of natural causes. So, my cover story was that I'm headed up there for the funeral to pay my respects, representing the club, but also to deliver compensation to his widow. It's actually something The Vikings do when the situation calls for it.

After we went over the cover story, Fry shook my hand and said, "Good luck. Don't get yourself killed."

"I'll try not to," I said, and I petted Scout one last time. Then, I got on the bike and left them there on the side of the road.

I rode into town, sunshades on, acting like I was just another biker without a care in the world. Which was how I already lived my life, minus the motorcycle. I have to admit that riding this machine with the wind in my hair and the rush of the speed and power gave me a feeling of being free. Maybe I should get a motorcycle? It'd make traveling around a lot easier. Then again, it's another thing that comes with maintenance and insurance and regulations and gas and storage.

Where would I keep it? Suddenly, I'm buying a house just so I can have a garage to store a bike that was supposed to make me feel free. Motorcycles are just a different version of the same trap, an alluring trap, but still a trap.

The people of Gasper seemed so used to guys on motorcycles roaring through the town that no one batted an eye at me. The streets were busy with people walking to their work or destinations. Children were in their last days of school before the winter break. I saw a coffee shop, the only one in town, and thought about stopping for a quick cup of joe, but I had a mission to accomplish.

I rode through the town and saw various members of The Phantom Sons. I saw motorcycles parked and some on their bikes. None of them waved at me, but each of them stared me down like I was in hostile, enemy territory. Suddenly, I hoped that Fry and Callesy's information was correct. These motorcycle gangs are territorial. If I wasn't friendly and was stepping on their turf, I could be put down before I even confirmed that Kara and Christopher were still alive.

I drove around town for nearly an hour, getting the lay of the land, and establishing myself—making my presence known. I didn't want to show up at the compound without being seen in town first. I wanted the word to get back to them. I was here, and I just didn't automatically show up.

Plus, there was the verification issue by phone thing with a guy I never met from the real Vikings. I didn't like the sound of it. I needed to get into the club alive. Dead did nobody any good, especially me. Also, I needed to get in quickly. Kara and Christopher's lives were on the line. I didn't have time to go through a whole rigmarole about trust. I needed to earn trust instantly. So, I came up with my own plan. I'd been an undercover agent with the NCIS for sixteen years. I knew how to get into places. The best tactic to infiltrate an organization quickly like The Phantom Sons wasn't to show up on their doorstep, like the new guy who mysteriously shows up right as the drug bust is about to go down. The best way to get access was to be invited.

So, I stopped several times and talked to the locals. Each encounter went the same way, with the same set of questions. I asked for directions to the compound. I pushed locals to tell me about The Sons and what businesses they might be involved in. A criminal motorcycle club was like any other criminal organization. They made tons of illegal money and they needed some place to funnel it through. What I learned was that The Sons owned more than half the town. Which meant that their fingers were in a lot of legitimate pies, so they could wash their money through the local businesses. It was a win-win for everyone involved. The business owners get protection, plus significant percentages. And The Sons got to clean their money. It helped the local economy.

The locals were apprehensive of me, but they told me basically the same information. They gave me directions and hinted at the economics of The Phantom Sons' existence. Everyone seemed to approve of them being there.

The last piece of information that I heard twice was that Berghorn liked Cuban cigars. So, I made one last stop. This one went the same way as the others, but with a twist. I'd tried at a few different Phantom Son-tied businesses to get someone to take the bait. This guy took it.

The last business owner I visited was a guy selling vape pens out of a cigar store. He had no customers. So, I parked the bike out front and stopped in. There was a piece of information that Fry gave me I figured would be useful.

The cigar store was in a long line of stores that faced the street. There was plenty of street parking. The place looked empty. It was next to a furniture store with *Going Out of Business* signs plastered in the windows. The inside of the store was drab. There were shelves behind a long counter with glass tops. Various items were displayed throughout the place. The items for sale were mostly vape pens and vape pen cartridges. There was one of those old-timey Native American statues. There were cigars and cigarettes and lighters as well, but the vape stuff took up most of the shelf space.

The guy behind the counter was wire thin, like a coat hanger all bent straight. He was tall, an inch shorter than me. His face was like sandpaper, but he was clean shaven. He said, "Can I help you?"

"Yes. I'm looking for The Phantom Sons?"

"The Sons? You ain't one of them?"

"Do I look like one of them?" I asked, and I showed him the emblem on the back of my jacket.

He plucked his gums like he was hiding something in there. And I realized he was chewing tobacco. He lifted an old coffee mug to his lips and spit. He said, "Sorry, friend. I thought you was one of them."

"No. I'm an outsider, looking for them."

"What you want with them?"

"That's not your concern. I just want directions."

"Well, you see that road there," he said, and pointed back to the road I was just on.

"Yep."

"Take it to the right about a mile, and when you pass the drugstore, take a left and go straight out of town. You can't miss it. It's the only thing on that road."

I nodded and said, "Okay. Thanks. I'd also like to get a box of Cubans."

"Cubans?"

"Yeah. The cigars. You sell cigars, right? Not just these weak-ass vape pens?"

"This is a cigar shop. Of course, I sell cigars. But we ain't got no Cubans. Cubans are illegal," he said and stared at me with beady eyes.

"I was told that Berghorn likes Cubans."

He said nothing.

I said, "Since you're the only cigar shop I saw in this poor excuse for a town, then you must carry them, or you get them for him?"

The guy looked me up and down and then back in my eyes. He said, "You a cop?"

"Do I look like a cop to you?"

"No. But you better know what you're doing. Berghorn don't like tricks. Wait here," the guy said, and he went into the back. He came back out a minute later with a large cigar box with a painting of a woman on the front and red trim around the bottom. The box had writing on the front. It read: *La Aroma de Cuba*, a brand of Cuban cigars I'd heard of before. The box had been opened previously. He set it down on the counter, opened it, flap to me, and took out a black .38 revolver. He pointed it at me and said, "Who the hell are you?"

I stayed where I was. I didn't raise my hands. I didn't flinch.

The guy stared at me. His hands shook, just a little. It was subtle, but I noticed it. I stared him down dead in the eyes, right over the barrel of the gun. I looked the barrel down just as much.

The guy repeated his question. "Who the hell are you?"

I said, "You know how to use that thing?"

"I know how to use it. I served this country."

"You did? What branch?"

He went quiet.

I said, "Tell me about your service."

"I did two years in the National Guard."

"The National Guard?"

"Right here in North Carolina."

I mocked him and said, "Right here? In North Carolina?"

He nodded.

I said, "Did you get a lot of action? How many combat tours did you do? Got any medals?"

"National Guard doesn't deploy like that. At least not back then."

"When was that?"

"Back in the nineteen sixties."

I paused a beat. Something dawned on me. I asked, "So, you deployed to the local schools?"

"No. What for?"

"You one of those segregationists? Did you spray little black kids with fire hoses to keep them from going to school?"

He said nothing.

I was just trying to rattle him. Being from Mississippi originally, I knew all about the kinds of racism attached to the old South, but I wasn't sure about North Carolina. I made a mental note to read up more on the topic.

The guy gave himself away. He said, "I never took part in that sort of thing."

"But you did something related to it. Didn't you?"

He stayed quiet.

I listened. I was waiting for a particular sound. It didn't come. Not yet. So, I said, "You never answered me. You know how to use that gun?"

"I told you. I served. Of course, I can shoot a gun."

Then, I heard the sound I was looking for. Just then, a low rumbling noise came from down the street. It was faint at first, then it grew louder and louder. The rumbling turned into loud roaring. Suddenly, there were motorcycles on the street out front. They swept in a large swarm, like locusts in a Biblical plague.

The guy wasn't really planning to shoot me. He was distracting me until The Sons arrived. He called or texted them when he was in the back, getting the "Cubans" out for me.

The rumbling continued. Several bikers drove past the store windows. They stopped on the other end of the road and created a blockade, directing traffic to go the other way. They did the same thing on the other side of the street. This move confirmed what Fry had already told me. The Phantom Sons have got Gasper's cops and mayor in their back pocket. Outside of Gasper, they were outlaws. Here they were the law.

Six bikers pulled up to the store. They parked their bikes in front of the store window, turned them off, and dismounted. They stayed outside and watched.

The store clerk said, "Now you're in trouble. Shouldn't be running your mouth."

I said, "You think they'll save you?"

He glanced at the window. The bikers stood there. They didn't enter the store, not yet. They stood there like they were watching how it all played out first.

One of the pieces of information I got when I was asking around town, making myself known, was that the cigar shop owner was the weakest link in the chain. He was not in Berghorn's good graces. A bar owner on the other side of town told me the cigar shop owner was *on the chopping block.* Those were his words.

The cigar shop owner kept the .38 pointed at me and turned his head and called out to the bikers. He said, "Hey! Come in! I got him at gunpoint!"

The bikers all wore slight variations of the same black leather jackets or vests. They each put their own spin on their biker *uniforms*. One of them was a guy about my age. He was white, but looked slightly Italian with thick, black hair. He wore a red bandana as a headband. His hair was slicked back above it. He approached the store windows. The others moved out of the way for him. He wore black sunglasses. He kept them on and leaned into the window and put one hand over his eyes like a sun visor. He stayed there, watching.

The cigar store owner glanced at him. He shouted, "Are you coming in? I got the guy right here at gunpoint! What are you waiting for? Come get him!"

I glanced at the guy staring in through the window and asked, "Is that Berghorn?"

The cigar store owner nodded a quick nod, like he forgot about our situation.

I said, "If you're going to shoot me, you need to pull the hammer back first."

The cigar store owner glance down at the hammer, giving me the second I wanted, and giving me the audience I wanted. So I exploded at the hip and snatched the .38 from his hands, reversed it, and shoved it into his face.

Berghorn and the others stayed where they were, watching.

The cigar store owner guy stared at the empty air where his gun used to be, like he missed the whole thing. Then, he stared at me, down the same barrel that I had stared down. He raised his hands up near his shoulders. Before, he slightly shivered. Now, he violently shivered because his life was going to end right here and right now. If I wanted it to.

He begged for his life, over and over. It was a whole, pathetic display, which was what I hoped for. He really sold it. I couldn't have hired an actor to play the part better. The guy gave Meryl Streep a run for her money. Then, he looked at Berghorn and asked, "Are you going to help me?"

Berghorn stayed where he was, watching, waiting, letting the scene play out.

I said, "They're not going to help you."

"They'll kill you if you hurt me."

"What they do to me after you're dead is none of your concern."

The cigar store owner begged some more.

I cocked the hammer back, aimed at his face, and asked, "How much for two cigars?"

The guy nearly peed his pants, but he answered, "They're two thousand."

"For two?"

"Each," he said. But then added, "Free for you. Of course. Just please don't shoot me."

I raised the gun to point at the ceiling and smiled at him. I opened the cylinder and rattled the bullets out. They clattered on the floor, like dropped marbles. Then I closed the gun, reversed it, and set in on the glass countertop. I said, "Deal. Hand me two cigars."

The guy looked at me, confused. I wasn't sure, but he might've pissed his pants. He nodded and wrapped the cigars up for me in paper and put them neatly into a Ziploc bag, and sealed it. He handed it to me. I thanked him and walked out of the store.

Outside, the bikers were on the street. Berghorn and the five from the window circled around the entrance. As I walked out, they surrounded me from one hundred and eighty degrees. And these were big boys. I looked around, scanned them and the riders crowding around on their motorcycles, and the ones blocking the street. None of them were small. They were all huge, with either muscles or fat or both. The muscle bikers had big arms and the fat bikers had even bigger arms. They didn't need big arms or muscles or strength to end me because each of them was packing. Some had pistols stuffed in the front of their pants. Others had gun butts sticking out of their jacket pockets. And the ones who didn't have visible guns, dollars-to-donuts their guns were concealed somewhere on them.

Berghorn stood at the top of the curve, at the twelve o'clock position. Three guys stood to my left and two to my right. Each took a position on the dial. The rest of the crew were spread out at the ends of the street. The motorcycles roared, except for the six parked bikes.

My bike was behind the two guys to my left. I carried the Cubans in one hand, by my side. I took off my sunglasses and tucked them into my shirt collar. I said, "Hello, brothers."

One of the bikers, the guy to Berghorn's left, at the two o'clock position, asked, "Who are you?"

I stayed quiet.

The two o'clock guy said, "I asked you a question."

I said, "Are you Berghorn?"

The two o'clock guy said, "No."

"No offense, but I only want to talk to Berghorn."

The two o'clock guy went for a gun holstered at the small of his back, tucked under his shirt. Berghorn put a hand up and the two o'clock guy stopped, but kept his fingers on the butt.

Berghorn said, "You've got some nerve coming into our town and stirring up things."

I said, "You Berghorn?"

"I am. Now who are you?"

I held up the Ziploc bag with the Cuban cigars inside, showed it to him, and said, "I got this for you. It's tribute."

He asked, "Tribute from who?"

In undercover work, the best lies to keep are the easiest to remember. And the easiest lies to remember are closest to the truth. So, I told the truth. I said, "I'm sorry. Where're my manners? My name is Jack Widow."

He didn't bat an eye at the name. None of them did because they hadn't heard it before. They may have heard John Capone, though, from Shay, if he was still alive. But they didn't know my name, which was good.

Berghorn said, "Mr. Widow, what are you doing here?"

I lowered the Ziploc bag down to my side and said, "I'm here on a Pilgrimage."

Berghorn raised an eyebrow and asked, "You're with The Vikings?"

"Yes."

"And you're going where?"

"New York. One of our elders died."

"Which elder?"

I paused, sifted for the name from memory, from Fry's information. I retrieved it and told him.

He nodded and said, "He died? I'm sorry to hear that."

"He was old. Not a big deal. It's the way it goes. I never met him. I was selected to go. It's short straw situation."

Berghorn said, "I heard your inner circle had lost interest in him. Still, he used to be something. Sorry he died. My condolences. So, you're going on your way then?"

"Actually, I was hoping to seek shelter from you. Just for the night."

Berghorn said nothing. The two o'clock guy said, "Shelter? What for?"

I stayed quiet. The two o'clock guy looked angry.

Berghorn said, "Answer, please."

I said, "I had a previous mission to ride to Texas. I'm coming straight from that. Been driving for two days. Alabama to Dallas and back this way to New York."

The two o'clock guy said, "So get a hotel room."

I stayed quiet.

Berghorn said, "Answer."

From the cover story Fry and I came up with, I said, "I can't. I'm a little hot right now."

Berghorn asked, "You got heat? For what?"

"FBI's snooping around for me. They're investigating a murder."

"And they suspect you?"

I shrugged.

Berghorn said, "Of course, we'll check this all out."

I stayed quiet.

Berghorn looked me up and down. He said, "I like how you handled yourself with Mr. Baker." He pointed to the cigar shop behind me. "And The Vikings are our friends. At least, they used to be. We've not spoken to you guys in a long time. How's Toucan Sam?"

A test. He was giving me a made-up nickname. It's a classic move. I'd seen it a hundred times before. You give a suspected cop a nickname that sounds too ridiculous to be true, and it's not. But it's close enough to a real nickname that if you were telling the truth, you'd recognize the mistake and correct the person asking.

I said, "I never heard of a Toucan Sam. Do you mean Tony Tiger?"

Berghorn nodded approval slowly, but just enough. He said, "Right, Tony Tiger. That's who I meant. How is he?"

"Not good. He's dead. Died two years ago. Motorcycle crash."

Berghorn nodded and smiled. He raised his arms up like he was seeing an old friend and said, "Jack Widow. Welcome to Gasper. You need refuge for the night? No problem."

* * *

THE PHANTOM SONS' compound was mostly as the cigar shop owner described. It was a large area of land, nestled into the base of low mountain. The land covered numerous acres. But the street to it wasn't empty. The Phantom Sons had neighbors. They were all farmers. I wasn't sure if they were all growing the same crops or various crops, or a combination of products. But there were some decent-sized operations nearby.

I followed Berghorn on my bike. He rode in front, and his inner circle, the guys who stood around me on a dial, rode two in front of me, between myself and Berghorn, and three behind me. The other bikers rode in the back, with one exception. There was a single biker who rode way out front, like a recon scout. He was charged with scoping ahead for ambushes. Apparently, that was a real fear. Fry told me that's how Sabo died. He rode in front of the others, as their leader. But one day he rode over a roadside bomb in a broken-down car. The whole thing was a ruse to get him near it. Then someone blew it up, killing the guy. Fry said the fireball was so huge that Sabo was burnt to a crisp. The funeral was closed casket. Fry said there wasn't enough body parts inside the casket to identify him properly.

We rode to a high iron rod gate attached to a high brick wall. The gates were wide enough for delivery trucks to drive in. There was a guy at the top, like on the perimeter of a medieval castle. Only there were security cameras along the corners, pointed at the road and the grounds out front. The gate squeaked open, and we rode through it fast. Berghorn didn't slow down, like he knew the gates would open in time. Autumn leaves swept up behind him and dashed across the faces of the riders surrounding me. None of them flinched or braked or recoiled. So, I didn't either. They rode with blind trust, with faith. The gates were automatic. I saw the gears and belts behind it.

In the compound's front, there was another long, two-lane driveway. It was paved, but old. The concrete was splitting and cracking all over the place. But on the bike, the road felt smooth. This feature wouldn't last forever. Eventually, they'd have to blacktop it. I guessed the reason they hadn't already was because that would require allowing an outside crew come onto the grounds, where they kept their secrets.

The clubhouse, as it was called, was far back from the main road. It was more than a football field from the gate. The grounds were unique. There were children playing on a playground with various toys and games and expensive equipment. There were women with the kids, like teachers at a school. The kids must be homeschooled. There were large hedges, trimmed into different animals and dinosaurs. They lined the driveway on both sides, like grassy guardians. On the opposite side from the playground, there was a large, plush garden. Rose bushes lined a low brick wall. But all the flowers were dead because of the season, or they were on their way out. There were long rows of fruit trees, all with different produce. In the back of the garden, there was an apple orchid. Enormous trees grew throughout it.

There was a greenhouse in the center of the whole thing. Marble statues of various Greek and Roman gods surrounded it. Many of them were on stone pedestals. Some statues were missing limbs.

We blazed through the driveway. Forty yards from the club-house, Berghorn slowed his motorcycle and the rest of us followed suit. We came to the end of the driveway, which looped into a big circle with a large fountain in the center. The loop circled back to the driveway, leading back out to the road. There was a large parking lot to the right of the club-house entrance and four huge open bay areas, like at the biker shop back in Charlotte, only these were big enough to drive a monster truck into. I knew that for a fact because there was a monster truck parked inside of one. It was painted blue with red flames along the bottom. The tires were huge, small enough to climb, but big enough to break a leg if you fell off one.

Big, ugly steel bars shone from the undercarriage. The front of the monster truck was all chrome. The chrome grill looked like dinosaur teeth. If the thing was coming straight at you, you might think you were facing down the prehistoric mammoth shark called the megalodon, only on land.

The clubhouse was huge. They called it a clubhouse, but really it was a converted mansion. There was an east and west wing. I counted four different chimneys. One of them smoked like someone was using it. There were several dormers and gables and three cupolas. The clubhouse had massive stone columns on top of front steps, also made of stone. They led to an enormous stone porch and a gigantic front door. The building was a combination of old and new. There were huge bay windows with sparkling clean glass and the stone columns. But everything was covered in graffiti, various spray can paint mixed with regular paint. On paper, it sounds like the building was vandalized, but actually it looked planned. The symbols and paints covering it weren't by mistake or happenstance. Everything looked like it was well-thought out. It looked like they commissioned Jackson Pollock to paint the entire place with cans of spray paint.

The Phantom House was painted above the door. Outside, between the garage and the kids' playground, there was a large barn. The doors were open, but there weren't any animals.

We drove around the loop to the bottom of the stone steps, where dozens of young, beautiful girls waited. Each was in their late teens or early twenties. The oldest was probably twenty-five. There were a few black girls, two Asian girls, and the rest were white. They were all tattooed with face piercings and mostly big hair. A few had short hair. One was buzzed down to stubble. She had a huge tattoo over her scalp. The girls all wore jackets and blue jeans because it was cold out. But they had little on under the jackets. Some had ripped t-shirts. Others wore crop tops. Several of them wore just bras under their jackets. Most of them had glazed eyes. Several of them held opened beer bottles. And several of them held two bottles of beer, one for them, and one for whichever biker they were standing there for.

They stood on the steps like they were part of a welcome home party for sailors returning to shore after a war. If we were part of a rock and roll band, they could be groupies waiting for us to get off our tour bus.

Berghorn parked his bike out front and got off. He stepped to the bottom of the steps and held his arms open. Two of the girls scrambled down the steps to greet him. They wrapped their arms around him and kissed him, like he was irresistible.

Then they kissed each other with their arms wrapped around him.

I stayed on my bike, behind two of his inner circle. The other three stayed behind me. Our motorcycles rumbled. The rest of the crew rode off to the barn and vanished inside it. Moments later, they all came strolling back out without their bikes. The barn was where they parked them. It wasn't for animals. It was for motorcycle parking spillover.

Unsure what I was supposed to do, I waited.

Berghorn carried on kissing the girls for a long minute. Then, he finished and patted them both on their butts. He walked over to me and stopped a few feet away. He said, "Widow, this is our home. And I grant you asylum for as long as you need. Why don't you park your bike in the barn? Gus will show you where. Then meet me back here."

Berghorn nodded to one of his guys, who was called Gus. Gus looked at me and said, "Follow me."

He reversed his motorcycle and rode toward the barn. I followed him. The other four guys rode their bikes to the club-house's garage. Berghorn joined them. He didn't have someone else park his bike for him. Bikers don't like someone else in their saddle, even to park it for them. It's one of their tribal things. *One man, one saddle.*

Gus led me into the barn. The inside wasn't like a barn at all. The place was gutted and renovated to look like a half garage, half game room. There was a bar and lounge area and motor-cycles parked neatly in rows. There were dozens of motorcy-cles and empty spots. There were bikers and biker chicks lounging around the game room. Some played pool at an expensive billiard table. Others sat at the bar. There were girls making out in more than one corner with other girls. There was even a jukebox on the wall. It blasted music. I think it was AC/DC. There were a couple of bikers with their shirts off, working out in a small gym in one corner. There were space heaters in the bar to keep it warm.

Both bikers working out had huge tattoos across their backs. It was The Phantom Sons' emblem. The tattoo pieces were serious business. They were large with all-black ink.

Gus pointed out a parking space for me to use, and I did. I parked my bike, and I walked back out, following Gus on his motorcycle. We left the barn and Gus said, "Wait for me," and he rode to the garage to park his motorcycle.

Berghorn, the other riders, and the girls had all vanished. They returned to inside the mansion, to do whatever it was they did. I walked to the base of the stone steps and waited. A moment later, Gus returned from the garage with two of the other inner circle guys. The three of them together were built like footballers, preparing to line up for the next play, only in leather biker outfits.

Gus took off his shades, pocketed them into his jacket pocket, and held his hand out, palm opened, like he expected me to hand him something. He said, "Give me your gun."

The other two bikers crowded around behind him, one to his left, one to his right. They stared at me and put their hands on the butts of their own guns, not unlike what a police officer does in a dangerous situation.

I glanced at Gus, glanced at the guy to my left, glanced to the guy to my right. Slowly, I drew the M9 out from under my shirt, out of the waistband of my jeans. I held it with my fingers across the slider, nowhere near the trigger, and I reversed the weapon and handed it over. Gus took it and holstered it into the waistband of his own pants.

I thought about the hygiene of sharing the M9 after that. None of these guys struck me as Mr. Clean. On their daily agenda of priorities, I doubted showering was near the top or even the middle of the list.

Gus stepped back, the other two did as well, and he pointed to the front door. He said, "Lead the way."

I nodded and climbed the stone steps and pushed the front door open. It was heavy. It slid open, exposing some of the interior on the back end of the door. It wasn't the typical door on hinges. It opened weirdly. It was a type of door called a pivot door because it pivots open and doesn't open on door hinges.

I entered the clubhouse. The interior was like the exterior. The ceilings were twenty feet high. The floors were all smooth concrete, an industrial style. The furniture was leather everything. The walls were covered in expensive, dark art, like paintings of sacrifices and violent depictions of war and cannibalism. They were pretty good, morbid, but well-crafted. It wouldn't surprise me if the paintings on the wall were stolen out of the Louvre in Paris, France. There were more sculptures and statues everywhere. There was no graffiti on the walls. That was the only difference in exterior and interior styles. The house looked like it could belong to some kind of strange European art-collecting billionaire.

Gus and his counterparts escorted me to a main living room area. There was a huge fireplace on one wall. It was all stone and rock. A fire roared inside it. The logs crackled. Heavy metal music played softly in the background. Which struck me as a blaring contradiction. It was like smooth jazz turned all the way up and blasting the roof off.

On a massive leather armchair, Berghorn sat. He'd traded his jacket for some kind of fur and leather coat hybrid. He'd lost his undershirt. His torso was exposed. His feet were bare and out. And he wore black leather pants. He still wore the bandana as a headband. Two completely different biker girls cuddled around him. They sat on opposite arms of the chair. He looked like something out of a rock music video. He looked like an adolescent boy that someone gave the keys to the kingdom to, and he never grew up.

Berghorn stared at me over his shades and said, "Widow, I'm afraid you've come at a busy time for us. We've got some internal things happening."

I said, "I hope it's nothing too serious?"

"It's nothing we can't handle."

"Well, I appreciate you letting me stay."

"Don't mention it. The Vikings are our brothers-at-arms. Besides, I called them," he said, and paused.

My shoulders tensed up. I made fists and squeezed them tight. My fists were like hammers. I could do serious damage with them. I glanced to my right. Gus stood there. He took the M9 out of his waistband and walked to Berghorn, and handed it to him. The other two bikers kept their hands on their guns and stared at me. I felt it even through their sunglasses.

They had me at a disadvantage. I was unarmed. I ran war-games in my head. The four of them were armed, but three of them wore their sunglasses indoors. And it was dark inside. That had to give me some advantage. Plus, the two quiet escorts smelled of liquor and weed. They had natural inhibitors working in their bloodstreams. Gus had his own gun, but it was out of sight. It'd probably take him longer to draw it out than the others. Berghorn had my M9 out and ready to rock, but he overestimated his own abilities. I knew that without even knowing what his abilities were. He was arrogant, which almost always led to mistakes.

I asked, "What did they say?"

Berghorn stared at the M9. He flipped it, studied all sides of it, like it was the first time he ever held one. He said, "They vouched for you."

I relaxed my shoulders and released the squeeze in my fists.

Berghorn said, "We're going to keep your gun. It's just a precaution. You'll get it back when you ride out."

I stayed quiet.

"Gus will show you to your room. Treat yourself to anything," he said, and he wrapped his free hand around one of the girls on the arm of the chair. He squeezed her butt. "And I mean anything you want, Widow. It's yours. We're a sharing community."

Then he kissed the girl. She kissed him back. It was all tongue and open mouths. I cringed, but stayed quiet. They finally stopped, and Berghorn said, "Partake in drugs, girls, or whatever else your heart desires. Just play nice."

Two women sat on a sofa opposite Berghorn. They eyeballed me. One of them licked her lips.

I said, "Honestly, I'm beat. I'd like to settle in."

"Of course. Gus will show you."

Gus elbowed me lightly as he passed, as a signal to follow him. I did. He led me up a grand staircase and to the second floor. He took me down a long hallway, past bedrooms and a den and a huge library, which actually had a lot of books in it.

At the end of the hall of the east wing, he opened a door and peered in. The room was empty of people. It was decorated with a king-sized bed and dark furniture. Everything was dark oaks, and the floor was carpet.

He showed me in and said, "Get comfortable. If you need anything, just come on out and help yourself. You can wander about freely, but after dark, stay near the clubhouse. You can leave after the sun comes up tomorrow. Questions?"

"Why can't I look around after sunset?"

Gus grinned slowly, ear-to-ear, and said, "Armed guards patrol the perimeter at night. I wouldn't want them to mistake you for a cop and shoot you dead."

With that, he was gone, and I was left alone.

26

I LOOKED around my room and the closet and the private bathroom. The accommodations were nice, better than most hotel rooms I've stayed in. But I wasn't there for the room service. They told me I could roam the property during the day. There was a couple of hours of sunlight left. So, I left the room. I strolled the mansion, checking out different rooms, but only the doors that were open. I didn't want to appear like I was snooping around. There was nothing upstairs of interest. Nothing that would lead me to a clue about Kara.

I ventured back down to the first floor. The two girls from the sofa, including the one who licked her lips at me, said hello to me. I politely returned the greeting, but I moved on. I didn't want them or anyone else offering to escort me around. I found the kitchen. Like every other room in the house, it was huge, really oversized for a kitchen. Unless there were dozens of people living in your house, which it looked like there were. I'd counted thirty heads so far. But I was losing track because a lot of them looked alike—bikers and biker chicks. Most of them were stoned. Most of them were drunk or drinking. Most of them were interchangeable.

I suspected some of them were doing more than smoking pot. Several of them seemed like they were dabbling in worse narcotics. Several of the women were too skinny. Lots of them acted spaced out. None of them were overboard. There were no drug addicts. I supposed once you looked like you were addicted, then you were a liability to the group. Berghorn was running an organization, a criminal business, but still a business. They couldn't have half the crew strung out on drugs. They had to function. But there were some borderline cases.

I kept my distance where possible. I needed to blend in and be overlooked. So I went into the kitchen and popped open a massive refrigerator. I peeked in and scoped out a lot of beer, with plenty of choices. I grabbed a bottle of Corona, popped the top on a bottle opener magnet off the fridge. In the refrigerator door, I found cut limes. I stuffed one into the bottle and took a few swigs in front of people. I needed them to feel like I was one of them.

Bikers nodded at me. Girls said hello. Many of them were overly friendly. Which I imagine was their obligation. Although, some of them seemed quite happy there. I didn't judge. *Live and let live* was my motto. I was only here for Kara and Christopher. I wasn't about to add to the list of sad cases I had to rescue. Maybe Callesy could convince the FBI to step in after I left. I made mental notes of every infraction I saw.

Down the hall from the kitchen, I found an alarming one. There was a large room built like a metal workshop, only it was filled with guns. There were assault rifles, grenades, shotguns, sniper rifles, and various handguns, some of which were modded out to fire full auto. Then there were the bullets.

Lined along two long walls, there were crates filled with boxes of ammunition. There were all kinds and types—sniper, rifle, and handgun bullets. There were explosive rounds and explosives.

I arched an eyebrow. There were bikers in the room counting bullets and writing everything down on a clipboard, like they were inventorying. They looked up at me and I smiled and left.

At the other side of the hall, there was a large room with a cell door that was open. inside it there were stacks of more crates. There were bikers in there too. But there weren't guns and ammo in the crates. Now, I knew why everyone seemed high, like drugs were in abundance. The crates were filled with bricks of cocaine. At least, that's what it looked like to me. The bikers glanced at me same as the other ones. I nodded and walked out.

The rest of the bottom floor was more bedrooms and dens and lounge areas. I found the backdoor and walked outside. The backyard was vast, like the front. Far in the distance, I heard gunfire. I looked and saw more bikers shooting guns at steel targets. It was a shooting range. It must've been at the tail end of the property to help subvert the noise levels. There was a long track to get there and a parked golf cart. There were more golf carts parked at the shooting range.

Directly behind the house, there was a large pool with slides and diving boards and two bars. There was a fire pit and multiple barbecue pits. There were more girls in bikinis around the pool and several bikers with them. They drank and laughed.

There were several outdoor heaters near them to heat them up. There were girls in the pool. I guessed the pool was also heated.

This place was something else. I could see how lost young men and women could be lured into a place like this. When you're young with no plans, no prospects, and you come from a broken home, a place like this could be attractive. It's the same premise that cults operate on.

I moved through the pool area, taking swigs from the Corona for appearances. The girls and the bikers eyeballed me as I passed.

The pool was decorated with the same statues as the garden, making the whole place look like a drug kingpin's home in a Hollywood movie. Which, in reality, it kind of was.

I walked the rest of the grounds, chatting with members, scoping the place out, and getting the lay of the land. I saw nothing else of interest. No Kara. No Christopher.

Then, I returned to the house and checked out the barn again. Inside the barn, there were the same bikes and the same people. However, this time I saw something I didn't notice before. There was a door in the back of the barn. I grabbed a second Corona from the bar and trashed the old one. Then I made small talk with a couple of bikers and biker girls lounging around. They hung out and talked about the Carolina Panthers and the season so far.

After a while, I got up and wandered over to the door. I opened it. It led to a staircase that went downward. I glanced around and saw no one paying attention to me. So, I went down them. At the bottom, there was a two-room cellar. The first room was temperature controlled. It was humid. There were a couple of lounge chairs and a table with a large ceramic ashtray. There were smoked cigars in it. Behind the chairs, there was a small shelf with cigar boxes and various cigars on display. I perused the brands and types. There weren't just Cubans. There were other expensive, imported cigars.

You really do like your cigars, Berghorn, I thought.

The rest of the room was storage for various things. I figured it was used for storing the cigars, plus excess items. I moved on to the second room. That's when I found something. The second room was split into two rooms. It was divided by a row of bars. It was a small jail cell.

On my side of the bars, there was a table and a chair and a security camera, mounted in the wall's corner. It pointed directly at the jail cell. It didn't move. It didn't react to my presence. Just in case, I stayed out of its view.

Inside, there were two beds and a toilet and a prison mirror. Built into the bars was a feeding tray, where a jailer could slide a plate of food in without opening the cell door.

The cell was empty, but this was where they'd keep Kara and, maybe, Christopher.

I looked around and studied the cell. I searched for ways to open it in case they were in it that night. I could spring them and escape. But there was no way out except through the cell door. I'd need the key to get them out.

I returned to the storage room and sat in one of the chairs. I took out the burner phone Fry gave me and called him. It rang, and I glanced around the room, making sure there were no security cameras or obvious recording devices. I saw nothing.

Fry answered, "Widow?"

"Yeah. I can't talk long."

"Go ahead."

"I searched the grounds. They're not here yet. But I found a jail cell."

"Jail cell?"

"Yeah, it's beneath the barn. In case something happens to me, they'll be kept in here."

"Okay. Are you good?"

"Yeah. It's weird being here, but I'm good. I just want to get them and get out."

"Understood. We're set up a few miles back down the street. I'm staying at the closest motel."

"Alright. How's the dog?"

Fry paused a beat, and then he said, "He looks sad. He doesn't know me, and you're gone."

"Just remember to feed him," I said, then I heard a sound coming from the stairwell. "Gotta go. Call you tonight."

I hung the phone up and went back out through the door. I ran right into Gus.

He stared at me and asked, "What the hell are you doing down here?"

"Looking for the bathroom."

He stared daggers into me and said, "It's not down here. It's back upstairs, near the bar door is the closest."

"Thanks, man!" I said and tapped him on the chest like we were old drinking buddies. Then I marched past him and back up the stairs.

* * *

I spent the rest of my day drinking Coronas and trying to blend in. I chatted with various people, but not for too long. And I only spoke when spoken to. Gus and the other four from Berghorn's inner circle kept eyeballing me. I ran into one of them every hour. I saw Berghorn here and there, but avoided him. I wasn't here to make friends.

That night, I took an unopened can of soup to my room with a spoon and ate from the container. I threw the trash in a bin in the bathroom. I locked the door from the inside and stayed in my room for the rest of the evening.

The bedroom had two windows looking out over the front of the house. The barn was in my line of sight. I opened a window, pulled an armchair up close to it, sat in it, and looked out all night for Kara and Christopher.

I fell asleep in the armchair. Around four in the morning, the sound of heavy tires on pavement woke me, and I saw headlights coming down the driveway. I sat up and stared out the window. There were two vehicles approaching from the farm road. One was a big, black pickup truck with chrome everything. And the other was a black panel van. Both vehicles were covered in dirt around the tires, like they'd been through some weather after a long drive. It had to be Kara and Christopher, with the guys who abducted them and were also responsible for killing Coger, my friend.

I watched from the darkness. The vehicles came to the front of the house and looped part of the circle. The van stopped behind the pickup and reversed to the barn. It stopped just in front of the barn doors.

I heard voices below me from the front door. I craned my head and looked. Berghorn, Gus, and the rest of his inner circle came out the front door. They walked to the truck first. The truck's doors opened up and three big bikers stepped out—all in The Phantom Sons' jackets with The Phantom Sons' coat of arms on the back. They met with Berghorn and talked for a moment. I couldn't hear them.

Berghorn, Gus, the other four inner circle guys, and the three big bikers met and walked toward the barn. They stopped about three yards from the van's grille. They stood silently in the headlights and the gloom. Their faces were covered in darkness, above the headlights' beams.

At the van, the driver left the engine running and the headlights on. He got out, and a passenger got out of the other side. They met the other nine guys. The van's cargo door slid open. And two more bikers hopped out with two figures. One the size of an adult female. The other the size of a six-year-old boy. Kara and Christopher, right there in front of me—alive. I breathed a sigh of relief.

They looked exhausted and a little malnourished, like they had eaten nothing in thirty-six hours. Their hands were zip-tied behind their backs. Terror blanketed their faces. But it was outpaced by the exhaustion because they hadn't slept in thirty-six hours either. The two bikers at the cargo door hauled them both out and stood them up and marched them around to the van's grille. They marched them out in front of the headlights and forced Kara to her knees. Her and Christopher were a yard from Berghorn and his guys. It was the first time in his life that Christopher ever saw his father.

Berghorn stepped out into the light. He approached Kara and spoke to her. I couldn't hear them, but I'm sure it was threats and accusations and terror. I clenched my fists. But all I could do was watch. In my head, I was making plans to rescue them. I could sneak out of here, make my way to the armory, steal some guns, and position myself in one of the windows close to them. I could unload enough firepower to kill them all, or at least scatter them, so Kara and Christopher could make a break for it.

Those thoughts were shattered a second later because Berghorn had Kara picked up and forced into the barn. Gus picked up Christopher and hauled him in. All thirteen bikers followed them into the barn. They were all armed. They were all dangerous. And now, they were in cover. I had to come up with a new plan.

I took out the burner phone and called Fry. I wasn't sure if my room was bugged or not. It didn't matter. What were the odds someone was listening to me now, at four in the morning? Probably near zero. I took my chances.

The phone rang and Fry answered it almost immediately. He said, "They're here?"

"Yes."

"I saw the van and the truck blasting through town. I figured it was them because there hasn't been another car on the street after midnight. Not in front of my motel."

Fry said, "So, how's it look?"

"Not good. But they're alive."

"Visual confirmation?"

"Yes. Thirty seconds ago."

"Okay. So, what's the plan?"

I said, "Most of the house is asleep, but Berghorn has a bunch of bikers with him and he's with Kara and the kid. They've got them inside a barn. I lost sight of them. But there's a cell in a cellar down there. I saw it earlier."

"What do we do?"

"Right now, nothing. There's thirteen armed bikers with them."

Fry asked, "No chance of sneaking them out?"

"Maybe. It's hard to say. Right now, I couldn't even get near them. I lost sight of them. And thirteen armed bikers are going to be near impossible to get through."

"Any chance you can wait until they're clear?"

I said, "That's about all I can do."

"They'll be executed, and soon. But probably not right now. Not this second. It'll most likely be in the morning or during the day, maybe in the evening. Like I told you, it's part of a ritual. Kara is a traitor to the club. They'll do something horrible to her in front of the club. They'll make an example of her for the others."

"What about the kid?"

Fry said, "They'll make him watch, or worse. Since he's Berghorn's son, he'll probably live. They'll want to raise him to be like one of them. But he'll be scarred for life."

"What's *worse*?"

"They could make him take part."

"Jesus. They're really like that?"

"Yes."

"Sounds like a fate worse than death."

"It is. So, what're we going to do?"

I said, "Let's wait two hours. It'll still be mostly dark out. I'll keep watch, but most of those bikers should clear out of there. Some of them were up all night drinking. I saw them myself. They'll want to sleep. Then, I'll call you and sneak in and get them out before the rest of the club wakes up."

"Okay. I'll be ready," Fry said, and he hung up.

* * *

FOR THE TWO longest hours of my life, I watched the barn. Fear boiled in the pit of my stomach. I listened, but never heard a thing. And no one ever left. Six a.m. rolled around slowly, and the sun was still down. It was time to move, thirteen armed guys or not. So, I prepared mentally and snuck out of my room. In the hallway, there was no one, and no sound but the stillness of a big sleeping house. I went down the stairs, casually but quietly. I could walk the house, but I didn't want to wake anyone.

Several people slept on sofas and armchairs and on the floor, like they'd gotten drunk or stoned and passed out where they were the night before. There was a person awake here or there, but no one paid me any attention. I snuck down the hall to the west wing, past the kitchen to the armory. I needed to get some firepower. *If* I was going to make my way to Kara and Christopher, then I'd more than likely be shooting my way in and shooting my way out.

I got to the armory door, but it was shut and locked, and two bikers stood in front of it like guards. They recognized me. They were holding shotguns.

They saw me walking down the hall. So, I couldn't turn back around. Not without looking suspicious. I kept walking forward, casually. They saw me and stepped out into the hall, shotguns lowered, not aimed at me, but at the floor in front of me.

I said, "Morning, guys. I need my gun back. I'm heading out early."

One said, "No can do. Turn around. Don't come any closer. This area is off limits until Berghorn says otherwise."

"Relax guys. I told you I'm headed out now."

Both guys pumped their shotguns and raised them at me. The one said, "Final warning."

I stopped. I was too far away to engage in hand-to-hand combat. And they were armed with shotguns. Stalemate. I did the only thing I could do. I raised my hands in surrender and said, "Hey. No problem. Relax. I'll come back later."

I backed away and turned around and went back to the living room. I would have to do this without firepower, which was a suicide mission. But I'd been through those before and came out alive. Why not press my luck a little further?

Then I exited the house and stepped out onto the massive stone porch and stopped behind the columns. I scanned the driveway. There were various bikers and girls up and walking around out front already. Some of the school children were already outside and playing. I couldn't start a firefight out here anyway, not without risking serious collateral damage.

I stared at the barn. I didn't know what to do. It seemed my only option was to wait for a better opportunity. But would I get one?

I went back inside, found a window on the first floor in an unoccupied nook, and stared out at the barn, waiting for a chance. But I didn't have to wait long because Berghorn, Gus, and the other bikers came out of the barn, dragging Kara and Christopher along with them. Their hands were still zip-tied behind their backs. This time, they were gagged with duct tape. The bikers loaded them back into the van. They were taking them somewhere else.

I glanced around. No one was in earshot. I took out the burner phone and called Fry.

Fry answered, "Now?"

"Fry, they're moving them. They're loading them up and heading out."

"Shit! They must have another location in mind."

"What do we do?"

Fry said, "Get out of there. We'll follow them. I'll be waiting off the farm road."

"Got it. Meet you out there," I said, and clicked off the phone. I threaded back through the house and out the front door.

Out front, I ran into Berghorn, Gus, and the others. Kara and Christopher were already loaded into the van. Their escorts also loaded up into the van and the pickup. The other bikers came out of the barn on their motorcycles. The engines roared. Berghorn rode out first on his bike. He saw me and rode over to me.

He said, "Widow? Where are you going?"

I said, "Morning. I gotta get an early start. I figured it was best to get going now. What's going on here?"

"Nothing. It's club business. Sorry to see you go. I thought you would stick around longer?"

"Nah. I really should hit the road."

"Okay. Well, it was a pleasure to meet you. Good luck on your pilgrimage."

I nodded and turned to go to my bike in the barn.

Berghorn called out to me. He said, "Wait."

I spun around.

He said, "You'll need your gun back."

"Right," I said and smiled.

Berghorn looked at Gus and said, "Give him back his gun."

Gus was on his bike near Berghorn. He nodded and reached into his inner jacket pocket and pulled out my M9 and reached it out to me. I walked to him, but Berghorn stopped me again.

"Wait!" he said. "Why don't you join us?"

I looked at my M9. It was right there. I almost had it in hand. Then, I glanced at Berghorn and nodded slowly like I was thinking it over.

"Yeah. Join us. It's going to be a show. You can see how The Phantom Sons handle our business. See how we handle sensitive things."

"What things?"

"We're taking care of an old problem. Tying up a loose end. Come along. I think you'll enjoy it. Plus, you can stay for breakfast. You can leave after. Come, meet our leader."

I froze for a beat and asked, "I thought you were the leader?"

"Hardly. Look at me. Do I look like the face of a thriving business?" he asked, and held his arms out, presenting himself to me. "I run the day-to-day. Come meet the wizard behind the curtain."

I thought about Fry. Thought that he'd warn me to turn down the offer. He'd say it'd be like going straight into the viper's pit. But wherever they were going, Berghorn was giving me a free invitation. It could present an opportunity to rescue Kara and Christopher. So, I said, "Okay. I'll follow on my bike. I'll need it to leave after."

"Of course," he said and glanced at Gus. "We'll keep your gun until after."

Shit, I thought. But I didn't protest.

I went to the barn, got on the Harley-Davidson FXDL, fired it up, and met them on the driveway. Berghorn smiled and ordered us to ride out. We rode back down the driveway, circling the van like we were giving it a police escort. We rode into the rising sun. The Phantom Sons. All armed. And me. Unarmed.

27

OUTSIDE THE COMPOUND, we rode in tight formation. The Phantom Sons rode together in perfect unison, like wild horses running together all of their lives. I was the only one who stood out. The six guys on motorcycles knew their places exactly. It was automatic to them. It was graceful, like synchronized swimming. I stayed near the rear. I was just trying not to fall off the bike.

We drove the farm road. I searched for Fry, but didn't see him.

We entered Gasper and wound through the streets. Everyone looked at us, but no one stared at us. It was like they couldn't help but look. Who wouldn't? A violent motorcycle gang rides through town, people will stare. The locals were conditioned not to question The Phantom Sons. Therefore, they looked, but didn't look. The people that looked had no judgement in their eyes. If you got caught staring at a Phantom Son the wrong way, he'd be the last thing you saw. Even if you didn't know, you knew because the gang oozed it.

We buzzed through the town. Two police cruisers drove by us. The cops inside nodded at Berghorn, like Disney security guards nodding at the head of the studio.

We passed through the town and still no Fry. It wasn't good. I had no idea where they were taking me.

On the outskirts of Gasper, right where Fry and I entered the town the day before, we turned north into the mountain range. We rode for twenty minutes into the mountains. The roads looped and wound. Deer sprinted across one section, forcing us to slow and wait. Other areas were slow to traverse because we climbed and looped steep curves. I glanced in my side mirror several times. Still no sign of Fry. Either he was an expert at following and staying out of sight, or he completely missed us. I assumed the latter, which meant that I was on my own with thirteen armed bikers, taking me to an unknown location.

We kept going until we were on a large mountain. Finally, Berghorn slowed, and the others slowed too, along with the truck and the van. We came to the start of a long track, covering a hundred acres of unspoiled land, with *Keep Out* and *Private Property* signs posted at the end, like Coger's place.

Berghorn turned onto the track first. The pickup truck and the van followed. Gus, myself, and the stragglers followed behind. Dirt plumed behind our tires. I pulled the scarf that Callesy gave me up and wrapped it over my nose and mouth to keep from inhaling all the dirt. I thanked her quietly.

Riding behind the others, the clouds of dirt were like passing through a sandstorm that didn't move. My sunshades kept it out of my eyes.

We rode for another fifty yards, then came to an obstruction and stopped. When the dust settled, I saw a guard hutch and a gate. This one was smaller than the one at the compound.

Berghorn talked to a guard posted in the hutch. They knew each other. The guard wasn't dressed like a biker. He wore a casual black suit with an earpiece dangling out of his ear. A wire curled out of it and tucked into the collar of his shirt, like a Secret Service agent.

I thought, *Where the hell am I?*

The guard knew who we were and why we were there. He exited the hutch and manually pushed open a gate with two parallel metal arms. He stepped aside and waved us through. Berghorn went first and the rest of us followed. I glanced back in my bike's side mirror. The guard pushed the gate closed behind us.

So much for Fry backing me up, I thought. Short of shooting the guard, he probably wasn't going to talk his way onto the property. He's a nice guy, but not that smooth of a talker.

Through the gate, we rode further down the track, across acres and acres of beautiful rolling hills and green pastures. Wild horses ran free across the property. Then, we rode under tall trees with thin layers of snow on the leaves.

We came out of the trees and there was a beautiful ranch house. It was two stories with a couple of rock chimneys and huge bay windows and thick brick walls and wood beams, and a three-sixty wood deck built around it. Sunlight sparkled in the windows. The place looked like a pristine hunting lodge out of a Stephen King book. It was something only the super-rich could afford.

There were a couple of hundred-thousand-dollar trucks parked out front. No one waited for us on the deck. No one came out of the ranch house as we pulled up. I had no idea who lived here.

We parked the bikes and the pickup and the van. I glanced back down the long track. There was no going back now. Three bikers opened the van's cargo doors and hauled Kara and Christopher out. I stayed at the back of the cluster of bikers. I kept my head down. I didn't want Kara or Christopher to notice me. They might accidentally acknowledge me with a nod or a smile, giving me away.

It didn't work. Kara spotted me. She saw me and her face lit up with a flutter of hope. Our eyes met and connected and locked. We hung there for a long second. I shook my head, gently, inconspicuously, and broke our gaze. She did the same.

The ranch house was built on a hilltop. Trees surrounded the place. To the side of the house, there was a wooden staircase that led down into the trees. It spiraled down the hill.

The bikers dragged Kara and Christopher down the stairs. They vanished off into the trees. I stared at them as they went, clenching my fists. Anger welled in the pit of my stomach. But I stayed quiet.

Berghorn and Gus walked toward the house. He called to me, "Come on, Widow."

I followed behind them. The rest of the inner circle followed behind me. The rest of the bikers followed behind Kara and Christopher. They were all armed. Everyone but me had firepower.

We stepped up onto the deck and the porch and entered the house. Berghorn didn't knock. He didn't ring a doorbell. He just opened the front doors and entered. We followed behind him.

The ranch house was majestic. Leather and dark oak furniture covered the various rooms of the house. There were soaring ceilings with large beams. The floors were wide-planked hardwood. There were huge windows and numerous skylights. A large rock wall fireplace climbed the height of the wall in the main room. A fire roared in it, unattended and forlorn and lonely. The place looked more expensive than the clubhouse and far more lifeless. Stuffed animal heads lined the walls. Some had antlers. Some did not. Most were hunted in North America, but some were from Africa. There were big cats and grizzly bears and wolves.

There was a large kitchen with two giant refrigerators and a pantry big enough to be a bedroom and a bar top long enough to seat all the inner circle comfortably.

The air smelled smoky and full of cinnamon, like burning incense. I guessed there was service staff, but I saw no one.

Berghorn gestured for me to sit by him on the sofa of the main room. He sat first, and I joined him. Gus moved behind me. He stood behind me, out of my sight. I didn't like my back turned to him, but what choice did I have?

The rest of the inner circle lounged in various places between the main room and the kitchen. Some of them got beer out of the refrigerator, making themselves at home. But they did things a little differently than they had at the clubhouse. They acted a little off, a little more uptight, like they were at ease but also on their best behavior. Berghorn sat up straight. He didn't put his feet up on the furniture. He didn't relax quite the same as at his own domain.

The others were the same way. The ones with open beer bottles put them on coasters. They all sat up straight. They behaved like we were at their momma's house.

We sat in silence. Finally, I turned to Berghorn and asked, "Where are we?"

He said, "You'll see."

"Okay. Who was that kid and woman?"

Berghorn smiled at me. His sunglasses stayed on. I couldn't see his eyes. I couldn't see if he was mocking me or being sincere. He said, "That's the problem I told you about. Don't worry. All will be made clear soon."

We sat there, staring out the huge bay windows, and lounging for a half hour before anything changed. The windows looked out onto a vast, green valley below the hill.

Suddenly, we heard a sound coming from the sky. The sound came from something outside, above the trees. I watched it. There was a small dot flying above the land. It flew toward the ranch house. It neared, and I saw it.

A small, silver helicopter came flying from the horizon. The rotor blades *whopped*. It was a Robinson R22, a single-engine, two-seater helicopter normally used as a workhorse for small companies and private charters. The helicopter continued to close in the distance between it and the house. I focused on the spot it was headed to and saw there wasn't a large, constructed helipad, but there was a circular patch of concrete on that side of the house with landing zone strips painted across it.

The helicopter slowed just above the house and descended to the ground. The grass around the helipad waved in furious gusts. The helicopter landed and Berghorn stood up. He removed his sunglasses. The rest of the inner circle did the same. I followed suit.

The helicopter landed, and the engine switched off and the rotor blades slowed until eventually they stopped spinning. The cockpit had one person inside, the pilot. He opened the door and climbed out.

The pilot wore a typical rancher's outfit. It was all western style. He wore jeans, boots, and a leather vest. Before he climbed out, he exchanged the helicopter headphones for a cowboy hat.

The only thing on him that wasn't western was a bomber jacket. The guy was white and bald. He lowered his head as he moved past the slowing rotor blades. Which was completely unnecessary because the guy was short. He was barely taller than Kara.

He came away from the helicopter and climbed a set of steps up to the house. We stayed there, waiting. He made it inside and walked into the main room, took off his hat, and hung it on a coat rack behind the door. That's when I saw what I missed from the window. The left side of the guy's face was badly burned. Half of it was scarred like crumbled paper. His left eyelid struggled to stay open because it was wrinkled and scarred so badly. His eye was greyed over. He was blind in it. The other half of his face was pretty normal.

The bikers stopped what they were doing and walked toward him. They gathered around him in a half-circle and did something I wasn't expecting.

They all knelt in front of him, like he was the King of England or something.

I stayed where I was, confused and estranged.

Gus saw I stayed standing and said, "Kneel!"

I stayed where I was.

Gus stood and walked to me, like he was going to force me to kneel. But the pilot spoke first. He said, "Gus, it's okay. He's not one of us. He's our guest. Rise, my sons."

He spoke in a cryptic and strange tone, because half his voice box was burned. I saw the scars on his neck. The burn scars vanished down the collar of his shirt.

Berghorn and the bikers rose from their knees. The pilot threaded through them and came straight to me. He put a gloved hand out for me to shake. It was his left hand. An inch of burned skin appeared in the space between the glove and his jacket sleeve. I took his hand and shook it. He said, "Butch Sabo. It's a pleasure to meet you."

It was Butch Sabo, Kara's dead father—only he wasn't dead. He stood here, in front of me, as alive as I was. He survived the roadside bombing. Kara never knew because she ran before it happened. No one knew. Fry didn't know. They all thought he was dead. But he wasn't. He was right here, still breathing, still leading The Phantom Sons.

"Jack Widow of The Vikings. Nice to meet you."

Sabo took his hand back, stepped closer to me, put his hand on my shoulder, and said, "Come, join us."

He walked first through the main room and down a back hallway. We came out on the deck around the back of the house.

The views were just as stunning as the front. It was all mountain tops and lush green plants and trees. The trees were thick
and dense. A platoon could sneak up to the house and Sabo
would never see it.

He stopped on the deck and leaned on the railing. I followed.
Berghorn, Gus, and the others followed behind me. Berghorn
and Gus stopped behind Sabo and me. The others flanked
around us. Sabo stared out at the land and put his hand out,
palm open, like he expected someone to hand him something.

Berghorn reached into his inner jacket pocket and took out
the two Cuban cigars I got for him. Then he took out a cigar
cutter, trimmed the tips of both, pocketed the cutter, took out
a lighter, and placed the cigars in his mouth, two at a time like
he was going to smoke them both. He lit the ends and pocketed the lights. He took puffs to ignite them both. Afterward,
he handed them both to Sabo.

Sabo took both cigars, smoked one, and handed the other to
me. He said, "Go on, Mr. Widow. Take it."

I took it.

"Smoke it with me," he said.

I nodded and puffed on the cigar.

I said, "This is friendly of you."

"Please, you're my guest. I appreciate visitors, especially a
Viking brother," Sabo said, and puffed on the cigar. He
grinned with it in his mouth, revealing blackened teeth and
melted gums on the burnt side of his face.

I said, "Sorry to bring this up, but I heard you were dead."

"Yes. Well, if anyone asks you, I am," he said and laughed. The bikers joined him in laughing.

I stayed quiet.

He puffed more and said, "You know? I owe you a great deal, Mr. Widow."

I wanted to keep up the illusion. So, I puffed on the cigar and asked, "How's that?"

Sabo stood straight, moved away from the railing, and stared at me with his one good eye. It was cold and menacing. Gus sidestepped, moved around Berghorn, and stopped directly behind Sabo. He towered over the man. He drew my M9 and pointed it at me from behind Sabo's shoulder.

Sabo said, "For returning my daughter back to her family."

I puffed on the cigar, glanced at Gus, at Berghorn, and then at the other bikers. Several of them drew their guns. Not all, but some. Even if I had a gun, I couldn't get them all before they shot me dead.

I asked, "When did you know?"

Berghorn said, "After you killed Shay's guys."

Sabo said, "But before you showed up today. Campbell told us of course. Come on. You think we're stupid?"

I stayed quiet.

Sabo said, "Follow me. I want you to see something."

He passed by me, close enough that I could've grabbed him and snapped his tiny neck before the others could shoot me. The opportunity tempted me, but I did nothing. Berghorn stepped up to me, took the cigar, and left it on the railing. Gus shoved me with my M9 in Sabo's direction.

I followed Sabo, and the others followed behind me. We walked around the deck to the front of the house. They led me to the stairs that led down into the valley and the trees. We walked a long stretch of land. The trees were thick enough to cast a dark shadow over the ground. I glanced up and barely saw the sun through the canopy of leaves.

At the bottom of the stairs, we came to a clearing and crossed it, passing underneath a tree stand with another guard in it. He wielded an AR-15 rifle with a scope on it. He glared at me as we passed. We walked further, down a dirt path until we came to a sight that sent horror through me. A cold feeling ran down my spine.

There was a large, circular area of concrete. It was designed with large stone steps circling it. Each ascended higher than the last, like a concrete stadium. There were heavy marble and wooden benches around the first level, like VIP seating. There was a giant fire pit in the center. The fire pit was custom-built. Large stones circled the bottom. At the center of the pit was a tall pole, like a stake. A large iron hook stuck out of the pole about six feet off the ground. It protruded outward, like it was waiting for something. The metal was dark and ashy like it'd been in many fires.

Off to one side, there was a large DJ station with stereo equipment. There were outdoor speakers setup in the trees surrounding the concrete stadium.

Gus stepped around me and pushed the muzzle of the M9 behind my ear.

I asked, "What are you going to do?"

Sabo said, "What we always do. We're going to protect our family and punish those who cross us."

He glanced at Berghorn and nodded. Berghorn looked at one of the other bikers and said, "Bring them out."

The biker nodded and vanished down a small path leading away from the fire pit. He returned a moment later with the three bikers who rode in the van. They had Kara and Christopher, still gagged, and bound. Now, their wrists were zip tied in the front.

Kara was half-naked. They'd stripped her of her clothes and slipped her into some kind of loose cotton pants and a top. They took her shoes. She was barefoot.

Christopher was dressed the same way he had been when they abducted him. He kicked and screamed, but his screams were muffled by the duct tape. Berghorn grabbed him, jerked him up, and dragged him back to watch.

Kara fought to stay with Christopher. She reached out him. Tears streamed from her eyes. She was terrified, like she knew what was going to happen.

The bikers grabbed Kara by the wrists and jerked her back, away from Christopher. Several bikers surrounded her. They dragged her to the fire pit, hauled her over the coals and rocks, lifted her up, and hooked her zip ties over the hook in the stake's front. She kicked and struggled, but it was no use.

The bikers backed away and circled the fire pit.

Christopher fought and kicked. Berghorn slapped him across the face. The kid went quiet after that.

Gus pushed the gun harder into my head and whispered, "Don't even think about it."

A biker came from behind the pit. He held a gas can. He popped the lid and poured it all over the coals under Kara. When the gas can was empty, he stepped back and nodded at Sabo.

Sabo stepped to Berghorn, held a hand out, and asked, "Lighter?"

Berghorn pinned Christopher to his chest with one arm around the kid's neck. He fished the lighter out of his pocket and gave it to Sabo.

Sabo went to the fire pit, puffed on the cigar, and tossed it into the pit. Nothing happened. He flicked the lighter until a flame came out the spout. He looked at his daughter. She rocked her head in protest.

Sabo looked at her and said, "I'm sorry, daughter. But you turned out to be a witch."

Then Sabo turned around and faced me. He asked, "You know what we do with witches, Widow?"

I said, "Don't do this."

"We burn them at the stake," he said, and tossed the lighter into the pit. The gasoline went up and fire blazed at Kara's feet.

28

MISTAKES. There were plenty made and plenty of blame to go around for them. I made them and Fry made them. I made them by not seeing Campbell for what he was. And for leaving Coger alone. He died protecting Kara and Christopher. Fry made a mistake by putting his faith in me. And now Kara was going to burn alive in front of her son, in front of me. There was nothing I could do about it. Not without taking a bullet to the head. I was pretty sure that I was better than Gus with a gun. But I didn't have a gun. He did. It was pressed against my head at point blank range. Even a blind man could hit a target that close.

All I could do was watch.

Sabo lit the fire pit, and the gasoline ignited, and flames burst up to the coals at the bottom of the stake. The fire rose higher and higher. Kara danced her feet up fast, interchanging them, one for the other. She hopped from foot to foot like a person walking over hot coals. She barely avoided the fire, but it was just getting started. The flames were right below her toes, inching closer and closer. It wouldn't be long before the stake caught fire, before she'd have nowhere to go.

She screamed under the duct tape. She wrenched her head from side-to-side. The combination of her screams and the heat of the fire loosened the adhesive on the duct tape. And it half-peeled off her mouth. Her screams became audible. They were no longer muffled. She begged and pleaded with her father to free her. Her words fell on deaf ears. The fire got so hot the duct tape slid off her face and burned up in the flames.

She shouted at Christopher to close his eyes. He did, but Berghorn grabbed him violently by the chin, shook him, and forced him to open them.

Kara's eyes squeezed shut tightly, like she was pretending to be somewhere else. Terror turned her face ghastly white. Her lips moved like she was whispering, or praying.

I glanced around. I rode in with six bikers on motorcycles and three in the van and four in the truck. There were thirteen bikers from The Phantom Sons. Plus, Sabo and his guard at the gate and the one on the tree stand with the AR-15. They totaled sixteen, but the guard at the gate wasn't here. He was at the gate. So, I faced fifteen armed, competent gunfighters. Some of them were a little inebriated because they had been drinking and probably smoking pot. Maybe other drugs. But they were sober enough to drive here. Therefore, they were sober enough to shoot straight.

Plus, there was Christopher, who could become collateral damage if a firefight broke out. There was Kara who was seconds from burning at the stake. Plus, I was unarmed.

The bikers were distracted, watching, and waiting for Kara to burst into flames. But Gus was behind me with a gun to my head. Then there was the guard on the tree stand. He might be watching me too. Or he might not be. I couldn't turn around and see for myself because of Gus.

Sabo glanced at one of the bikers, who stood near the large DJ station. Sabo said, "Hey, turn on the music!"

It was sick. His own daughter was burning at the stake, and he wanted to celebrate by blasting music. This whole affair was twisted. It was like Fry had said. They got their rituals. I had no idea.

The biker nodded in the affirmative to Sabo's orders. He flipped switches and turned knobs on the stereo equipment. Rock music came on and blasted over the speakers. He cranked it loud. I could barely hear Kara's screams over it.

I stayed quiet and watched.

The bikers hooted and hollered like spectators at an underground cage fight. It was insane to watch. Then they started chanting.

"Burn! Burn! Burn!" they chanted.

My stomach turned. I felt desperate. *How was I going to save Kara?* It looked impossible. I needed help. I needed a distraction. Something. Anything. I needed a miracle.

Fry, where the hell are you?! I thought.

But Fry didn't step in. He didn't save us. He didn't turn things around. Someone else did. Something else did.

Just then, over the music, I heard faint wind rustling and heavy footfalls. It came from behind me, behind Gus. It got closer and closer. The bikers chanted. The music blasted. Kara screamed. Christopher cried for his mother. No one else heard what I heard. It came from beyond the music, the chanting, and the screaming. The bikers were too busy watching the horror unfold. They were distracted by the spectacle, by their own bloodthirst, by the chaos.

Suddenly, something charged us. Something big and black stormed up the path and crossed the gap and leapt several feet into the air and slammed into Gus, like a lion charging a gazelle. Gus screamed in pain. He went down fast and dropped my M9. I spun around and saw Scout chomping on Gus's groin. The biker's face swelled up in agony. He turned purple.

Time slowed. Two of the nearest bikers reacted. They drew their guns and aimed in Scout's direction. The others were still watching the fire, still unaware of what was happening. I dove for the M9, got to it, and scrambled to aim at them. But before I could, they were already aiming at Scout. Gunshots rang out. But not from their guns. Their guns never fired a single shot. Both biker's chests exploded in that red mist of flesh and blood. They fell backwards—dead.

I got to my feet.

Three more bikers spun around, away from Kara and the fire, and saw me on the ground with the M9. They saw Scout chewing their comrade to bits. And they saw their two other comrades fall down dead. They were stunned and confused. They thought I shot the two dead bikers. They aimed at me. I fired the M9. *Bang! Bang! Bang!*

The first bullet exploded one biker's head. His face caved inward on impact. It blew chunks of brain out the exit wound in the back of his head. The second one got it in the neck. Blood sprayed out like a fire plug cracked open. He dropped to the ground and writhed around helpless and desperate, until he bled to death.

I missed the third guy completely. The bullet meant for him slammed into a tree five yards behind him. Bark exploded off it. He aimed at me. Before he could squeeze the trigger, his head exploded worse than the first guy. He was hit with a much bigger bullet. Far behind me, I heard the *crack* of an AR-15 rifle. It was Fry. He killed the guy in the tree stand, took his place, and commandeered his rifle. He stared down the scope at us.

Gus screamed in agony. Scout kept up the pressure. The others turned back to see what the commotion was. They stopped chanting. Fry fired again from the tree stand. Another biker went down. His chest exploded with the red mist and a huge exit wound. I glanced toward Berghorn, saw him look confused. I aimed down the M9's iron sights at him and squeezed the trigger, but I released because he saw what was happening and scooped up Christopher and held him close like a human shield. I moved the M9 and aimed at the next closest biker and fired. Twice. *Bang! Bang!*

The bullets ripped through the guy like a nail gun through butter. He went down—dead.

Berghorn scrambled away with Christopher in his arms. He fired his gun in my direction. He got off three rounds. Two hit Gus in the chest and blood exploded from it, covering Scout in blood. The dog recoiled, turned to Berghorn's direction, and snarled. The third bullet went off into the woods.

Kara screamed, and the music blasted over the chaos. Now everyone knew what was happening, and the bikers scattered like cockroaches. They dodged this way and that, frantically seeking cover.

Two of them took cover behind Kara and the growing fire. They came out on one side and aimed toward Fry in the tree stand. I scrambled to my feet and dodged right and aimed and shot them both. *Bang! Bang! Bang! Bang!* Four gunshots from the M9 flew through the air with their names and addresses on the bullets. All four rounds hit their targets. Two bullets for one guy and two for the other. They went down—dead, joining their friends. *Thank you and goodnight.*

I glanced at Christopher. Berghorn, Sabo and one of the inner circle bikers stayed behind him. Fry had no shot. I had no shot. They scrambled backwards, crossing behind Kara and the fire, and vanished down a dirt trail into the trees.

One biker stayed to fight. He was stuck between the fire and a tree. Fry laid several shots at him, hitting the back of the tree. Bark splintered from each bullet. The guy leaned out to see what he could do. I pointed at him, looked at Scout, and said, "Kill him!"

Same as I had back at Coger's marina.

Scout released Gus's lifeless body and charged to the tree. The biker saw him and leapt out, trying to run away. But Fry planted three bullets in the guy's back. He went down in a heap of dead meat and red mist. Scout tore into him anyway.

I scrambled away and ran toward Kara. She shouted, "Widow, hurry!"

I glanced at the fire pit, at the stake, and at her feet. She was pulling them up, holding them as high as she could. She hung from the hook. Her skin was red from the heat. Her wrists were blue from holding her weight up.

I ran to the fire and tried to dash across it to get to her, but I couldn't. It was too hot. I glanced around for a fire extinguisher or something to kill the fire. I saw nothing.

The music blared in my ear.

"Widow, hurry!" she shouted.

Scout barked behind me. I spun around to the DJ station, the music still blasting all around us. There was one of the VIP benches in front of it. I ran to it and tucked the M9 into the waistband of my jeans and grabbed the bench. It was part wood and part marble, but it wasn't bolted down. I grabbed it and heaved it up. It was portable, but heavy. The marble parts were solid. It took both hands and all of my strength to lift it.

"Widow, hurry!" Kara shouted. The flames were on the stake now. They climbed faster and faster.

I dragged the bench down some steps and across the concrete. In the distance, Fry climbed down the ladder and out of the tree stand. He scrambled toward us.

I made it to the edge of the fire pit. Kara was barely keeping her toes out of the flames. I took a deep breath, held it, and deadlifted the bench and threw it on the fire. The flames burst up once, like throwing a log on a fire. They shrank again. I stepped onto the bench. My weight pushed it down into the coals. The flames sparked on the wood. I scrambled up the bench to Kara.

The flames nipped at my boots. I ignored it. I grabbed Kara and lifted her up over my head and off the hook. I slung her over my shoulder and leapt off the bench.

The flames burned the soles of my boots and engulfed the bench. We passed over the fire and landed on the concrete hard. We both rolled away.

I came back up on my feet and got to Kara, checking her for wounds or burns. She was frazzled. The skin on her feet was ashy. Her hair was disheveled, but she was okay.

I slipped the biker jacket off of me and dropped it around her. She pulled into it close and said, "You're on fire."

She was right. The cuff of my jeans was burning. I batted it away, and the flame went out. I asked, "Are you okay?"

"My son, Widow?"

"I'll get him," I said and squeezed her once more.

Fry caught up to us at that point. He huffed and puffed and grabbed at his chest. He had the AR-15 in hand. He said, "Wait! I'll come with you!"

I looked at him. He looked terrible. His brow was covered in sweat. I put a hand on his shoulder and said, "Fry, you had a heart attack. You look like you're about to have another one. Stay here with Kara. Protect her. I'll be back with the kid."

Before Fry could protest, Kara put a hand on his and said, "Please. Stay here with me?"

He nodded. And I stood up and took off running. I ran down the trail, where Berghorn took Christopher with Sabo and the last biker.

Behind me, Fry yelled, "Widow, get them!"

"Ten-four," I whispered to myself.

29

THE TRAIL behind the stake and fire pit was a beaten dirt path that led away from the concrete. The canopy of leaves above it was thick. Sunlight trickled in, creating sunbeams. The light fragmented and refracted, like staring into a prism. Scout walked directly beside me. He clung close to my legs, staying in pace. It reminded me of working with Marine dogs. I'd worked on SEAL missions where a Marine and his dog were embedded with us. They make great tactical team members. Dogs can sniff out bombs, armaments, and even hostages. They can track specific terrorists. They're invaluable to any good war effort. I didn't know Scout's background, just that he took his commands in German. But he seemed to get the gist of English. Or maybe it was the pointing he understood.

Coger was gone. Now, Scout took to me. But it wasn't because he substituted me for his slain master. It was because we had the same enemies. We wanted the same thing, to find and protect Christopher. We were on the same mission. We were teammates.

Scout sniffed the air, like he was picking up Christopher's scent. But he stayed close to me. He didn't run out ahead after Christopher without me. He knew we were a unit now. He'd been pretty good under pressure and in firefights so far. Coger did a good job with him.

We tracked down the path into the trees. I scanned and tracked with the M9. I went from tree to tree. There were countless places for them to be hiding in wait, before jumping out and ambushing us. I relied on sight and sound to avoid getting ambushed. But Scout had scent on his side. I realized it quickly. He knew no one waited in the trees. So, we picked up the pace.

We fast-walked for a long minute before Scout stopped, and slowed just before a clearing with a bend in the path. The bend veered drastically to the left. He didn't bark. He sat on his butt and pointed with his snout, and stared back at me. I remembered that in the field, Marine dogs aren't trained to bark when they find danger. They're trained to sit. When they locate a cache of weapons or a roadside bomb, they sit. They don't draw attention to the bomb. They sit so that if the bomb is on a trigger and the trigger is in someone's hand, that person isn't alerted to the bomb being discovered. That way they're not tempted to detonate it—killing everyone.

I looked at him and glanced ahead to the clearing. I asked, "Something wrong, Scout?"

He whimpered quietly, like a whisper. I stared into the clearing and saw nothing. There was nobody there. It looked empty, calm, and safe.

I stepped forward, closer to the edge of the tree line. Scout growled at me. I stopped. I looked again and saw nothing. No one waiting in hiding. No sign of anything there. I listened. Wind howled silently through the trees. The trees cracked and swayed gently. Birds chirped and wings fluttered. Then, tree branches rustled to the right, above me.

I exploded from the knees and raised the M9 and sidestepped left, and got behind a tree. Just then, the last biker shot at me from another tree stand. He didn't have an AR-15 like the first guard who had been posted in a tree stand—the one Fry killed. If he had, he'd have used it. He shot at me with a hand-gun. Which was why he waited for me to step into the clear-ing. The range and too many trees were an issue. He fired blindly at us in desperation. He hoped he'd hit me. Bullets slammed into the other side of the tree and into nearby trees. Bark exploded and splintered. Scout was smart. He stayed crouched behind another tree.

I returned fire at the tree stand, but I suffered the same problem as the biker. The range was not good. I had to get closer to make a difference. The biker slowed his return fire. He paused, waited, and then fired. He was being more conser-vative with his ammunition. He was probably running low. And he was waiting to get a better view of me. I leaned out, spotted him, and returned fire. Just a couple of shots because I was low on ammunition as well. I only had what was left in the Beretta's magazine. The best strategy was for me to shoot and move.

He was twenty yards away and twenty feet up. I ducked back behind the tree. The guy returned fire like clockwork. He fired, and I fired. It was predictable. The biker was stupid. His original plan would've been a great plan. If I had stepped into the clearing, he could've shot me in the top of my head as I passed. But I hadn't stepped into the clearing.

It's true that he gave himself the high ground. But now, he was a sitting duck up there. These guys were formidable shooters, but they had zero tactical combat intelligence. If he'd had an assault rifle or a sniper rifle, I'd be in real trouble. But he didn't. So, I did the easiest thing. I drew his fire and waited for him to run out of ammunition. I waited for him to have to reload. Which wasn't long because he kept blindly shooting at me.

He fired until his gun *clicked* empty. I heard it even from that distance. I stepped out, charged toward him, staying in the trees in case he was a fast reloader. He saw me charging. Scout joined me and we ran up a hill, under the trees, and straight toward the biker. He fished around in his pockets for a spare magazine. I shot him first.

I came out from under the tree line, into the clearing, aimed and squeezed the trigger three times. I shot three in case I missed one, then there were still two more chances. But I didn't miss one. All three bullets met their mark. Three bullets tore through his chest, neck, and face. Blood sprayed everywhere. He slumped forward in the tree stand and hit a metal railing and tumbled forward over the side. The guy fell the twenty feet and crashed into the ground. He landed on his head and broke his neck on impact. Which didn't matter, since he was already dead before he hit the ground.

I'd lost count of my bullets. So, I checked the M9. Now, I was out. I went to the body, checked his pockets for his spare magazine. But he had no extra magazines. I was unarmed again.

I left the biker's weapon and tossed the M9. Scout barked in the other direction, at the other side of the clearing. There was another trail. It circled back in the other direction. I joined him at the beginning, and we ran down the new trail. I didn't have to worry about being ambushed anymore. There were only two left—Berghorn and Sabo. I wasn't going to worry about the guard posted at the gate. Not yet.

Scout had already proven that he could sniff out an ambush. So, we picked up the speed and ran without worry. Plus, Berghorn, Christopher, and Sabo's tracks were on the ground, in the dirt, and obvious. If any of them veered off course, I'd see it. We ran straight after them and followed the trail as it wound and looped and passed under heavy, leafy canopies. I stayed loose and agile in case I had to dodge or leap off the track. But I didn't. We made it to the end of the trail. It looped back to Sabo's ranch house.

We came out to an open field between the trees and the house. Scout ran forward. He didn't wait for me. I looked at the house. There were a ton of windows. A sniper could be perched anywhere and have a huge advantage over me. It was a chance I was willing to take—for Christopher. I couldn't let Sabo get away with him.

Close to the house, but thirty yards from me, there was a pile of split logs, a tree stump, and a multipurpose axe left stabbed into the stump. I scanned the windows again. No snipers. I took a deep breath, held it, and ran for it. I ran hard. The run to the bottom of the house only lasted seconds, but it felt like an eternity. I made it to the wall and put my back to it and exhaled. There were no snipers, which was good.

I glanced around, but Scout was gone. He must've smelled Christopher and taken off toward the scent. I couldn't be mad at him. Christopher was his favorite. I was on my own now.

I caught my breath and grabbed the axe and jerked it out of the stump. I swung it a few times for practice. It wasn't a gun, but it'd do as a weapon until I could commandeer a new firearm. So, I took it and circled the bottom of the house until I found stairs leading up to the deck. But I didn't take them. That's where they'd expect me to go. I continued circling the house, until I found a set of open garage doors. I hugged the wall and peeked around the corner. I knew that Berghorn and Sabo had made it back to the house. They knew I was chasing them, but they didn't know I was out of bullets and had no gun. So, they'd hide out somewhere inside and shoot me in the back as I passed.

The added danger was they could've armed themselves with anything from inside the house. They'd had enough time to grab a couple of assault rifles or shotguns. Firepower was on their side. But I had stealth and sixteen years of Navy SEAL experience on mine. And in a situation of an unarmed SEAL versus two bikers with superior firepower, I'd bet on the US Navy every time.

There was no one in the garage. I entered, staying quiet and walking slowly. I scanned every corner and every doorway.

The garage had three bay doors. Two of them had five motorcycles parked inside. They were all different brands and models and years. They looked old and expensive, like antique models. I could've been staring at millions of dollars' worth of rare motorcycles. I had no idea.

The third open bay had various land and yard equipment cluttered about. There were two riding lawnmowers, three weed eaters, and a bunch of other yard work tools. In one corner of the garage, there were work tables built into the wall. There were racks of various tools and equipment. On another wall, there were shelves filled with various supplies. There were a couple of snowmobiles for the coming winter months.

I threaded through the vehicles and over to a set of concrete steps that led to the only door into the house. I stepped behind the door, grabbed the knob, and turned it slowly. I eased the door open and paused and listened for anyone on the other side. I heard nothing. So, I pulled it open and left it open. I stepped into the house. The floorboards creaked under my footsteps. The creaks *boomed* under my weight. Only they weren't, really. It was that thing when you're walking on hardwood in the middle of the night, but trying not to wake everybody else in the house. It sounded loud to me, but it wasn't. The whole house creaked and cracked in the way that huge timber houses do.

I walked into a pantry, passed through it, and entered the large kitchen I'd seen earlier. I saw no one. I stayed close to the wall, in case someone was hiding out behind a corner. I passed the long counter and went into the living room. This was where they should've set up an ambush for me. I was out in the open and unarmed. I'd been walking into a shooting gallery. I would've been an easy target, like shooting fish in a barrel. But there was no one there.

I threaded through the leather sofas and furniture to a U-shaped staircase. It had floating stairs with expensive iron work for railings and wires. Just past it, there was a long hallway with more doors. I glanced down the hallway, thinking that's where I should check first. Then, I heard creaking upstairs. *Footsteps.* I turned and headed up the stairs. There's no real way to sneak up floating stairs, not when there are two armed hostiles who know you're coming. I did the best

I could, but the key was to just get upstairs as fast as I could. I made it to the top of the stairs. No one ambushed me. I figured the reason that no one stepped out to shoot me yet was because they thought I was armed. And they probably thought Fry was with me. Hell, they probably didn't know how many guys were with me. They tucked tail and ran away so fast. Maybe they didn't realize it was only me and an over-the-hill former Marshal with a bad heart.

The ranch house was enormous. A lot bigger than I thought. The upstairs split off into three different hallways. And each was winding and long. Scout was nowhere around. So, I had to rely on my own senses. I picked the rightmost hallway and turned and walked down it. I held the axe back, ready to swing, ready to strike.

I passed an open doorway and glanced in. There was a huge upstairs den. An old fire burned in a fireplace. There were several armchairs and a large oak desk and more animal trophies on the walls. The room was too big to glance in and be sure that no one was hiding in it. But I had a lot of ground to cover. I didn't have time to waste searching every nook and cranny of every room. So, I stood in the doorway for a long second, glancing at everything, trying to be sure without wasting time and energy.

Suddenly, I heard a creak behind me, down the hallway. Out of the corner of my eye, I saw movement. I darted into the den. And a gun went off. *Bang! Bang!* Two gunshots rang out. The bullets slammed into the doorway. Drywall exploded and dust clouds filled the doorway.

I dodged right and reversed and reared the axe over my shoulder. I stood back, behind the door, and waited. The shooter chased me into the room, like I hoped. The first thing I saw was a Glock and a hand in a black suit. It was another guard. One I missed. He was like the one from the gate or the tree stand. I forgot they had those secret service ear pieces. This one had probably gotten suspicious when the guard on the tree stand wasn't responding. And, for sure, he heard all the gunshots. He must've tried to check in with the tree stand guard. Only that one was dead. So, now he was checking the house for Sabo, his boss. Because that's the only person who mattered to him.

The guard entered the den. Unsure of where I went, he first scanned the corners and the furniture, like I had. He probably expected me to duck and cover behind a sofa. it was the most obvious place. But I was right there, behind the door. He felt my presence and reacted. He sidestepped and spun around to face me, to shoot me. But he was too late. I swung the axe down and chopped his gun hand clean off, right at the wrist. The hand and the Glock flew, splattering blood across a Persian rug. The hand rolled back out into the hallway. The Glock was still in it. The severed hand's index finger was still on the trigger. The guard grappled at his wrist and bloody stump desperately, like he could will it to grow back. His mouth opened to scream, but I didn't wait for that.

I swung the axe again hard and chopped his head off at the neck. The axe blade stuck into the doorframe. Blood slid off the blade and dripped onto the floor. The guard's head lobbed through the air. The curly wire from the secret service earpiece got cut in half. It dangled out of his ear. The head plopped onto the hardwood floor and rolled away like the Glock, but it rolled the other way into the room. It rolled and stopped and got wedged under an armchair. The guard's last facial expression was now frozen that way forever.

The lifeless, headless body stood there for a long second, like it was still alive and in shock. Then, the knees crumbled and folded forward. The body thumped on the hardwood. Blood spilled out of the hole in its neck, where its head used to be.

I jerked the axe out of the doorframe and stepped over the body and back into the hallway, over to the guy's gun hand. I planned to pry the Glock from it. But I never made it, because Berghorn stepped out of a room at the other end of the hall. He was holding a fat, black shotgun. He smiled at me and fired it. The muzzle flash filled the dark hallway. The blast filled the silence. He missed and hit the wall. Various paintings that hung along the corridor exploded into paper confetti.

I ducked and ran the other direction, back to the U-shaped staircase. Berghorn walked after me slowly and with confidence, like he knew I didn't have a gun. Which he did. If I'd had one, I wouldn't be using an axe as a weapon.

He wasn't aiming at me properly. If he had taken the time to aim properly, then he would've hit me the first time. His confidence was as good as arrogance. And arrogance is overconfidence. His overconfidence spoiled the opportunity to kill me. Still, he had a shotgun. I didn't. He was shooting the shotgun from the hip. He pumped the action, and the fired shell casing clattered to the floor. He walked calmly after me. He was still overconfident. He hadn't learned his lesson. If you get the chance to kill me, then you'd better pull the trigger.

I scrambled to the stairs and down them. He fired again. The shell blasted the iron railing. It clanged from the impact. Metal shards splintered and dusted behind me. He pumped the action again. Another shell casing clattered to the floor. He picked up the pace and ran to the top of the stairs and leaned over the railing and fired it again. I clambered to the first floor and dove. The last shotgun blast barely missed my legs. The bottom two steps dusted wood splinters from the shell impact. I scrambled to my feet and ran back through the kitchen.

Berghorn pumped the action and loped down the stairs, skipping every other step. He reached the first floor and followed me. He fired again at me. I dashed through the kitchen. A large bay window just next to me exploded from the shotgun shell. Wind gusted in through the hole.

He barely missed me. I changed course mid-run to avoid it. I darted to the left and went back through the same pantry I snuck in through. The door to the garage was still open. I dashed through it and turned and stopped between two parked antique motorcycles. I took an athletic pose, raised the axe over my shoulders, rested it on my back, held the tip of the handle with both hands, and waited. I watched the open doorway.

Berghorn walked through the doorway into the garage confidently, arrogantly, and carelessly. The shotgun was still at his hip. He saw me and saw my arms over the back of my head. I saw his eyes. I kept eye contact with him. He smiled and turned the gun's barrel in my direction. With full-force, I swung the axe forward from over my back and over my head and I released it at the arch right above my head. The axe spun through the air.

Berghorn shot at me once. The shell slammed into one of the antique motorcycles. The headlight shattered, and the tire popped from the shell's impact. I wasn't hit. And he never shot again because the axe spun through the air and the blade slammed into Berghorn's center mass, right between his rib cages into his solar plexus. He flew back off his feet like he'd been hit by a boulder from a medieval catapult.

The shotgun dropped out of his hands and clattered down the concrete steps. I threaded between the motorcycles, returned to the steps, and scooped up the shotgun. I pumped the action, replacing the empty casing with a new shell. The shotgun only held seven shells. He'd fired five. So, I had two left.

I climbed the steps and pointed the shotgun at him in case he was still a threat. But he wasn't. He lay there. Blood trickled out of his mouth. His hands were around the axe's handle, trying desperately to pull the blade out. But it wasn't coming out.

I stood over Berghorn. He cursed at me. It was mostly illegible because his mouth filled with blood. I stared into his eyes and put a boot on the hammer-back end of the axe blade. Terror crossed his face. I thought of the look on Coger's face again. The look he had on that pike, just before he died. And I leaned on the axe's head. I put all my weight on it. The axe blade sank further into his chest. Blood oozed out of the sides of the wound. Berghorn was dead seconds later.

Suddenly, I heard Scout barking fiercely. He was outside the ranch house, back on the front driveway. A big engine roared to life. Then, I heard tires peeling out on the driveway. I left Berghorn's body and the axe and ran back through the house and out the front door onto the deck.

Kara stood in the driveway, screaming frantically. Fry was beside her, still winded. Scout took off running behind a cloud of dust and gravel, spat up by big tires.

I looked up and saw Sabo take off in one of the pickup trucks. And Christopher's face was in the window, staring back at us. I ran to the deck railing and leapt clean over it. I landed hard in the grass, but kept running. I ran past Kara and Fry, who stood there not knowing what to do. I leapt onto my motorcycle, fired it up, held the shotgun in one hand and the handlebars in the other. I took off after the truck.

Gravel and rocks spit up into my face from the back of his truck's big tires. I leaned and dodged the clouds of dust as best I could so I could keep eyes on the rear of the truck. Sabo saw me in the rearview mirror and punched the gas to the floor. It was obvious because the truck was flying at top speed. He was getting away. Dust clouded everywhere. I took the bike up as fast as I could. We blasted past trees so fast that one false move and I'd crash into one, evaporating into a ball of fire.

We floored it down his long driveway, back to the private road. More wild horses ran in the distance. We weaved the turns and loops and corners. I tried to get closer, but the truck was fast. I stayed as close as I could. Christopher stared at me through the back window.

We'd left Scout behind in a cloud of dust, but I still could hear him barking, far behind me. He ran flat out at his top speed and wasn't giving up, and neither was I.

I glanced at the fuel gauge. It was low. I couldn't give chase for very long. I doubted I'd even make it on the mountain roads. I had to catch Sabo here and now.

Sabo slowed the truck to take a huge curve ahead. I didn't slow. I sped up. He took the curve and braked hard and skidded through it. Now, I was on his bumper. I had a real chance. The driveway straightened out, and I tried to move closer to the passenger side.

Sabo turned the steering wheel hard, and the truck swerved toward me. I skidded to the right, barely missing a head-on collision with a huge tree. I returned to the road and stayed on his bumper. He swerved again, trying to slam me into his big back tire. I dodged right again. Then I swerved violently back to the left to avoid another tree.

Dust filled my lungs. The scarf Callesy gave me went flying off me because of the speed and the wind. I stayed tight to Sabo's bumper. I tried to get a shot at his back tire with the shotgun, but he swerved again, and I lost control of the motorcycle. I braked hard just before I nearly pancaked into another tree.

I got back on the track and accelerated. Sabo's truck gained ground on me and he floored it. I still had the shotgun, but there were only two shells left and he'd put more distance between us. So, I sped up all the way. But I was too far back. The fuel gauge was nearing empty. The bike would sputter out of fuel soon.

I was going to lose them. Once he crossed onto the mountain roads, there was no way I'd keep up with them. But then, I lucked out. I thanked Fry in my head because ahead of us, I saw the gate and the guard hutch. The gate was blocked off and the guard hutch crushed and the guard inside was dead. Fry had rammed the hutch at full speed with the rented car, killing the guard inside. Fry left the car parked across the driveway, acting as a barrier. It blocked both lanes in and both lanes out. Sabo was stuck inside the compound with us.

Sabo saw the wreckage and braked hard. I might just catch him before the fuel ran out in the bike. But that hope was dashed when Sabo turned the wheel and accelerated the truck off road. The tires bounced and dipped over the grassy, hilly terrain.

I followed behind him, keeping the motorcycle at top speed. I pushed it as hard and fast as it'd go. The motorcycle wasn't built for off-roading like the truck was. So it was much harder for me than him. But I kept up the chase anyway.

Christopher bounced around the interior of the cab violently. He crawled to the passenger door and tried to open it. The door cracked open an inch. Christopher pushed it open. I saw his little hands grabbing at the door pillar. He tried to leap out and escape. But Sabo grabbed him and hauled him back in. The passenger door flew open. I kept the pressure on. I was only a few yards behind them.

Suddenly, more wild horses stampeded across the trail, out in front of his path, and he jerked the wheel again. He missed the horses. They ran wild in the other direction. The truck turned and sped off into the trees. I followed. The truck's big tires kicked up dirt and grass everywhere. But he kept going forward. We dodged more trees and bounced over hills.

The path ahead was getting tighter. But Sabo kept on. The fuel gauge on the bike passed *E* as I glanced down at it. I was running on empty. I had to make a bold move, or we'd lose Christopher forever.

A cluster of trees came up. Sabo slowed to weave through them. I sped up and got alongside him, barely missing several trees. One-handed, I fired the shotgun at the back tire. We both hit a dip and bounced up into the air one after the other.

And I missed the tire and hit the well above it. The truck's metal shell dented from the shotgun blast. The shell impact sparked the metal skin. I rode through the gun smoke.

I took my hand off the handlebars and pumped the action. The motorcycle sputtered. I was out of gas. I was coasting now. The trees flew past us, making *whooshing* sounds because of the speed.

Sabo's truck went faster, and I was slowing down. Two-handed, I took aim over the shotgun and fired the last shell.

Bullseye. I hit the back tire. It exploded in a ball of compressed air and torn black rubber. The truck dropped onto the axle. Sabo countered the lost tire, trying to compensate for it, and jerked the wheel the wrong way. The truck swerved and pulled violently. Christopher flew out of the passenger door. The door broke off and went too. It slid across the grass. The kid followed it. He rolled five yards away and stopped in a heap of dust and grass.

The truck slammed into a tree, cracking the tree, and wrecking the engine.

I skidded to a stop. The bike was out of gas. It wouldn't accelerate anymore.

I got off the bike, dropping it and the shotgun. It was empty and useless now. I ran to Christopher. I grabbed him and spun him over. I scanned his whole body. He stared at me. There were some bruises and a wicked cut over his forehead, but he was okay.

I asked anyway. "Are you okay?"

"Yes, sir," he replied.

I pulled him to me and hugged him tight, like he was my own son. I couldn't help it. He was important to me. He must've felt the same way because he hugged me back. We stayed like that for a long minute. Then I pulled away from him. We heard Scout barking frantically. I let go of Christopher and stepped back. He got up on his own. Scout came running at us from out of the trees. He was panting like he might drop dead from running so fast and so far.

He ran right up to Christopher and jumped on him and licked his face. Christopher cried like he had lost his own dog, and now, had found him. They were reunited.

I stepped away from them and looked at the truck. The engine ignited and a small fire started. Smoke plumed up from it. I heard Sabo grunting and struggling.

I looked at Christopher and said, "You both stay back here."

The kid nodded and Scout barked at me.

I left them and went around the rear of the truck and passed the shredded rubber. It dangled from the axle. I passed between the bumper and the motorcycle and walked around to the driver's side door.

The front of the truck was smashed inward. Half the engine was on fire and the fire was inching into the cabin. The other half of the engine was smashed into the cabin. Sabo's legs were crushed under it and the mashed steering column. He was pinned there. His legs were broken. His chest was half-folded in on itself. The good side of his face was all messed up. Now, the burnt side was the *good side*. His nose was smashed in and broken. His bad eye was blood red instead of grey. The other eye was completely bloodshot. His ear drums were busted. Blood trickled out of his ears. More blood gushed out of his mouth. He stared at me, helpless.

He said, "Widow! Get me out of here!"

I stayed quiet.

He said, "Widow, the engine's on fire!"

I stayed quiet.

He said, "Please, don't let me burn up! Not again!"

Silence. I stared at him. There was no sympathy on my face.

He said, "Please! Save me?"

I said, "Save you? But you're a dead man. You burned up in a car bomb. Six years ago. Remember?"

And I backed away. He reached out to me with his hand weakly. He grabbed at me, like if only he could grab me, then he could save himself. I turned and walked back to Christopher and Scout.

"No! Widow! Help me!" Sabo shouted. I ignored him and kept walking. The fire grew and burned and got bigger. He screamed and howled desperately.

I got to Christopher. Scout licked my hand. I petted his head. I looked at Christopher and asked, "Can you walk?"

"Yes."

"Okay. Let's go back to your mom."

Christopher reached up to me and took my hand and squeezed it. I looked down at him. He said, "I'm supposed to hold an adult's hand when I'm on a strange road. My mom's rule."

"That's a good rule," I said, and I walked him back the way we came, back to his mother. Scout followed alongside us.

Halfway back to the ranch house, Fry and Kara stopped on the private road to pick us up in one of the other trucks. They'd taken a key from inside the house. Kara jumped out of the passenger side and ran to us and scooped up her son and hugged him in a long embrace. Scout rubbed up against her legs, like a cat, and kept trying to get in on the action. I stayed where I was.

Eventually, we climbed into the truck and drove out of the ranch. We saw the flames and smoke of Sabo's truck from the road. Before we left the ranch and turned onto the mountain roads, we heard an explosion.

Kara asked, "What was that?"

I said, "Just the past catching up to the present."

We left the ranch, drove back down the mountain range and through Gasper. We got a lot of looks from the locals. But we didn't stop. We got back on the interstate and drove back to Charlotte.

Fry took us to a hotel, a nice one. And he put us all up in a suite with three bedrooms for the night. I sent Kara and Christopher upstairs in the elevator and walked Fry back out to the truck. On the way, we talked.

I said, "Something's gotta be done about Campbell."

"What do you mean?"

"He's dirty. Sabo mentioned him to me. He knew my name. Campbell told him."

Fry said, "Jesus!"

"He's the reason Coger is dead."

Fry stayed quiet.

I said, "You thinking of arresting him?"

"It's the right thing to do."

"Fry, they cut off Coger's head. Stuck it on a pike."

His shoulders sank and his skin turned ghostly white, thinking about his dead friend. He said, "I know."

I paused a beat. We passed through the hotel's double doors and back onto a downtown Charlotte street. He opened the door to the truck and hopped in, and closed it. He buzzed the window down. I leaned into it and said, "I could visit him."

He looked at me and said, "No. That's not my style. I'll take care of it. The FBI will take care of it."

I stayed quiet.

He fired the truck back on and said, "I'm exhausted. But I got to go see Callesy. I gotta explain all this to her. This is the FBI's affair now. Kara and Christopher are safe and free. Let her deal with Campbell. He can rot in prison. By the way, Shay didn't make it. I got the call this morning. So, you don't need to worry about the Irish mob."

"I wasn't worried. They'll go after John Capone."

"Right."

Fry paused a long beat. Then he asked, "What about you?"

"What about me?"

"Where will you go?"

* * *

EVEN THOUGH KARA had worked for six years as a waitress in a small-town diner, she'd stashed away a lot of cash. She invested it in something called *Cryptocurrency*. And she'd made a small fortune. She tried to explain it to me, but I didn't understand it. Not really.

I spent the night with her in the hotel in Charlotte, North Carolina. And she told me about her dream of moving to a beach in Mexico and raising her son there. She wanted it to be somewhere not touristy. Christopher and she could learn Spanish. He could go to school and grow up there.

Scout stayed in Christopher's bed that night in the hotel suite. He slept like a baby. And he never left the kid's side again. They became best friends.

Kara invited me to go with them to Mexico. So I did. The least I could do was to see them there safely.

Kara bought us a car. We drove back to Arizona, where she had stashed their passports in a safe deposit box. We picked them up and crossed the Mexican border, drove down to the beach town that she had dreamed of living in. I stayed with Kara and Christopher.

Scout took very well to the kid, but he missed Coger. I saw it in his eyes. That would fade with time. *Time heals all wounds,* so they say.

We got situated. And Kara rented a little house on the beach. The water was blue and clear. The sand was nice. We were so far south, even the winter months were warm enough for bikinis. I saw Kara in a lot of bikinis.

One day, she got a text from Fry. There were no words. It was just a web link. She clicked on it and showed me. The link was to a newspaper article about Campbell being arrested for corruption. It included another link to an article about The Phantom Sons Motorcycle Club being murdered by a rival gang. The FBI was investigating. *I* was the rival gang. So it was just a ruse fed to the media by Callesy to send them off my trail. If I'd left a trail.

Overall, we were all happy for a spell, like a little family unit. Even I was happy. But I grew restless. And one day, I asked myself a simple question. *Is it time to move on?*

KILL PROMISE

S C O T T
B L A D E

A **JACK WIDOW** THRILLER

**KILL
PROMISE**

COMING 2022

Widow made a promise. And he intends to keep it

A WORD FROM SCOTT

Thank you for reading THE PROTECTOR. You got this far —I'm guessing that you liked Widow.

The story continues...

Look out for *KILL PROMISE*, coming 2022.

To find out more, sign up for the Scott Blade Book Club and get notified of upcoming new releases. See next page.

THE SCOTT BLADE BOOK CLUB

Building a relationship with my readers is the very best thing about writing. I occasionally send newsletters with details on new releases, special offers, and other bits of news relating to the Jack Widow Series.

If you are new to the series, you can join the Scott Blade Book Club and get the starter kit.

Sign up for exclusive free stories, special offers, access to bonus content, and info on the latest releases, and coming-soon Jack Widow novels. Sign up at ScottBlade.com.

THE NOMADVELIST
NOMAD + NOVELIST = NOMADVELIST

Scott Blade is a Nomadvelist, a drifter and author of the breakout Jack Widow series. Scott travels the world, hitchhiking, drinking coffee, and writing.

Jack Widow has sold over a million copies.

Visit @: ScottBlade.com

Contact @: scott@scottblade.com

Follow @:

Facebook.com/ScottBladeAuthor

Bookbub.com/profile/scott-blade

Amazon.com/Scott-Blade/e/B00AU7ZRS8